INSIDIOUS INTOXICATION

Suddenly Miss Faith Hamilton realized how much she had drunk at the ball, spurred on by the warmth of the room and the pace of the dizzying dances. Now her head was spinning as she stood in the garden with the tall and elegant earl.

How surprised she was when his full, cool mouth came down on hers, so surprised that she didn't even react when he gathered her close to his body!

How long that kiss lasted, she did not know. But when she felt his body grow warm against her, and felt his grip tighten with harsh urgency, she woke to what was happening.

"No!" she cried in alarm, desperately afraid it was already too late to stop a man who had a reputation for getting what he wanted. . . .

*Introducing a new
historical romance by Joan Wolf*

DESIRE'S INSISTENT SONG CARRIED THEIR PASSION THROUGH THE FLAMES OF LOVE AND WAR . . .

The handsome Virginian made Lady Barbara Carr shiver with fear and desire. He was her new husband, a stranger, wed to her so his wealth could pay her father's debts, an American patriot, sworn to fight Britain's king. But Alan Maxwell had never wanted any woman the way he wanted this delicate English lady. And a hot need ignited within him as he carried Barbara to the canopied bed, defying the danger of making her his bride tonight . . . when war could make her his enemy tomorrow. . . .

Coming in July from Signet!

The
INDIAN
MAIDEN

Edith Layton

A SIGNET BOOK

NEW AMERICAN LIBRARY

NAL BOOKS ARE AVAILABLE AT QUANTITY DISCOUNTS WHEN USED
TO PROMOTE PRODUCTS OR SERVICES. FOR INFORMATION PLEASE
WRITE TO PREMIUM MARKETING DIVISION, NEW AMERICAN LIBRARY,
1633 BROADWAY, NEW YORK, NEW YORK 10019.

SIGNET TRADEMARK REG. U.S. PAT. OFF. AND FOREIGN COUNTRIES
REGISTERED TRADEMARK—MARCA REGISTRADA
HECHO EN CHICAGO, U.S.A.

SIGNET, SIGNET CLASSIC, MENTOR, PLUME, MERIDIAN AND NAL BOOKS
are published by New American Library,
1633 Broadway, New York, New York 10019

First Printing, June 1986

1 2 3 4 5 6 7 8 9

PRINTED IN THE UNITED STATES OF AMERICA

ONE

*T*HE LADIES SAT beneath the trees and spoke in voices as light and murmurous as the slight breeze which stirred the vault of leaves above them. The oaks and beeches still wore their frivolous yellow-green spring foliage, though it was close enough to the change in season for those who sheltered beneath them to wish they instead already bore the broad, serious leaves of summer. That might have provided a deeper darkness than the thin, shifting, dappled shade they rested in. So some put up their parasols, and others kept their faces downcast to avoid the touch of the shards of sudden dancing light, so ruinous to the complexion, so sure to increase the already unexpected warmth of the day.

Since these were very young ladies who took their ease beneath the towering trees, they did not sit upon chairs as their watchful chaperones did, where they were ranged, further back, almost out of sight (though never out of line of sight), right in front of the trunks of the great trees. Nor did they stand, as some of their attendant gentlemen did, nor did they rest gingerly upon little spread squares of handkerchief linen as some of the more foppish of those fellows did, nor never, of course, did they squat or sit Indian style in emulation of some of the other gentlemen, either. No, servants had brought them various small rugs, and paisley throws and plump cushions and knitted patchworked stoles to protect their skirts from the grass and they rested on them as they languished on the close-cropped lawn, and fanned themselves lightly and complained softly about the warmth of the day.

A lone gentleman had been riding slowly along a high bridal path that ran between the long avenue of twinned trees, and when he came upon the gathering it seemed to him that they all were ranged beneath him in a hollow of the land in tableau, specifically for his viewing. Thus the young ladies in their light gauze dresses, upon their vari-colored seatings, appeared to him at first to be almost like a bowl of blossoms shaken down from some fabulous tree and newly settled upon the greensward. It was such an unexpected sight and such an amusing sudden thought that he checked his horse and gazed down at them with the pure simple pleasure of the unseen, uninvolved observer.

Although he was a man who valued progress and although he fully appreciated the scene before him, for a moment, because of his love of the theatrical and his connoisseur's eye, he almost wished he could have come upon such a scene a generation before. Then it would not have only been the cloths and cushions and blankets that pied the landscape with brilliant color, but the ladies themselves in their billowing gowns would have been spectacularly set off against the grass, surrounded by yards of rich fabric and brocade. But modern fashion in this year of 1816 had all the females clad in the lightest, narrowest wisps of gowns. And these young ladies were, if no other thing, fashionable.

Yet, though they lacked the antique splendor he might have preferred for art's sake, there was enough that was piquant about their appearance to keep his interest. In their pale and drifting gauzy garments, they looked to him like wan sprites riding on fantastic Arabian carpets.

He would have only rested there for a moment and looked his fill before moving on with a smile and a sigh for the ephemeral visions and joys of youth, if he had not then, with assistance from a fractious wayward breeze, heard them speak.

"Well I don't think," protested one pastel pink vision atop a fat green striped pillow, "that just sitting here helps in the least."

"And I think Sallie's entirely right," mewled another young lady from her island of puce satin-pieced rag rug, "there might be a breeze by the lake. And it least, it *looks* cool there."

"The reflection, however, from the waters," a very fair young creature upon a wine-colored silk runner commented in as ominous a tone as her spidery voice could manage, "might produce glare. *Glare* causes more harm than the sun itself does, Mama says," she added in baleful tones, with an emphasis on "glare" that made it sound like she considered it some hideous contagious disease.

But so it seemed did all her listeners, for a nervous silence fell over the group after her pronouncement. Though the observer had heard quite enough, since what passed for conversation in the assembly below was beginning to bore him as heartily as their appearance had captivated him, he did not move his mount forward lest the sound of its passage ring out in the quiet and trap him in his tracks, a penalty he discovered he disliked more than the unknown young lady dreaded glare.

"I say, let's do go," called out a youth whose spirited voice was at odds with the stocky figure it issued from, as he hunkered near a young creature in an apricot gown and fanned her absently and unproductively with her matching fan. "It would be far better than sitting here and roasting. It's a bit of a trek, to be sure, but there are willows there. Willows have acres of shade."

The observer edged his mount on a few paces as a general concensus was taken of opinion on this startling suggestion, but he halted his mount abruptly when the glare-hating female silenced the discussion by insisting in highly dire accents, "But *things* drop from willow trees. If you sit beneath them, they drop right on your head."

As the stout young gentleman began to exclaim the innocence of all things dropping from willows, with the energetic assistance of a lanky young man who became so exercised at the discussion that he leaped to his feet shouting, "Catkins! That's what they call them, and they haven't any legs at all, they're not even properly alive. Catkins is what they are, Caro, don't be a flat," the horseman blessed the empty-headed chit who'd started the altercation and under cover of the resultant clamor, moved his horse quite a few unnoticed paces along the beech-lined avenue.

The level of intellectual discussion raging beneath him was exactly what he'd expected to hear from the group he'd spied, which was the chiefest reason why he'd no intention of stopping to pass the time of day with them when he'd seen them. He'd been too far away to make out any individual faces then, but there was not a doubt that the gathering consisted of the daughter of the owner of this great estate, and her entire court of friends and suitors. Since that gentleman, the Duke of Marchbanks, had a young daughter, and she, the Lady Mary Bolton, had been acclaimed this past Season's "Incomparable," the solitary rider had a fairly good idea of exactly what and who her retinue consisted of. And he shunned the thought of consorting with them in every bit as lively a fashion as the unknown young lady below resisted having her head used as a landing site for unspecified many-legged creatures.

He was eyeing the distance to a curve in the beech avenue and estimating how long it would be before he could get there and then let his mount gallop, since the hindquarters of a horse are scarcely recognizable enough to give anyone an excuse to flag a fellow down, when he heard the sudden lack of voices as loudly as he might have heard a scream.

"I said," a clear, carrying young female's voice then asserted on the empty air, "that nothing, absolutely nothing, would induce me to wander through a forest. From my experience of such ventures, Miss Timmins's willow-dwelling thingies are as nothing. But you go on, I won't mind waiting here in the least. Here, it's at least safe, so far as I can see."

There was something about the voice, before he even digested the content of the words, that made the rider pause. The little speech had been clearly enunciated, but there was something odd in the intonation. All thought of imminent escape vanished. The rider sat still upon the rise, the only motion that might betray his presence in the shifting shimmer of sunlight, his beast's head dropping to crop the grass and its tail idly switching as its master looked down with a new interest at the group he had now gotten close enough to see clearly.

"I assure you, Miss Hamilton," the plumpish young man declared, rising to one knee in front of the young lady he'd been fanning as though he were going to declare something quite different to her rather than addressing the young woman who'd spoken, "there is nothing in the forest to upset you in the least. The duke would not permit it," he added pompously, and by craning his neck, the rider could see what the voice would have told him anyway, that it was the absurd young Lord Charles Holland, who'd been trying to get into the four-in-hand club for a year, paying court to what must have been one of the Swanson girls, obviously the latest model to reach the market, that nose was unmistakeable, even at a distance.

"Charles is right, Faith. Daddy would never tolerate anything dangerous in our home wood," an anxious voice said immediately. Yes, the rider thought, his lips curving in an involuntary smile of tribute and acknowledgment, it was a fair designation, for if she wasn't exactly "incomparable," the speaker's appearance came close to the meaning of the word. Her hair was cool sunlight, and her features fulfilled the faultless, flawless classic expectation of what a well bred, wealthy titled young female ought to look like. If there was not enough animation and charm there to suit the silent horseman's own preferences, he reminded himself that those quirks that personified loveliness to him were often considered antipathetic to beauty by the arbitors of the *ton*.

A trim looking, spruce young man with a blunt, open countenance stood beside the Incomparable, and though his face was unknown to the horseman, his accent was not. When he said, with the smallest hint of threat, "Come along, Faith, it's only a short walk; I hadn't thought you such a poor sport," the rider's smile widened, he'd been right, the party contained some more interesting specimens of humanity than he'd thought at first stare. But the sound of the next voice wiped his smile away.

"My dear," a gentleman drawled in amused mellow tones, "we rid ourselves of dragons centuries ago. Or is it possibly unicorns you fear? It's been, to my shame, decades since I had anything to worry about from them, but from what I've been given to understand, although you might meet up with one if there were any at all left in the realm, you, at least, would have nothing to fear from that encounter."

A great deal of tittering arose at the comment, but it had been so adroitly phrased that even the chaperones didn't stir more than their fans at his words. But then Robert Craig, Earl of Methley, was a gentleman noted for his wit.

The only surprise was that he would be exercising it here among these infants, the rider thought, bending forward and growing more involved in the chance-met party.

"Heavens no," the clear young female voice replied without missing a beat, "I don't fear unicorns. They are only horned beasts. Females never worry about the wearing of horns so much as the gentlemen do, you know."

This was sailing very close to the wind, and the rider, grinning, leaned forward to get a good look at the young creature who'd just created a buzz among the chaperones as well as a giggly stir among her contemporaries. But the gentleman blocking his view, the Earl of Methley, was not contemporary with most of the other young men. The earl had recently left his third decade behind him, even as the rider himself had lately done.

That wasn't the only thing that distinguished him from the others in the party. It was odd, almost jarring, to see him here in the green outdoors, since he was so much a creature of the salon. And if he were set on maintaining his reputation as a man of taste and dangerous wit, the rider thought critically, he might do better to remain there. London suited the earl's style, the drawing room was clearly his milieu; this particular fish appeared very much out of the social swim here. In a salon his extreme height was a distinctive and impressive sight; beneath the trees it was reduced to a trifling oddity. In a ballroom the marked contrast between his stark white skin and straight jet hair seemed dramatic, rather than unhealthy. But standing outlined against the open landscape he looked merely thin instead of aristocratically slender, and overall, attentuated rather than elegant. He no more belonged upon a lawn beneath a limitless azure sky than did one of the gilded, spindly chairs he customarily arranged his narrow frame upon.

And yet, his silent critic admitted grudgingly, the man was never a fool. For those light gray eyes sparkled with the same intense intelligence here in sunlight as they did in candlelight, and he dominated the scene here as easily as he did in Town. He loomed so extraordinarily tall, and even with his spareness cut so commanding a figure in his signature garb of stark black jacket, breeches, and boots, that he was like a blot on the pastel canvas the company seemed posed upon. So much so that when he stepped back to execute an overdone bow of complete submission to the young woman who'd silenced him, it was to the unseen rider as though a dark cloud had drifted away from the face of the luminous, shining moon.

He couldn't compare her to the sun. Such brilliance was left to fair beauties like her hostess. This girl, surely no more than a girl, the rider thought, glowed rather than shone. Almost demure in her green sprigged frock, she sat upon a patchwork throw, and he could see little of her slender form save for the fact that it was, like the rest of her, pleasing. But then, he was busy absorbing every detail of her face.

She was nothing at all like such an acclaimed beauty as her hostess, though he found her far more entrancing. Her hair wasn't blessed with the frizz and curl of fashion, but was absolutely straight and drawn back in a glossy slide of amber, so light a brown that it shone like honey in a glass jar in the glancing spears of sunlight. Her face was a clear oval, never the coveted color of milk, but rather the more ivory hue of cream. Her nose was small and straight above lips, acurve with secret laughter at her triumph, the exact flushed shade of bruised raspberries.

It was while the rider was sitting startled, wondering at why so many of his thoughts of her had come couched in edible terms, that the earl, rising from his bow, both hands out to either side to show he was unarmed, capitulated further by asking sweetly, as though he knew she meant him to, "But then, my dear, why hesitate to stroll through the wood with us?"

"In my country," she said, very much in the manner of a governess telling a tale before bedtime, and since her listeners, for all their affectations, were most of them not too far from that stage of life, they responded by unconsciously settling back to listen, "one does not venture into a forest without good and sufficient reason. It is not," she said sternly, "a thing lightly undertaken."

"Red Indians, of course," the earl said dulcetly.

"Of course," the young woman answered readily, "but," she added on a gusty sigh, "if only that were all."

"I should think," murmured the dashing Harry Fabian

to his friend Charlie Bryant, "that a slew of Red Indians would be enough to discourage any picnics."

"Oh but you see," the young woman promptly answered what she'd overheard, "they aren't such a bother, really, since we can post sentries to warn of their coming. Although, one has to post a sentry to watch the sentry, you understand, since Red Indians creep a great deal, and as they shoot arrows, and carry knives, and pad about in deerskin boots, one never knows the sentry has been gotten until one sees him fall."

At this, Lieutenant FitzHugh, the local squire's third son, who'd got himself a bit deafened by cannon at Salamanca and who'd been listening in desultory fashion, now left off admiring Miss Protherow's necklace as he'd been doing just to see her blush and leaned forward to pay closer attention to the young narrator.

"It's that which we can't post sentries for, those creatures and things that lurk in our great forests, that we most dread. But if you really wish me to come along with you now, and can assure me that there are no such things here in England, why then," she said, rising, with the earl's immediate assistance of a hand beneath her elbow, "I should be pleased to go along with you."

"Hold on a bit," demanded Lord Greyville, who'd been on fire to go to the lake a moment before, "what sort of things do you have lurking?"

"Poison bushes and snakes, ticks and leeches and poison spiders," the young lady said pleasantly, and since she'd only gotten to her knees, she shook off the proferred hand and remained there, looking blandly at her inquisitor.

"We've ticks and leeches," the young gentleman pointed out patriotically.

"Nettles, too," one of the ladies put in ruefully, remembering one unpleasant encounter in her youth.

"Do we have any poison spiders?" one of the Washburn sisters asked fearfully, even as her twin left off fanning herself and looked down, examining the rippling surface of their satin coverlet anxiously.

The horseman sighed. These young persons were the cream of society's young eligibles, in the pink of health and blush of youth. Yet still, he thought, very much like the three old fates the ancients had said passed one eye around between them, this group would be lucky if they had the equivilent of one full brain to share among the lot of them.

But then, he shrugged to himself, they weren't expected to invent new machines, write great works, or compose beautiful music. Their primary task was to attract a mate, and breed in the true line to carry on their noble names. And this, in all fairness, he had to admit, they could do, and were actually now in the process of doing. This little gathering was all in the nature of a rite to advance those worthy purposes, and he should not have expected to hear anything very much more profound than the excited babble and argument that now arose over what noxious dangers America possessed that England did not. Actually, he mused, the fact that the conversation had risen above neckcloths and frock lengths to attain such dizzying heights as the nature of poisonous reptiles was likely entirely to the unknown young American female's credit. But if she were a guest here, that, he thought sadly, was likely all he could credit her with, no matter how he tried.

She'd spoken in the unmistakeable accents of her native land. That, and her remarkable face, of course, like the original sight of the entire party, had made him wish for more and feel this curious disappointment at finding two illusions unmasked within the same hour. Because if she were not a member of the idle nobility, then having been made welcome here, she was either related to one of them, or was herself extraordinarily wealthy. And that would make her a member of the newest aristocracy. That happy circumstance could buy her all the older class's rights and privileges, only if, that was to say, she were fortunate enough to attract a true nobleman to help her spend all her money.

Undoubtedly, that was why the earl was here, as close to her as her elbow. It was well known that though his line was as long as his limbs, his fortune was thin as they were as well. And though his intellect ran deep, his pockets were shallow. He doubtless deserved it, but still, the rider thought, it must be a bitter thing to sell oneself to a ninny to save one's heritage. But the earl was never a fool, and what's a soul as weighted against a castle, two manor houses, and a hunting box? the observer mused, as he prepared to knee his mount to a walk. Then he had to leave off his reflections as the pitch of the discussion below intruded upon his thoughts.

"Nettles," young Lord John Percy insisted, his face becoming even redder than his tight high shirt points could account for, "are very nasty. Why, on Oak Day in my home district, the boys fight with them, do you see, and anyone who gets swiped with one ends up with blisters for days." He crossed his arms and glowered, daring anyone to gainsay him, as though he were feeling the sting of the nettles even now, upon this green and blameless shorn lawn.

"Weeks," the young woman said flatly, unemotionally. And as young Percy turned to listen, she added, "The ivy has such a volatile poison within that merely breathing in its vicinity causes internal blisters that last for weeks. And it looks exactly like harmless ivy, the sort I see growing everywhere about here. There's oak, too, that look like these we sit beneath only not quite as tall, that produces even larger lesions . . . that ooze." She drew out the last word as though it were so delicious she could scarcely bear to let it leave her mouth.

As she prated on, about the snakes that pleased themselves by coiling around those deadly oak limbs, some that rattled a tune you had to dance to before they struck, and others that wrapped themselves around persons and promptly hauled them up, screeching, to the treetops, the group she addressed shrank back from her as though she could produce these horrors from a pocket in her skirts.

The young American gentleman, who stood as if on guard at the Incomparable Lady Mary's side, bit his lip and gazed up at the trees as though he wished something, serpent or otherwise, would come and haul his compatriot up and away from the enthralled throng. And the earl stood back, eyes shining, and beamed upon the young woman as she happily launched into descriptions of other venomous attractions commonly found in American gardens. It was then that the rider knew that if he was the only one who could stop her narrative, he must, for her own sake.

He leaned far forward in his saddle to verify his impression. Yes. If at first he'd found her lovely, and at second look believed her as unexceptional as the rest of the company, this final close scrutiny confirmed what he'd suspected at last when he'd seen the earl's reaction. For whatever his multiple sins, the earl was certainly no fool. The girl was in high spirits; she could scarcely conceal her amusement. She was enjoying herself profoundly by pulling the legs of the assorted company so far that in a moment, she'd have them all down flat on their rear ends, howling in distress—and then for her blood. There was the sum of it. And that was the danger in it, for it wouldn't be mere sport in the end; in this company, as he well knew to his own sorrow, ridicule was a blood sport.

Clearly, she'd been bored with them, their amusements and their conversation. And so here she was entertaining herself by spoofing them. But as a stranger, she did not know, could not know, how they valued their self-esteem more highly than any Oriental potentates might or how very much they'd resent having been gulled, nor the extent and the nature of their revenge when they discovered the deception. Oh Methley knew, doubtless he knew, doubtless, the rider thought as he urged his mount forward, he knew to a fraction how easy it would be to woo even a very wealthy young woman who had no other friends, a young female no one else would deign even to speak to without scorn.

And so as a complex act of charity, with revenge and self-service intermixed with it, the rider on the creamy stallion burst from his place of concealment in the beech avenue and rode down the sloping lawns to spoil sport. Only to all the onlookers who immediately turned from the American storyteller to view the intruder, he looked more like a knight of old come to slay a few dragons in order to rescue the fair maiden than a fellow hell bent on silencing the damsel as soon as he could. But the simple fact of his sudden appearance turned the trick nicely before he even drew his mount to a stand several feet from the young lady. For she left off speaking and stared at him as though he were the most wondrous thing an English forest ever disgorged, nettles, dragons, and unicorns included.

There was nothing odd about her reaction, for after all, American or not, the chit had eyes. So all of the other young females, and quite a few of their seniors as well, responded when they saw him. It was not just the fact of his sudden appearance that thrilled them, it was he, himself. He might well have produced the same excitement in their ranks if rather than flying down the slope on a blooded stallion, he'd come strolling along, negligently, hands in pockets. His was that sort of presence.

He didn't need the great steed to show off the long muscles in his legs nor close-fitting riding clothes to display the athlete's torso which grew from trim hips to broader chest to broadest shoulders. Nor did he need his mount's brushed light coat to point up the light golden tan that gilded his own smooth skin on the sensitive hands that held the reins, or on the strong-featured face which smiled reassurance at his startled hostess. Nor did he even require the steed to nudge the errant memories of some of the gentlemen to make them remember their long neglected, gladly forgotten classics lessons and suddenly think, "Centaur!" when he bowed his tousled, tawny head in greeting.

The hair was overlong and thick, and streaked blond and baize and all the several colors that the sun will turn a thatch the color of taffy to begin with when it is left to have its way by constant exposure. And when the dutifully bent head lifted, it was a pair of long hazel eyes which looked out at his impromptu audience, and beneath the long straight nose the mobile lips parted to show a flash of strong white teeth again before the cool voice said evenly, "My lady, greetings. I was visiting with your father and, having missed seeing you at home, I am, you may imagine, delighted to find you here. I cannot believe my good fortune," he added, when it seemed that his unknowing hostess could not reply at once.

The Lady Mary might be forgiven for coming to a stand and remaining at one as her company recovered themselves and pressed forward, eager, in some cases avid, for an introduction. Barnabas Stratton, Lord Deal, might be a neighbor, she might have seen him, or more honestly speaking, looked to see him, many a dozen times along the local roads, but he'd never been delighted to see her, nor missed not seeing her, nor considered it good, bad, or even indifferent fortune to see her, so far as she knew. He was, as everyone knew, almost a social recluse. But now he was here, and Lady Mary had had an excellent upbringing, and besides, everyone was staring at her now. So she swallowed down her fear of his mockery and her surprise at his arrival, and doing homage to generations of British governesses, curtsied and then quietly and without one slip introduced him to her party.

". . . and this," she concluded, several moments later, having come full circle, "is Miss Faith Hamilton, who is visiting with us from America, and this, as I am sure you know, is Robert Craig, Earl of Methley. Lord Deal," she breathed at last as she finished up.

"Yes, of course, we've known each other forever," the earl said pleasantly, though his eyes remained cool.

"Servant, Methley," Lord Deal replied quietly, giving the tall gentleman a level look.

"I could not help but overhear your somewhat spirited debate as I approached," Lord Deal turned and said at once to the entire company, "and I couldn't fail to be impressed at how all you fellows tried to paint this green and pleasant isle as a jungle, even as Miss Hamilton made surviving in her country for over a day seem an incredible feat."

The assembled young people began to relax. The gentlemen, seeing the absurdity of their position and moreover feeling fractionally better because the new arrival made the American girl's boasts seem as foolish as their own so that they knew there could be no winner or loser in the dispute, could now begin to chuckle. The ladies cheered up enormously. Just knowing, one of the Washburn twins whispered to the other contentedly, that there weren't really such ghastly things afoot in the world was a very great relief. The other young American, whom Lady Mary had introduced as a Mr. Will Rossiter, seemed relieved as well. But the earl wore a thoughtful expression, and a quick glance over to Miss Hamilton made Lord Deal wince. Some of her wilder countrymen, he remembered learning, committed massacres when they looked as she did now.

"I understand," he said quickly, "that the fact that you were planning to go through the wood to the lake precipitated the discussion. And as I rode over from that direction this morning," he lied, "I can tell you it's a very good idea, since there was a cool breeze blowing there that was very refreshing. I tell you what," he said with great false spontaneity, "since Miss Hamilton, as a newcomer, quite reasonably has some trepidation about our English woods, I'll take her on my horse, and then we'll all meet there, that is," he bowed to the chaperones who stood at the outskirts of the ring around him after they'd come down the hill to be introduced, "if it is quite all right with you ladies."

It was clear to Miss Hamilton that the chaperones would have considered it quite all right if he'd requested permission to remove her head. And when he put out his hand to her, and Will faithlessly came to her side and cupped his hands to give her a lift up to the saddle, she was very tempted to invent an instant fear of horses. But she did want to ride on this visit, and she didn't want to give this fellow Lord Deal, who was already wearing an irritatingly challenging smile, any further reason to belittle her. So she turned and gave the earl a helpless lift of her shoulders, and he returned the smallest lilt of his dark brows to show he understood, and she found herself raised up until she sat before the new arrival on his magnificent horse.

It was not until they'd pointed out the path to the others and then paced on ahead down the pine-needle-covered narrow track, that he spoke to her.

"You see," he breathed, and no matter how she held herself upright there was no getting away from the fact that they were so close she could hear his faintest exhalation and she even fancied she could feel the glow of his body warmth behind her as palpably as a touch, "no snakes twined about the trees, not a bird of prey gorging on unwary travelers. Mind, there's a man-eating rabbit lurking in the rhododendrons, but don't stare or he'll give himself airs."

"Why," she asked, still staring straight ahead at the tunnel of pines they were passing through, "are they allowing you to ride off with me, alone? I'd thought that wasn't done."

"True, they'd never let me so close to a well-brought-up female unattended if we were on the ground, or on any other piece of furniture for that matter, except a saddle. We're great equestrians, we English, but there are some things even we don't do on horseback. Don't worry," he said all at once, quite seriously, seeing how stiffly she held her slender back, how high her head, "it's not because they think an American girl isn't worth protecting. It's only because a great many things that are unthinkable any other time are quite permissible in summer. It's such a brief, rare time. We relax then, you see. Why," he asked calmly in turn when she made no comment, "did you tell them all that nonsense back there?"

"Oh," she said, beginning to think that the strangest thing about the conversation was not that it was being held with someone behind her back, but that she was losing her anger at his interruption of her fun and chatting with a stranger as though he were a long-time acquaintance, but it was easy, and she saw no harm in it, "I don't know, they were talking such claptrap. All they were doing was flirting and teasing and maneuvering for attention. The ladies were only interested in fixing the gentlemen's interest, or posing for them, and all the gentlemen were doing the same. I became bored, I suppose."

"You're not interested in finding a husband then?" Lord Deal asked with some amusement, remembering the earl's long measuring look as he'd watched them out of sight.

"No," she said at once, turning so that he could at last look directly into her smoldering gray eyes, "for I haven't lost one, you see."

Oh lord no, he thought merrily, even as he threw his head back in delighted laughter, he'd been entirely right, the earl certainly was no fool.

TWO

THE SOUNDS OF the horse's hooves were muffled by the needle-covered floor of the narrow path, and the evergreens crowded so close to the trail that it was obvious that only repeated shearings kept them from jealously closing up entirely around this hole within their heart. They'd been cropped only recently, or so Faith thought, for their cool spicy scent was a sharp contrast to the warm floral aroma of the day she'd left outside their perimeters. Here it was dim, for the evergreens touched tendrils high above their heads where the shears had not yet chastened them, and here it was also cool and quiet and more peaceful than any place she'd yet visited since she'd set foot in England, fully three weeks past.

Although she was not alone now, as indeed, it seemed she'd not been let alone unless she was asleep or in her bath since she'd arrived here, the gentleman she shared the horse with did not, at least, seek to entertain her or quiz her endlessly about her home, as so many of the people she'd met so far had done. In fact, even now, after passing the last week with them at this house party, she found it difficult to separate most of them from the mass of them in her mind, she'd been so overwhelmed by their attentions. There was Lady Mary, her hostess, of course, and her family, and some few others who were different enough to be remarked upon in any crowd, like the earl and the Washburn twins, but in all they were still a jumble of voices and faces to her, all alike in that they all appeared to be equally astonished by the one salient fact of her being an American.

It couldn't just be because she was an alien, or even because her country had lately been at war with theirs. After all, they seemed to take French people as a matter of course, they spoke of Russian princesses as though they were not half out of the common, many of them had servants of several European nationalities, and they mentioned Austrian and German cousins without a blink. But from the moment they heard her speak, or heard of her home country, they were wide-eyed and curious to the point of being ill-mannered. Even more galling, they didn't seem to think that she'd notice, or know enough to mind if she did notice their rudeness. Perhaps they expected her to wear feathers or carry a spear or eat her mutton raw, but it seemed they watched her every move and were vastly pleased and entertained by every difference they did discover in her.

That was why she'd finally broken and told them such a tale back on the lawn. And that was why she'd been so angry at the fellow she rode with now, for she'd just been getting into her stride, and was wondering how far she could go with the tale she'd been spinning, when he rode in and ended it all. She hadn't minded the interruption at first, for in truth, he'd been a thrilling apparition, cutting into their lethargy like lightning enlivening a breathless day. But not only had he ended it, but then he'd clearly let them know they'd been being hoaxed as well. And she'd been just about ready to tell them about the dangerous wild opposum hunts.

Now she remained silent, for she hadn't the measure of this man who companioned her at all. Though he was so astonishingly good looking that she scarcely dared to meet his eye, he spoke to her as naturally as she wished everyone else would do. Yet he'd responded to the greatest set-down she'd ever given a fellow as though he considered it vastly entertaining. Ordinarily, she would have begged pardon for her rudeness to him immediately, she'd never gone so far in incivility and knew there was no excuse for it. But since she suddenly realized that, clearly, she didn't understand any of these people any better than they did herself, she kept to a troubled silence.

"Well," the gentleman behind her now said casually, as though they'd just left off speaking rather than having ridden along mutely for several minutes, "since you're not searching for a husband, I infer that this visit to Marchbanks is in the nature of a vacation. Not," he added lightly, "that I think for one moment it's my business to know what any of your aims are. I assure you I don't mean to interrogate you. But you're obviously unused to our enchanting English customs. If your stay is only to be a matter of weeks, a summer idyll, as it were, then I won't bother to point out certain . . . pitfalls, in our society to you. For then it would scarcely matter, would it? You'd be off on a ship in a month and devil take the lot of us and what we think of you, or, more to the point, what we might do to you for inadvertently tripping over some of our hallowed institutions. It's only because I thought you might stub your toe painfully that I interfered today.

"But that's over now, and if you're just passing through, why bother to tease you with lessons in surviving in the *ton*? . . . I'll swear this is the coolest spot in the entire park, and unless someone's of a mind to submerge themselves in the lake up to their necks, they'd do far better just remaining here until evening, don't you think?'' he asked brightly.

"I hope to be gone by autumn,'' she said very softly, after a thoughtful pause, "but my grandfather, you see, has other plans.''

"Ah,'' Lord Deal commented, finding it interesting to try to read his companion's thoughts by watching the nape of her neck. It was a very lovely nape, to be sure, long and unblemished and shadowed now and again by stray wisps of honey hair that the wind sometimes caused to drift across it. It was a nape that he discovered himself very tempted to kiss in fact, not only because he wondered at whether that creamy skin would be as cool and fragrant as he imagined, but because then she would undoubtedly turn around and he would either be given a more classic embrace, or a deserved swift slap. But either way, he'd be able to see her face and her eyes, which he'd been enchanted to discover were gray as the first haze of dawn. Still, he could at least see her point.

Sitting quite properly side-saddle, if she gazed straight ahead of her instead of looking off to the front of the horse as she was doing, she'd seem aloof and unfriendly if she didn't incline her head that further fraction necessary to read his expression. Yet if she turned to him, since they were of necessity sharing the somewhat confined space of a horse's back, they would be, essentially, nose to nose. A delightful circumstance for him, but unless she were known to be very short-sighted, a very compromising position for her. He sighed.

"I don't mean to be cryptic," she said at once, misinterpreting the reason for the sound she'd heard. "It's only that Grandfather sent me here for exactly the reasons you'd suppose. He's the one looking for a husband," she said crossly, "for me. And as I love him, the least I can do for him is to visit here as he wishes me to do, for a while at least. I've been here almost a month. But I want to go home," she whispered very softly, and as she spoke it, he could swear he read that barely suppressed longing and loneliness for home in the dejected droop of her neck as well as he'd ever read it in anyone's face.

"You're quite sure then that you don't care to shop around and pick up a nice inexpensive English husband?" he asked pleasantly.

"Oh no," she replied at once, shaking her head in the negative so many times that several slips of hair slid loose to tempt him unmercifully.

"Is it anything we've said?" he asked in hurt tones, and then was about to explain his jest as he would to most young women, since they usually took him quite literally, when she pleased him enormously by saying at once, "I've nothing against the English, believe me. I just don't care to marry as yet. Not anyone, of any nationality. But knowing that you've been sent specifically for that purpose and having your hosts know it as well, makes it all that much more uncomfortable. I don't want Grandfather to think I haven't tried, and I don't want to actually deceive him. He knows how I feel, you see, but he's so sure I'll meet my match here . . . How long, do you think, would a person be expected to have to stay on before they gave up on such a search?" she asked.

"That depends," he said thoughtfully, "entirely on how old Grandfather is."

She chuckled. He was just as unexpected a person as his entrance had hinted at. He was very pleasant, one of the nicest gentlemen she'd met since she'd come here. So she turned her head and grinned at him. It was difficult talking with someone you couldn't see, but, on the whole, she

discovered as she quickly turned back to stare down the
long, dark arched tunnel of evergreens again, it was more
comfortable than keeping your gaze averted as he studied
your profile, and far easier than looking directly into those
kind and amused light eyes.

"I'll probably leave for home," she said, "in the autumn. I thought I'd wait until Will gets himself a wife, for
I doubt Grandfather would expect me to stay on here
alone. Will's looking for an English lady to call his own.
He's originally from London, you see, and came to America when he was very young. We arrived here together
because he's worked with Grandfather forever and now
he's made his fortune, he's come back here to settle down,
and Grandfather asked him to look after me. . . . Do you
know that I've told you more about us in a few moments
than I've ever told half the people who pepper me with
questions?" she said wonderingly.

"It's because I promised you something in return, don't
forget," he explained. "And I'm sure you didn't forget,
you're a canny Yankee trader. Now then, since you're
going to stay for an indefinite time, I think you might well
have use for that advice. Don't tease them, Miss Hamilton," he said seriously, "they'll believe anything you
choose to tell them so it would be too easy for a bright
young woman like yourself to mislead them. It's no sport
casting for fish in a barrel. But it's not your sportsmanship
I worry about, it's the fact that they have great power, and
can make you very wretched indeed if they've a mind to,
and if they're given the opportunity as well."

"What?" she said in amazement. "Are you funning me
now in revenge for my earlier stories? What can they
possibly do to me, my lord? Are you going to treat me to
tales of chains and dungeons in return for my stories about
snakes?"

When she was done laughing, he went on to say, very
clearly, very seriously, "They can give you a name,
Miss Hamilton, which is far heavier to bear than chains,
and they can tell tales about you which hurt more and are
more poisonous than those snakes you invented. They can
create you a dungeon out of the thin air by ostracizing you,
and taunting you, and excluding you from society."

"But I have friends whom I trust to remain my friends,"

she said, sitting up straighter. "And I've told you that I don't care about your society. So I don't believe I need any more advice. But thank you," she added, inclining her head as would a queen to acknowledge some courtier's small favor, an effect somewhat ruined by the fact that it could only be seen from the back by the one it was meant to dismiss. To show that she wasn't concerned enough to even be angry, she changed the subject lightly by asking, "And by the way, how did you know I was bamming them?"

"I've been to your country," he answered quietly, turning the horse sharply where the trail suddenly divided.

"Oh really?" she asked with lively interest. "When?"

"The first time? Four years ago," he said.

"But . . ." She paused. "As a soldier?" she gasped.

"Oh no," he said calmly, "I've never bought colors."

"Then," she said breathlessly, this time swinging her head around so swiftly, she felt a twinge, "as a *spy?*"

"No, Miss Hamilton," he answered with a trace of anger, "as a patriot."

They rode on in absolute silence for a few moments more, Faith now wondering why she'd been foolish enough to be shocked simply because a man had been true to his own country, and Lord Deal wondering why a girl whose grandfather had sent her to get an English husband would be angry at a gentleman for being English.

"Good heavens," she said at last, abandoning her bout with semantics and nationalism in an effort to normalize relations, "I'd no idea the lake was so far."

"It isn't," he replied, "we've only been going round and round the bridal path. See?"

And now, looking past his pointed finger, she could see that the evergreens were beginning to slope lower and grow farther apart until they gave way at their end to a wide and grassy meadow. Beyond that, she could make out the group of ladies and gentlemen they'd so recently left, looking as though they'd been raised up by some giant hand and deposited gently in this new locale, for they were ranged around on their cushions and rugs again, only this time on the banks of a disappointingly bland, obviously artificial, and perfectly round ornamental pond.

"And," he bent his head to whisper to her as they rode

into the clearing and he noted the back of her neck growing pink, "here's another unsolicited lesson in British
social niceties. Don't bother to be vexed with me for the
sake of appearances. They none of them will ask where
we've been. It's not only because, my dear Miss Hamilton, they believe you to be entirely moral. Neither is it so
much that they trust me to be highly honorable, as it is that
they know me to be highly eligible. And I am, I assure
you. For you see," he breathed, his whisper tickling her
ear as he brought his lips nearer the nearer they came to
her smiling hostess, "I just happen to be looking for a
fiancée. Because as it turns out, I *did* lose one."

Faith was lifted down from the saddle immediately by
the earl. Before she could get her balance back and take an
unwavering step on firm ground, Lord Deal had made his
abjectest apologies to the group, cited several pressing
matters, and with a show of reluctance so outsized it
bordered on mockery, he saluted them and was off again
and gone back through the evergreen passage he'd so
lately left.

"The fellow," the earl drawled, "certainly knows how
to make his entrances and exits. But how was the performance itself?" he asked Faith as they strolled back to
where her patchwork cushion had been placed upon the
grass. "Did he entertain you? He took such a time deliver-
ing you to us, we'd begun to wonder whether we'd have to
send either a search party or a vicar after the two of you."

Though the words caused Faith to feel guilt for no
reason at all, Lord Deal had said that no one would mind
their absence, and then too, the earl's voice held no more
than its usual boredom, despite his words. So she only
laughed and said dismissively, "You'd have done better to
send a gardener with pruning shears. I'd no idea that you
English kept timber on your land as impenetrable as our
deepest forests."

"Oh?" he said with a little interest lightening his gray
eyes, "like the ones with all those dreadful creatures lying
in wait within them? Why don't you tell us some more
about them? Lord knows we could do with some enthralling conversation. The company's gone into a decline since
you've left. As you can see," he whispered as he gave her
one long white hand in assistance so that she could grace-

fully settle down to her lawn seating again, "they're all positively wilting, and it isn't just the weather that's breeding ennui. We could use a little enlivenment from our intrepid young American visitor."

He smiled down at her, and from where she sat upon the ground, he seemed even taller, for to read his expression she had to tilt her head so far back as to look foolish. Perhaps that was why she decided to only shake her head in denial of his request, because it seemed silly to carry on a conversation with someone yards above you, and not, she told herself bracingly, most certainly not because she'd just been warned against indulging herself by telling more such tales. This day, she mused, she seemed to be being invited to the most awkward discussions with gentlemen she'd have otherwise enjoyed chatting with, for they seemed either to tower over her or sit behind her when they spoke.

That was why, after she noted the earl had removed himself a pace from her, she greeted young Lord Greyville with such a wide smile when he approached and then without ceremony plunked himself down beside her with a sigh, and hugging his knees, said disarmingly, "What a pack of dead bores you must take us for, Miss Hamilton. Your only excitement today was when the Viking took you for a ride, but then he dropped you off and went on his way again. And this Duke of Limbs," he whispered, gesturing with one raised shoulder to the earl behind him, "only says sweet somethings into your ears, and those, from two miles away. Poor sport! I'll wager you don't pass your afternoons in such no-account fashion back where you come from," he concluded, looking at her eagerly.

"Of course she doesn't, ignorant puppy," the earl commented laconically, causing the young gentleman to wince, since he'd only approached the American girl when it seemed that the older man had moved away from her and had been thoroughly engrossed with staring out at something across the waters. "But she doesn't dare tell you the whole of it for fear you'd drown yourself in the lake in shame for your lack of enterprise. Then too," he mused, "perhaps she's afraid the Viking will come bounding out of the forest again to repudiate her."

"The Viking?" Faith asked curiously, for she'd thought the first mention had just been Lord Greyville's jest regarding Lord Deal's dramatic appearance, but now the earl's continued reference to it confused her.

"That is our little name for Lord Deal," the earl commented, with a sidewise smile at Lord Greyville which was instantly reciprocated, "whose last visit seems to have silenced you."

"Oh too bad," Lord Greyville said with disappointment, "since I wondered at what American fellows did for fun on summer afternoons."

When Faith did not answer at once, the earl looked down at her indecision and said in kindlier fashion than was his usual wont, "You might as well tell him, Miss Hamilton, since he'll doubtless cling like a burr until you do. And I shouldn't worry about the Viking. I don't know how Lord Deal would be able to contradict you on the subject of American gentlemen and the way they spend their leisure even if he came down on a thunderbolt to interrupt you this time, since when he visited your nation last I imagine your countrymen had very few idle hours, and likely were all engaged in shooting at him in any event."

"Well," said Faith, looking up him, and raising her chin, she went on defiantly, "as it happens you're right both ways, your grace. I'm not worried about being contradicted, and my countrymen often pass their leisure time shooting, whether we are at war or not. Because, you see, there's so much to shoot at. For example, I'm sure you've heard about our great bears?"

"I'd wring your neck Fay, my dear," Will Rossiter remarked pleasantly as he took her arm and marched her a few paces ahead of the rest of the company that was straggling back to the manor, "if there weren't so many witnesses."

"But then you'd have to leave sweet Mary's side for an extra minute to do so," Faith replied just as charmingly and in just as low a voice.

They smiled at each other so prettily, and seemed so much in charity, that to the rest of the houseguests, who could not hear them, it seemed as it always did, that the two young Americans were brother and sister. They were a handsome couple, and it was generally agreed to be especially charming to see them when they conferred together. Though they did not exactly look alike, there was a likeness about them. She was nearing her twenty-first year and he was only four years her senior. Miss Hamilton had those long straight gleaming brown tresses, and Mr. Rossiter, a stylish crop only a shade darker. She had a shapely, graceful form, and he was trim and well coordinated. And though his eyes were the shade of deep brewed tea, and hers smoky gray, when they spoke together their accents made them seem as twinned as the Washburn sisters were.

Mr. Rossiter had been born in England, and it was true that each time he spoke with an Englishman he sounded more British, but like so many afflicted with unintentional mimicry, he seemed to lapse when he chatted with Miss Hamilton. What those two spoke in those oddly flat and nasal accents sounded so different from English as to be another language entirely, and yet what they said was comprehensible. Listening to them, as one amazed gentleman said, was more than amusing, it was like suddenly discovering you understood Latin, a thoroughly unexpected and delightful experience. Even now, some of the guests, seeing them deep in whispered conference, felt it was too bad that they were missing out on the fun, since no one could hear what the two were conversing about.

"Do you suppose," Harry Fabian remarked half-seriously to Jeremy Tuttle as they sauntered in the wake of the pair, "that all Americans act as though they're related to each other? Is that what they mean by the democratic principle they're always going on about?"

"I shouldn't think so," his companion replied quite seriously, since he seldom saw humor unless he could actually see it with his eyes, and Harry seemed to be straight-faced, "because I understand their population's growing and it can't be all due to immigration."

"I couldn't stop you once you were in full spate," Will went on, his pleasant smile for the company's sake at odds with the annoyance in his tone for her, "but you've got to decide whether you want to be received as a guest or an entertainer here. If your grandfather could hear you, my girl, he'd whack you. I would if I dared. You've got to stop spouting that nonsense. You're making it seem like we all grew up in haystacks, or just swung down from the trees."

"Ah, you're afraid I'll hobble your style," she said.

"It's you I worry about," he replied, before she cut in with just enough anger to silence him, "Bother it's me, my boy. I've got the pack of them eating out of my hands. It's your Lady Mary you're worried about. And as they're all tickled at whatever I say since they've been told it's a very rich American lady says it, she'll take you as you come, Will. You're not accountable for me."

"But I am, Fay," he said unhappily, his brown eyes so serious that she heard him out. "I promised to look after you while we're here, and you know I've offered more than that to you, many times. And not just for your money either. We're friends, and if you've changed your mind about it and dislike me making up to Lady Mary, tell me now, before I get too involved, because I tell you I will get more involved if you do not."

"Ah, Will," she said softly, "many times indeed. You've offered for me four times, this makes it the fifth, and I'll tell you again, no. And I know we're friends, just as I know it's only that between us, though you're right, there's no 'only' about such a nice thing. So court your lady and good luck to you, she's sweet and kind, besides being outrageously beautiful, and I'd like to see you make a match of it. Don't worry so much about me. I'll do fine for myself."

"Fine?" he asked with such emphasis that they stopped walking abruptly and the rest of the company had to meander on and pretend very busily that they didn't see the pair halt in their tracks and hold an argument in hushed whispers.

"Fine? When you present yourself as some sort of a . . . freakish thing, American or not, to amuse yourself or them, I can't say which."

"They bore me, Will," she said with quiet emphasis. "And when they're not boring, they're patronizing me, I can tell. Because I'm not one of them, and not even a 'lady' as they see it. Or even born English, as you are. But yes, sometimes I need to amuse myself and it gives me great pleasure, perhaps the only pleasure I've gotten since I came here, to see how far they'll continue to go, despite all the terrible things I tell them, simply because they believe me to be rich beyond their most pressing needs."

"But how can you expect sincerity from anyone when you refuse to be sincere in turn?" he asked.

"Well, I don't expect it," she snapped. "I don't expect anything. All I want is for sufficient time to go by until I can go home again."

"Oh Faith," he sighed, hearing how her voice broke at the last, almost making "home" a two-syllable word. "It's the first time you've ever been away, you'll get used to it. And I promise I'll take you home myself when it's time. But, at least, why not give it a chance till that time? Why not make some friends while you're here?"

"Well I have," she said, rubbing at her nose and searching for a handkerchief in her recticule so it would look as though she had to sneeze, for really, these waves of black sorrow which came over her so suddenly when she let herself realize how far from home she was, how surrounded with strangers she was in her new circumstances, were sometimes embarrassingly overwhelming. "There's Lady Mary, and the Washburn sisters, and that nice little Miss Protherow," she said, snuffling and abandoning the search for a handkerchief as she gained control again.

He took her arm and they began walking again, since he'd noticed the way the others were slowing their steps or frankly hanging back, and whispering together.

"I meant," he said softly, "gentlemen friends. Remember, you promised your grandfather to try."

"Yes," she admitted, "I did promise . . . to at least make friends. I will try. But Will, they're so stodgy and trivial and, except for the earl, they're all such jinglebrains, too."

"Even the dashing Lord Deal? The fellow you disappeared with for so long this afternoon," Will asked slyly.

"Dashing indeed. Precisely." She laughed. "Because Methley says he's almost a hermit, but when he does appear on the scene, he dearly loves to cut a dash. At least he's not boring, but there's nothing at all to take seriously about him, the earl says."

"And he?" Will asked curiously, looking to where the tall gentleman was strolling alone after he'd been relieved of Faith's company.

"He," Faith smiled, following the direction of his glance

toward the earl, "might well become a *friend*, Will. But that's all."

"I see," Will said, and he thought, Ah well, it's early days yet.

"Do you?" asked Faith, and she thought, I don't think so, my dear friend, I hardly think so at all.

THREE

AFTER DINNER A storm blew up. The ladies sat in the drawing room and made desultory conversation, and then, as though some composer with a fine sense of irony was orchestrating the night, even as the first gentleman set foot in the room to join them, a rumble of thunder drowned out his opening words. This, of course, gave the company a great deal of conversation immediately, and though she imagined she was, Faith was not the only one to bless the sudden early summer storm for the diversion of its unexpected appearance.

Timid little Miss Protherow was secretly able to dry her damp palms on the velvet seat of her chair and breathe a shaky sigh of relief. She'd been dreading the onset of evening all day, remembering that Mr. Haskell had begged her for a song last night, and then, when time, on her side for once, had ended their evening without her performance for the company, he'd vowed he'd hear her out this night. Since it was difficult for her to even chat comfortably with a gentleman, much less one she admired so much as she did Mr. Haskell, she counted herself fortunate that the noise of the storm spared her the agony of singing to him in public tonight. It was fortunate, too, that since the thunder caused the company to forego the pleasures of a domestic musicale, she never had the chance to discover that by the time he'd reached his room last night Mr. Haskell had forgotten both the promise and Miss Protherow entirely.

But there were, after all, fully twelve highly visible, highly eligible, and highly nubile young women at the house party at Marchbanks, plus some older sisters and a great many mamas, with a clutch of chaperones and a surfeit of accompanying maids, and not a few of these attendants of a sportive nature, so it was understandable that a fellow might be distracted. And as there were fourteen eligible gentlemen invited to be distracted by them (for since the ladies had the ordering of the invitations, they spited nature and drew the balance in a way to please themselves), plus a good many papas and uncles and scores of valets and grooms to go with them, it was not surprising that Miss Protherow should have dreaded performing before such a gathering. Still, although she considered it something on the order of singing at the Opera itself, her hosts thought the party merely a comfortable number for a country gathering. But then, they had a daughter to marry off.

Not that they had a thing to worry about on that score. The Lady Mary had been hailed as an Incomparable the moment her little satin-shod toe had touched social waters a few months before. She was titled and lovely, demure and obedient, wealthy and well-bred. The Duke of Marchbanks already had four excellent offers for her, in writing, on his desk and five other verbal ones waiting to be put to paper the moment he gave some encouragement. Or she did.

For the Lady Mary hadn't shown any outsize preference for any suitor and though her parents knew she'd take whomever they chose, it pleased them to wait on matters for a little while longer to see if there were any she or they particularly preferred. The noble Boltons were, as everyone in the *ton* knew, prepared to be liberal. They'd made clear that so long as a gentleman was enormously wealthy and of impeccable lineage, he might be considered for the honor of applying for their lovely daughter's hand. But there was no great hurry; she could remain available for at least a few more months. After all, a man with a full stomach can afford to peruse the menu and keep the waiter waiting. Then, too, there was the matter of the American girl, Miss Hamilton. The duke owed her grandfather a favor and showing off the chit with his Mary would do no harm, even though, as it became increasingly clear, it would do neither of them any especial good. But then, Mary didn't need any benefits from the relationship, and the American girl certainly didn't seem to want any.

For instance, the duke thought, looking over to where

the young people were congregated before he went off to the card room with some other gentlemen, look at the chit now. Unusual style, but pretty with it, and with a fortune coming from her grandfather to improve her all out of recognition. Foreign to be sure, American to boot, so not quite the thing for a gentleman with both name and funds to his name. But she might do well enough for some young sprig whose family would be pleased to see him finally settle, and settle comfortably at that.

And there she was, surrounded by the likes of young Greyville, who, granted, once was not worth a look, but who was now sure to be old Crowell's heir, and Gilbert North, a younger son but one with a fine estate in the Midlands, and Porlock and Trowbridge, both a bit rackety to be sure, but each with a manor and a townhouse in his pocket. And who were all her smiles for? The Earl of Methley, who had an old title, a castle, two manors, and a townhouse, but all mortgaged up to the rooftops and every bit of it for rent or sale to save it from the auction block including, obviously, from his presence here, the owner of these honors and properties himself.

The duke sighed; he'd told Godfrey he'd present his girl to society, and he had, but he couldn't prevent her from wasting herself. He was her host, not her jailer or banker. Perhaps, he mused, as he entered the card room with thoughts of more perfectly matched suits in his head, he'd have his own lady, or Mary herself, have a word with the girl before she ruined herself entirely. But had the duke lingered on longer, he might have changed his timetable a bit and hauled his guest away to have that word with her himself, at once.

"A real rattler," Lord Greyville said with some pleasure, after a roll of thunder had silenced the conversation in the room, "but don't tell me, Miss Hamilton," he sighed, "I know, you've got worse than this sort of thing going on every night at home."

He'd been a bit disgruntled since the American girl had so far bested each one of his boasts of the horrors and dangers his own home offered, especially when all he had to contribute were a few apocryphal ghosts, which he couldn't produce on demand anyway. Had he but known it and pushed the matter further, the spirits in question would have carried the day, or the night, and clanked away with the honors uncontested. Her homeland held a great many wonders but wasn't old enough to be properly haunted, a fact for which Miss Hamilton was profoundly grateful, as she didn't relish the thought of spectral visitations, feeling she had enough of her own phantoms to cope with.

Miss Hamilton was a fine looking female, Lord Greyville thought; he especially liked those large and speaking eyes. Though he'd always preferred blond and curling tresses, there was no denying she had a first-rate shape, or else he wouldn't have complimented her on her blue frock tonight; he wasn't a man to comment upon fashion unless manners demanded he explain his stares. But it made a fellow feel very small to be constantly told, even if only by inference, by a smashing young woman, that she thought he lived in a land as safe and tepid as her bathtub.

But Miss Hamilton surprised and gratified him this time by only saying quietly, in response to his challenge, "Oh no, I think thunderstorms are universal."

Mr. Rossiter, from where he stood at Lady Mary's side, smiled approval at this unexceptional answer.

"The weather then is the same?" the Earl of Methley asked, with one thin dark brow arched high in amazement. "But my dear Miss Hamilton, you were only just telling me how pleased you were with how temperate our blessed isle is in comparison to your homeland."

"Ah well," Faith answered with a sweet smile that took the curse off her words in Lord Greyville's eyes, if not his ears, "Our summers are hotter and our winters colder, of course, but—"

"It might just be a matter of latitudes," Mr. Rossiter put in quickly, "or longitudes, since we come from an area which is, I believe, several degrees both to the south and to the west of here."

And as he expanded on this dull theme, several of his listeners began to fidget with their fobs or fans, healthy competition being one thing, geography lessons another. So it was that there was a general murmur of gratification when he was done and the earl said, nodding just as though he might have understood the lecture, though due to its impromptu nature, even its author had not, "Still, how tranquil by comparison it must be for you, this vacation here with us.''

Before Mr. Rossiter could speak to intercept the comment that was aimed at Miss Hamilton, young Lord Greyville, clearly goaded beyond his limited capacity to endure, interrupted him by saying with patriotic zeal, ''Yes, damme, Methley, we all know the Yanks have blizzards in July and heat waves at Christmas and giant toads and whatall monstrosities to contend with every day, Miss Hamilton told us all about those. But it ain't as though they're safe as houses here, for we've had a war going on around us for donkey's years, and they have not. We've only had Napoleon slathering on our doorstep since forever,'' he sneered, ''and bless me but I'd rather face a dozen of Miss Hamilton's wild bears and opposums than the likes of him. So I, for one, think they ought rather to be grateful they were safe at home, *by comparison*,'' he concluded, shooting a triumphant look to the earl, ''until now.''

''Here, here,'' a few other young gentlemen said rousingly, as Lord Greyville, flushed with victory, downed the rataffia he'd only been holding for something to do in one gulp and didn't even notice to gag when he was done.

''Really?'' Miss Hamilton said sweetly, cutting across Mr. Rossiter's reply. ''How odd that you should think we ought to be grateful, Lord Greyville. For as I recall, and I've a shocking memory usually, we were very lately at war. At least,'' she went on as Lord Greyville's face started to become warm as he began to remember what he realized he ought never to have forgotten, even in his annoyance, ''*someone* burned down our capital city of Washington a few years ago, and I don't believe it was Napoleon, at least I can't recall that *we* ever had anything to fear from him. In fact, as I remember,'' she went on inexorably as Mr. Rossiter prayed for the lightning to stop playing about outside and immediately get down to business within the drawing room itself, ''it was Napoleon who kindly offered to help us at that time, but only to save our lives, you see, so I don't believe,'' she concluded to an absolute and deafening silence, ''that we had, or would have had, much to fear from him here, even if he weren't marooned on an island halfway to Africa now.''

*   *   *

Well, good, Faith thought after she dismissed her maid and blew out her candles and slipped into bed. Because likely now she'd be able to go home that much sooner. And from the looks upon the faces of everyone this evening, including Will and even her maid, that might be as soon as tomorrow morning, and probably too, she thought, on a rail, all the way out of town. With perhaps, she thought, lying absolutely still and staring into the darkness, a little bit of tar and a few feathers to speed her on her way.

Oh damnation, Miss Hamilton thought, as one warm tear fled her hot, embarrassed keeping, she hadn't meant a word she'd spoken and wished she'd cut her tongue off instead of spouting them. She didn't even like Napoleon. And she wasn't sure he'd offered help to her country, she'd only been sixteen, after all, at the time, but doubtless if he had, it was out of mischief. And neither did she blame Britain for the onset of the hostilities, since Grandfather had been a rabid Federalist who'd disliked President Madison almost as much as the war which had cut into his shipping and export business. He and his friends never called it anything but "Mr. Madison's War" anyway.

And lord, she thought forlornly, turning her face into her pillow, he'd be disappointed in her if he'd heard her tonight. Never for voicing her opinion, if it only had been her opinion—but it wasn't. It had only been that she'd been acutely aware of the fact that she was different, and since she'd arrived she'd been searching for insult in every comment addressed to her. And, at that, she remembered wretchedly, the comment hadn't even been meant for her.

That young dunderhead Lord Greyville had been brangling with the earl and she had taken him up on it. Then she'd proceeded to insult everyone in the room, including poor Will, who'd been trying so hard to impress his English lady. And all because she'd feared mockery. And partially, perhaps, she thought, stung by sudden guilt, because she wanted so badly to go home.

She longed for home with such acuteness that each sunset she dreaded facing the pillow she drowned in secret tears each night. But it wasn't because of the English, or the war. The war was over; however reluctantly it had been fought by the Federalists, or willingly waged by the War Hawks, it was done. And since no one had won, and no one had lost, it was better forgotten.

And how could she dislike the English? Their every spoken word reminded her of the one person in the world she adored, her grandfather. He had those same musical arched accents, as did so many of his friends. A great many persons she knew at home from his generation had originally come from the old world, and most of them still had their accents intact. In truth, what she'd heard since she'd come here sounded more like what she had grown up with in Grandfather's house than what she heard regularly in many quarters of New York, since half the city was immigrant and spoke in the dialects of a dozen lands. Hearing her hosts and their guests in conversation reminded her of long evenings at home when she'd been a girl, sleepily listening to adult conversation spoken in accents she'd come to associate with safety, wisdom, and love.

And no matter what her hosts might have privately thought of her, they'd been unfailingly polite. It wasn't their fault she'd been foisted on them anymore than it was that she didn't wish to marry any of them.

Faith turned in her bed, seeking a more easeful position. But as it wasn't her body but her heart and conscience that troubled her; there was no way she could arrange herself so as to be comfortable with herself. She was almost one and twenty, and unwed. Though she was content with that statistic, Grandfather was not. He'd known she didn't wish to marry as her mother had done; he understood she didn't seek a husband at all, indeed, he'd seen her turn up her nose at all the worthy young men who'd called upon her at his home. But still, though she thought he knew her as well as any being on earth could, he couldn't accept that this was her desire and not her dire fate. He'd believed it a lack in the young men, not in herself. He'd begged her to come to this, his England, thinking, no doubt, that if the long sea voyage didn't change her mind about his favorite, Will, then one of those glib young blades he remembered from his own youth in London would change her mind about wedlock itself.

But Grandfather had been forced to leave his homeland because of poverty, and so remembered those gentlemen with an aura of grace and graciousness that only envy could have gilded them with. For she didn't find them so beguiling. But then, she thought, suppressing the thought even as it arose as it so often did in the depths of night, like some leviathan from the unplumbed bottoms of her mind, she wouldn't, since love, marriage, and all it entailed was not for her, could not be for her, no matter if Grandfather had sent her to the heights of Olympus rather than to the countryside of England to seek a mate.

But she shouldn't disappoint him. That was poor payment for one who'd cared enough to take her to live with him those years ago, rescuing her from out the noisy, rancorous, frightening battlefield that had been her parents' keeping. No, she owed him far more than that. If she were a better girl, she often thought when in her deepest desponds, she'd marry just to suit him, no matter the sorrow to herself. She'd been tempted to do so many a time and would have done long since if it were not for the outsize terror that arose in her at the very thought.

At the least, she sighed, twisting her coverlets in her tossing until her bed looked as though it had been furrowed and plowed for a spring planting, she ought to have seen it out until a decent time had elapsed before returning home, as she'd agreed. She oughtn't, she knew, just like her countryman had cautioned, have given up the ship. And she was too honest to elude the damning suspicion that it was possible she'd known all that, but had gone ahead and ended it all anyway at the first opportunity and on the merest pretext, in the quickest, most selfish, convenient way possible.

Faith was so disappointed in herself that when she finally heard the faint tapping on her door above her stifled sobs, and thought for one moment that it might be all the assembled company come, bearing torches, to escort her to the town limits, she didn't blame them in the least.

She finally managed to sit up and whisper "Come in." When the tapping went on, she slid down from her high bed and crept to the door and cracked it a slit open. Lady Mary stood before her, shifting from foot to foot, her worried face seeming to float in a blurred nimbus of candlelight.

"Oh do let me in, Faith dear," she whispered, her breath causing the candle to dance and throw violent shadows across her lovely face and the wall behind her. "I dread being discovered out here in the hall, but I have to see you."

"I don't know why you should want to," Faith said on a sniffle. But she drew the door wide and Lady Mary came hurrying in, looking very like one of the ancestral spirits Faith was most anxious not to meet, with her long white dressing gown floating after her, almost catching in the door she closed quickly behind her.

"Oh dear," Lady Mary said, as she placed the candlestick on a dressing table. "Does that mean you won't forgive me either?"

Faith had wandered back to her bed, and was in the process of climbing up to sit on the side of it when her hostess's words stopped her in mid-motion.

"Forgive you?" she asked, turning her head and staring at the blond girl. "What in heavens name is there to forgive you for? I'm the one who's thoroughly disgraced herself. I ought never to have spoken as I did, and I tell you right now, Mary, I'm ashamed. But you needn't worry, I'll be ready to leave for home on the first fair tide . . . and Will doesn't have to come with me either."

"Oh no," the other girl wailed in distress before she clapped her hand over her mouth and whispered, "Indeed Faith, that's why I came here tonight. Father said he'd have a word with you in the morning, and Mama is so angry at Lord Greyville that he's been allowed to stay on with us only because the only way she could get to bed was by telling him his apology was accepted. That and the fact," she mused, "that Father went to school with his father. But it will be dreadful if you don't accept our apologies—it will be unthinkable. Oh Faith, please, it will all be forgotten in a day if you stay on, but if you leave us, Mama says we will look so . . . gauche, ah, no account, do you see?"

"I understand 'gauche,' " Faith said wryly.

"I've done it again, haven't I?" Lady Mary sighed. "It's only that I've tried and am trying to take such special care with you, Faith. I've never known any other Americans, except you and Will, and he,'' and here she paused and even in the inconstant light, Faith imagined she could see the other girl blush rosily, "is actually English, you know. It's simpler with French people,'' she explained sadly, "because they're so foreign, and you can always blame everything on their not understanding, but in your case, you do understand, and are so much the same as we are, but very different too.''

"I have the same problem,'' Faith replied, and hopping down from the side of the bed again, she came over to Lady Mary and said, with the first real warmth she'd felt for hours, "And I'm not angry at anyone, truly, except myself. And,'' she smiled, for the other girl looked so woebegone and defenseless in her white gown with her fair curls worn loose and tumbling down her back that Faith remembered she was three whole years her hostess's senior, and that eighteen was, or at least seemed to be in the case of English girls, or perhaps only this particular English girl, still very young, "I'll stay on, of course, and gladly, if you can assure me that you all truly want me to.''

Mary blurted in amazement, "Of course we do, how can you doubt it? But when you went rushing out of the room without a word, we feared we'd mortally insulted you. The War, you know. It never ought to have been mentioned. Is it,'' she asked hesitantly, "was it,'' she stammered, "oh I don't know whether you think it proper that I ask, but had you . . . lost someone dear to you in the confrontation?''

"Oh. No. It wasn't pleasant, of course, to know we were at war, and there was a scare when all the militia came to town because we'd heard we were going to be invaded. I was frightened then. But no, we were lucky. Grandfather was likely too old to join, even if he'd wanted to, my father was down in Virginia and only in a civilian patrol, and I've no brothers or uncles. No,'' Faith repeated, adding, since it seemed her hostess was still uneasy, "and it isn't rude to ask me that.''

"Oh,'' Lady Mary said, and then very quickly, as though she hoped to get the words out before she thought better of them, she said, "It's only that, you see, I'd thought perhaps that's why you'd never married, and that, you see, what Lord Greyville said upset you so much because it brought all of it, and . . . *him*, whoever he was, back to you," and having said this in a rush, she hung her head.

"Oh," Faith said softly, "that's lovely. But I'm afraid you've read too many novels. Or perhaps I haven't read enough." She laughed, feeling closer to her hostess for the first time since they'd met, but then, she realized suddenly, they'd never had such an informal chat, nor even had time alone together since that day. "No, there's no 'he,' and likely never will be. You see, I don't want to marry, that's why I'm not wed."

But now the other girl's eyes opened wide and she stepped back a pace, stumbling against a chair, and by catching onto its side, she unthinkingly backed herself into it. Then she stared up at Faith, and asked, with a certain amount of absolute incredulity coloring the shock in her voice, "Never wed? But Faith, whatever else will you do? I don't know about America, but here, if you don't marry, you dwindle to nothing. No, really. You have no home, unless it's with your father or your husband. If you can't get a husband, when you grow old and your parents are gone, you must live with a relative and make yourself useful, as it's not likely you'll ever have any fortune. Females seldom inherit, you know; your money usually comes to you in a settlement when you wed. No, there's no place for a woman alone here. Whatever do you do in America if you aren't married?"

Faith hesitated. This was difficult. Though she'd thought the problem through logically time and again, it was never easy to explain. None of her friends who were already wedded agreed. Grandfather refused to believe it, which was why she was here. And she'd tried to explain it to Will forever, but he simply didn't comprehend at all.

"It's not a great deal different in America," Faith began, but then said impatiently, "Well, no, it's not different at all, yet. But it will be. No, truly, because we pride ourselves on being daring and modern in all our ideas, at least, we aren't quite so . . . rigid in our customs as you are here. That is to say, and I've discussed this with my grandfather at length, someday I hope to help him run the family business. Ah, there, you see? You're horrified, I can see it in your face. But there's one whopping big difference between us right there, for we see nothing wrong with trade, and since I've come here I've noticed that you don't think any gentleperson should engage in it. But at home, we think everyone should, and if they make a great deal of money, well, more to their credit. Here, you don't even like to talk about how you make your fortunes at all.

"Though I have noticed," Faith continued on a smile, as she paced in front of Lady Mary like a lecturer, "that everyone whispers about how much money they think the other fellow's got."

Lady Mary smiled at that too, remembering the hushed conferences one so often overheard among the mamas and dowagers at every social occasion as they rated prospective suitors by their birth, appearance, and funds, although not necessarily in that order.

"I've a head for business. My grandfather is in shipping and trade, and I find it fascinating. He has a colliery, part ownership in several vessels, both river- and ocean-going, and deals in tobacco and cotton going to Europe, and china and linen coming from it. And he has no son, only my mama, who doesn't care for money in the least, she only likes to spend it."

Here both girls grinned, and then laughed together, thinking of similar females they both knew. As they laughed, Lady Mary thought with wonder at how nice Faith actually was, not at all alien or prickly as she'd thought she was until now, and Faith thought all at once about how sweet young Mary was, not a bit stiff or excessively mannered as she'd believed her to be all this time.

"My father's in business, too, but he lives down in Virginia," Faith said quickly, "and hasn't the slightest interest in anything but his plantation and his crops. So who's to carry on the family trade? Will's a partner, and Grandfather has others. But who will carry on in the family tradition? Well, I think I will.

"Because," she said at last, coming to the hardest part, "I don't care to marry. My parents, you see, dislike each other enormously. They haven't lived together for years. And for all he talks of marriage, I note Grandfather has been content to live a widower since before I was born. So why," Faith asked militantly, "should I wish to be told what to do, to be ordered about, and to spend my entire life at someone else's beck and call?

"After all," Faith insisted, wheeling about, hands on her hips, facing Lady Mary as though the girl were accusing her instead of sitting wide-eyed listening to what appeared to be her idea of blasphemy, "you were right. It may not be easy to remain unwed in either of our countries. But why should I spend my youth obeying my father, my adulthood obeying my husband, and then likely my dotage obeying my children? When then, should I be able to do what *I* choose?"

Since this was unanswerable, since indeed the entire concept was so . . . yes, Lady Mary thought dazedly, revolutionary, she could not speak at once. But looking at Faith, who stood waiting for a reply, and seeing how her eyes flashed even in the unreliable candlelight and how her long straight hair gleamed when it caught that unsteady glow, even bound as it was in its single bedtime braid, and how her nightshift drifted against her as she spun around, outlining her high breasts against her graceful, slender form, Lady Mary (who had read quite a few novels) said only, rather pitiably, as though she was holding on for dear life to the one sure thing she knew even as she'd hold on to a raft in a raging floodtide, "But what about love?"

"Ah," said Faith.

After a moment, when her words were carefully chosen, she said thoughtfully, "I'm sure it's delightful. I've never been 'in' love, and I daresay if I were, I'd wish to marry. But," she said at once, as Lady Mary began to grin in triumph, "I firmly believe that one doesn't 'fall' in love, as one falls into a pit, or a hole in the street, all unawares. One has to want to be in love, or need to be, to feel love for someone. Only look at all the old bachelors this old world holds! I don't see them tripping about, 'falling' in love, or apologizing for having not done so. No, they're far too concerned with their own comforts to be susceptible. And as I don't wish to love anyone either, I don't think that will be a problem."

"My nurse," Lady Mary giggled, "would say you've just dared the elves. She always told me to never say 'never,' since there are elves that live in cracks in the ceiling who listen to you and take you up at your word. She'd say that now you've guaranteed that you'll fall in love with the first fellow you see when you leave the room.''

"Good heavens," Faith gasped in great mock horror. "And with the way my luck's been running, I'll wager it will be Charlie Bryant!"

At that, both girls began laughing, for Bryant was a houseguest and though as well blooded as a brood stallion and twice as high on his own high horse, he was famous for having almost as long a nose as one of those fine steeds, and absolutely no chin at all. After they'd shushed each other for making so much din at such an advanced hour, and then promptly went off into more fits of smothered laughter, they smiled at each other. For though Lady Mary was more than a little shocked by her outspoken American guest, and Faith thought her hostess charming but more childlike than was good for her, each thought she'd found a good friend. The late hour, the shared laughter and stealth had united them.

And so when Lady Mary finally crept off to her chambers, with Faith keeping watch at her own door and barely suppressing her giggles when Mary stubbed her toe and hopped a pace, Lady Mary thought that though a great deal of what her American guest had said was absolutely terrifying and certainly seditious, it was, like everything else about her new friend, interesting, nonetheless.

And Faith, tumbling into her bed at last, and noting that it had begun to feel like her own bed at last, and moreover that now she hadn't the slightest desire to dampen that pillow with so much as one tear, thought that in all, Lady Mary was a very good sort of girl, and perhaps this visit wouldn't be as onerous as she'd believed.

But before sleep could come, Faith felt a twinge, because she hadn't been completely candid with her hostess. She'd told her the bare facts, of course. But since she was basically a straightforward person, she wondered drowsily as she sank into sleep whether she ought to have mentioned certain details. Such as, for example, the reason for her own name. And that the reason there had never been a "Hope" or "Prudence," "Clemency," or "Charity" to keep her company in the nursery as her parents had originally planned was because they seldom could get together in a bedroom without fighting for long enough to have produced one. Except of course, for that one time Faith knew of, but that, she thought suddenly, coming stark awake in distress as she always did at the thought, was foolishness, since it wasn't for anyone else to hear, know, or think about. Even herself, she decided.

As for those elves of Lady Mary's, Faith thought, the late hour and her own weariness calming her and helping her to store away untidy thoughts that sometimes came slipping out of closets where they'd been safely locked when she was too weary to take care which doors she opened in her mind, why, she didn't believe in spirits. She'd stay the summer here in England and she'd do the pretty with the gentlemen, and then she'd go home, heart-whole and whole-heartedly, to take up a useful life. And she'd leave no languishing suitors behind her either.

She'd already decided to pass her time with gentlemen who were no more serious or susceptible than herself. That way she could keep to the letter of her agreement with Grandfather and not harm anyone in the process. There were enough foolish young lordlings to tarry with here, and when their company palled, there was Will to confide in, and the Earl of Methley for humor and spice. That languid gentleman seemed to take nothing seriously, and if he had a heart that did more than lazily pump blue blood through his lanky frame, she'd be very much surprised.

When her last conscious thought of the night came—and with it, the vision of dappled sunlight and the scent of pines, for it was an image of the dashing gentleman the noblemen at the house party had called the Viking—she smiled. Though admittedly, his presence had been oddly disturbing, unlike the lusty fellows that name they'd given him implied, he'd seemed more intent on warning her to behave properly than set on ravishment.

Perhaps, she smiled into her pillow as the feathers in it winged her away across the night, they ought to have called him the Missionary instead.

The gentleman drew his dressing gown more closely together about his naked form and belted it around himself. Then he smiled, on a yawn, and picking up a crystal decanter, raised it and a tawny brow as well at his unexpected visitor.

"No," he yawned again, even as he poured out two glasses, "unfortunately you have not interrupted anything. This is the countryside, remember, sir. This is Stonecrop Hall. When I go to my chambers here, my bed is just as chilly and empty as my ancestral halls are at this hour of the night. It's odd, I grant you, but when I'm in residence in London where there are several hundred people I know and wish to avoid, I can take whomever or even whatever I choose to my bed because it is the City, and I'm not as likely to be remarked upon. But here, where my nearest neighbors are pheasants, I repair to solitary sheets, to preserve," he grimaced, "my good name."

Then he grinned as he presented a glass to his visitor, who was already seated at his ease in the library, and taking a twin goblet to his own lips, he drank before settling in an adjacent chair near the newly laid fire.

"Pheasants," mused his visitor, "and the Duke and Duchess of Marchbanks."

"On the whole," the gentleman mused, holding his glass to the firelight and watching the light dance in the amber liquid there, "I prefer the pheasants. They're wittier, and I can shoot them if I wish."

"But it is about Marchbanks that I've come," the older gentleman said softly.

"Really?" his host asked, running a hand through his tousled, varicolored hair. "Then I must be sleepier than I thought, or it's possible that I've not really wakened to find you here. Because I'd doubt very much if you'd make this trip down from Town to have me sniff out treason at Marchbanks. The duke thinks Prinny's the greatest radical he's ever clapped eyes on, and I'll wager all he knows about Napoleon is that he makes a 'demned fine brandy,' " he mocked in very much the same gruff accents as his neighbor the duke often employed.

"But he has an unwed daughter," the bland older gentleman said softly.

"Oh please, sir," Lord Deal said in what might even have been real terror, "not that. Anything for my country, but never that. I've had a glimpse at that house party, so loaded with eligibles of the *ton* for the young lady's delectation that I doubt there's a coherent word spoken from dawn to dusk there these days. I think the range of discourse runs from simper to guffaw to giggle and back, but that's the limit."

"Methley is there," the older gentleman put in.

"Methley," Lord Deal said, suddenly serious, "is badly dipped, so he'd likely be anywhere money was. But whatever else I may think of him, I doubt he's a traitor, although that well may be the only treacherous thing he's not."

"There's also a pair of Americans there, I understand," the other gentleman persisted.

"I know the breed. They're formidable," Lord Deal said, gazing at his glass in the firelight and now remembering where he had lately seen that exact shade of honey glimmering in the light, "but I didn't think a stray pair of them would be enough to terrify the foreign office."

"Ah Barnabas, my friend," the other gentleman sighed, "ordinarily not, and in this case, very likely it's a flap over nothing. But then, we chase wild geese over our desks as a matter of course in London. Then we send you chaps pursuing them around the country. Remember the beacons on the cliffs last year that turned out to be those boys and their secret meetingplace for roasting chestnuts? Or the odd merchant in Torquay who was nervous, it transpired, only because he was smuggling watered wine instead of the good sort we all buy?

"Now, true, we've got the duke's brandy-maker snug and safe at St. Helena, so you'd think we would relax. But there's always some who'd like to see him off for another tilt at the world. We hear there's a contingent from New Orleans, more than a pair of them at that, eager to give the fellow a boat ride around that little island, and over to their further shores. And we remember the time you were of some service in that far country, and how well you aquitted yourself, and how nicely you got on with those you met there. And lo, here's this new pair, right on your doorstep.

"I really don't think there's anything to it," the older gentleman sighed, "but rumors disturb my sleep even more than I interrupted yours tonight. The young woman, I understand, is supposedly here to find herself a noble mate. But why should a rich young female I hear is as lovely as a summer's day need to travel all this way to find a suitor? And if she has, I wonder why it is, then, that I've heard she discourages the gentlemen's interest rather than angling for it? And since her companion is a handsome, likely lad, I wonder why she didn't settle for him? It puzzles me. So if you'd be so kind, I'd like it if you'd make their acquaintance, if only to oblige an old gentleman.''

''Only for you, sir.'' Lord Deal sighed. ''And is there anything else you'd care for, a quart of my blood perhaps?''

''A bed for the night, so I can be gone before dawn,'' the older gentleman said. ''And my thanks, Barnabas, though not my sympathies, for she's most attractive, I hear.''

''And so was Delilah, and so was Eve, and so was Salome, and so was Helen of Troy, and so was Jezebel, and so was Lilith . . .'' recited Lord Deal as he rose and led the other gentleman up the stairs to the room his servants always prepared for occasional visitors.

''And,'' Lord Deal paused at the top of the stairs to ask, with a show of uncertainty, ''correct me if I'm wrong, sir, for you're the classical scholar, but wasn't there also some talk about that other lovely foreign lady, Lucretia Borgia?''

And then, despite the lateness of the hour, their unbridled laughter drifted down the stair.

FOUR

SOME OF THE YOUNG people wanted to play at lawn bowls, just as that amusing young American Miss Hamilton suggested. But several mamas frowned at the idea, and not a few of the young ladies who wished to be styled as "fragile" resisted as well. No one wished to go riding, as the older gentlemen had done hours ago, since no one could come up with workable, amiable groupings for the venture. They had picnicked the day before, similarly, croquet had already been deemed a bore, and only three persons voted for an archery match. Everyone was growing irritable, and as one guest remarked, it didn't even have the decency to rain and cancel all their options. No, it was a beautifully sunny day they had somehow to get through until night. The night would bring a dance party, but it was fully eight hours away no matter how you wound your watch, another guest grumped.

Someone suggested that they get blankets and cushions and sit out on the lawns again, but the mere thought filled Faith with loathing. She couldn't understand how it was that they all looked forward so to the dancing this evening, when most of the people who would be in attendance there were already sitting about in the same room together right now, obviously bored to pieces with each other already. She'd been told that several of the young persons had serious intentions toward several of the others in the room, but, she wondered, how could they contemplate a life together when they could scarcely pass a summer's afternoon with each other without dozing?

"It isn't afternoons that they think about spending together when they think of marriage," the earl said languidly after she'd whispered her query to him. Even as she flushed, he added, "It's settlements and annuities, my dear—why, you're blushing, you naughty thing."

She grinned at him. Lady Mary was unavailable, since as hostess she must not closet herself with any one guest. And as Will was desperately attempting to alter that circumstance and so hovered around her shoulder more closely than a shawl, Faith had been left to herself. She didn't wish to make any further blunders and so this afternoon avoided dangerous chatter with the more flighty members of the party, since exhibitions of lack of wit sometimes goaded her to excess, while a companion with too high spirits might carry her away. But the earl, as always so cool, laconic, and entertaining, was the perfect gentleman to linger with.

He stood beside her now, or lolled there, she corrected herself, smiling bemusedly and observing the follies of the company through half-closed eyes. He was as different from the rest of them as she was, although as an earl of the realm he had every reason to be precisely like them. But not only was he a head taller than any in the room, in his habitual night-black raiment there was no doubt he was paler and thinner and more elegant, and much older than any of the others, as well. Perhaps it was that which linked them, Faith thought. For where she was an outsider in an alien land, he appeared to be an alien within his own circle.

There was nothing romantic in her friendship with the earl, the mere thought of that was absurd. Not only was she a girl who steadfastly resisted such nonsense, but even should she indulge in foolishness, she thought, this sardonic, elongated, and distant nobleman was not the sort of fellow to stir those sorts of notions. There was nothing in the least loverlike in either his attitude or his conversation. She thought of delicious quips when she watched those pale thin lips, not kisses, and no more considered the possibility of being caught up in his long-limbed embrace than she would have entertained the idea of sparring with the gentleman. Neither did he ever treat her in the least as though he considered her a woman in the sense of the word which would have made her nervous.

Actually, she hadn't the slightest idea of why he should be included in this company, keeping her company. But then, she couldn't be expected to, she wasn't English after all. It might, she thought nebulously, have something to do with his friendship with the duke. The fact of his bachelorhood did not weigh with her, for he didn't play the cavalier with any of the young ladies present, neither did he seek the company or conversation of any of the younger men, just as he assiduously and with killing politeness, avoided contact with the mamas and chaperones. But he was exceedingly witty and scathingly clever, and he was always available for a chat with Faith, which was just as flattering to her as it was amusing. In sum, she thought him an excellent companion.

One of the young women interrupted Faith's thoughts and electrified the company by calling out rather breathlessly, as though she herself was so staggered at the thought that she'd had such an idea that she wanted it out and aired before her poor wits forgot she'd begotten it, "I say, let's decorate the ballroom!"

Lady Mary clapped her hands together and turned such a radiant face to her companions that Faith actually saw poor Will draw in his breath at the vision she presented.

"How clever of you, Anne," she said delightedly. "We can get flowers, and . . . no, no, first we'll think of a theme, and each of you will get a chance to suggest one, and then we'll vote on it, and—"

"But my dear," the duchess said reprovingly from the corner of the vast saloon where she'd been holding quiet court with a number of visiting mamas, "have you forgotten? We already decided that this evening was to be a celebration of Midsummer's Night and I've already tended to the decor."

"But Mama," Lady Mary said, so carried away by the idea of a scheme that would fill up the entire long afternoon that she forgot herself so much as to dispute her parent, "we only have a few vases of flowers and the usual greenery draped over a wooden trellis near the musicians, just as we always—"

"Mary!" the duchess interrupted in grim accents, rising to her feet as she did so, looking very like a startled pigeon in her purple gown with her white fichu rising and falling rapidly over her swollen breasts with each new outraged breath she drew. It was a constant wonderment to the *ton* that the short, plump duchess and her rotund husband had produced such a beauty as Lady Mary. Even her brother, the marquess, had been known affectionately as Owl in his schooldays because of the goggle eyes his father had passed on to him along with his noble title. But though friends might warn besotted gentlemen that the Incomparable might produce surprises when she produced offspring, it was impossible for them to think of such heriditary dangers when they looked deep into her beautiful blue eyes. Although it must be admitted that not a few of them had found themselves hesitating before they'd made their offers, at the exact moment that they'd tried to look the most sincere and had gazed into the duke's wide, bulging, but otherwise quite similarly hued, bright blue eyes.

"But Mary," the duchess now huffed, "you cannot remember, you admired the idea very much originally and," she added with a broken laugh to assure everyone of how foolish young girls were, "we cannot redecorate the room each time time hangs heavy on your hands. Why don't you all go for a stroll?"

"Yes, Mama," Lady Mary said dutifully, as, Faith realized, she always did. When she rose and put her hand upon the arm of a surprised and gratified Will, she looked very much like the sort of girl Faith had taken her to be when they'd first met: a lovely, lifeless, and passionless creature. So she always seemed in the company of her parents; it was as though they leached the life from her.

Yet, Faith remembered, in the company of her own parents she too was transformed. But that pair usually made her into a wild and volatile thing, which was why she'd gone to live with her grandfather all those years ago. Perhaps it was better to rage than buckle, Faith thought, looking at the vapid creature so unrecognizable from the spirited girl she had giggled with last night. Although thinking of herself and of how she sat in a room three thousand miles from home, against her will, even though she did it through love, not blind obedience, Faith couldn't feel she exemplified the virtues of any sort of behavior right now.

"A brief rebellion, quickly doused. Be thankful, Miss Hamilton, that Lady Mary was not one of your forebears, or we'd still be countrymen right now," the earl commented as Faith rose to go for the required stroll. It was at such moments, when she felt sympathy for one of his victims, that Faith felt least in charity with her companion. But if he noticed her lack of response to his sally he didn't mention it, and that was one of the other things Faith liked about him—he demanded very little from her.

Though Lady Mary had capitulated instantly, there was nevertheless a good deal of muted mumbling as the various other guests arose and prepared to go for the stroll that no one save the duchess, who didn't have to go at all, had desired. And even that lady gave her daughter an ill-favored glance for her abortive attempt at disobedience. So it was an out-of-sorts, disappointed, and rebellious group that turned, as one, when the butler entered the salon they were just about to vacate, to announce a visitor.

And he, standing just behind the servant, had a moment of sudden, irrational discomfort, seeing the mass of ill-tempered people looking up glumly at his arrival. But even as the butler pronounced, "Lord Deal to see you, Madame," the faces brightened, shoulders were thrust back, and smiles appeared. The gentleman could be forgiven if he'd been puffed up at this miraculous transformation at his entrance, but there was no need of such charity, he'd long since learned to ignore the reactions of this set of persons.

"Your grace," he said at once, coming into the room and taking the duchess's plump, beringed hand in his, "your pardon if I interrupt something."

He waited only long enough for the sound of her disclaimers to die away before he said, with a shake of his tousled head, "I am a gudgeon, my dear lady. You kindly sent me an invitation for the festivities tonight, and like a chucklehead, I sent back my regrets." He hadn't needed to check this detail with his secretary. It was a thing done as matter of course, since that worthy young chap had seen the invitation in the trash with others of the sort where they always were deposited by his employer immediately after being delivered, and he'd fished them out and written polite regrets, as he always did whenever he discovered them crumpled there.

"But I was too hasty, and have come to tell you that the urgent affairs which required my presence tonight happily have already been taken care of. Is it possible, my dear duchess, that I am still welcome?''

It took several minutes for the duchess to finish telling Lord Deal the many ways in which it was not only possible, but desirable and vital to the course of all her future happiness in life that he come this evening to her little soiree. Lord Deal might be a recluse, he might have a decidedly odd reputation, but he was a nobleman, he was a neighbor with a matching estate, he had more funds than she could count, and he was notoriously single. And even though he had all these virtues, she and the duke had never considered him as a possible match for their daughter. Because never in a thousand years had they ever thought he would actually come to one of their parties.

After she'd done with assuring him of his welcome, the duchess paused and frowned. It was one of the few times in her life that she regretted an earlier decision she'd made. For here the young people were already reluctantly beginning to leave the room upon her express orders, and there her daughter was about to stroll off with an obscure American, while the greatest catch in the shire was left to stand with her mama. So it was understandable that she looked forlorn when he made his good-byes, claiming that duties prevented him from going along on that fascinating promenade with the houseguests. She brightened when she realized that he would, after all, be returning with the dusk, but her upturned lips compressed into a rigid slit when she saw him pause to have a word with her other American guest before he left. Thus, for the first time in her life, the duchess of Marchbanks became political, as she decided that there was a new nationality in the wide and unworthy world to dislike.

As Lord Deal made the most perfunctory bow to the earl's chillest smile of greeting, Faith realized that the two were almost of a height. Yesterday, Lord Deal had been astride a horse, and somehow the earl's extreme lankiness made him appear to be so extraordinarily tall that no man in the company seemed his equal. Perhaps it was so, but gazing up at the pair now, Faith could see that the sun-streaked locks of the other nobleman came almost to the earl's own dark brow. It was only that Lord Deal was so balanced in proportions that unlike the lofty earl, the first thing that struck one about him was not his height. Even as Faith's eye registered this, her ear took in the fact from the merest of civilities being exchanged, that the two were on the barest of speaking terms.

But then Lord Deal bent his full, white, warming smile upon her. After she'd noted bemusedly how his tanned cheeks creased symmetrically just to the side of his lips when he did so, he smiled again as he told her how well she looked, how he looked forward to seeing her this evening, and how regretful he was that he could not accompany her on this exciting excursion around the grounds of Marchbanks. He left them then, and Faith in turn smiled after him as she realized that even when he spoke insincere social nonsense, when he spoke without censure or warning, it was very pleasant to hear.

"Charming, charming," the earl said softly, watching her reaction to Lord Deal's departure. Then taking her arm and walking her out the long french doors to join the sullen strollers, he went on to say negligently, "Our Viking has some manners, to be sure, though he's quite out of practice. Fancy him attending the dance tonight though. One would have thought he'd had his fill of debutantes, but then, perhaps a decade of avoidance may have whetted his taste for them again."

When Faith looked up, interested in hearing more about the gentleman but not wishing it to seem so, the earl, as he always did with gossip, obliged her by going on to say without prompting as they paced onward, "Oh yes, it's been a while since he was in society. For all the outdoor glow, my dear, he's of an age with your humble servant. Yes, he's got two and thirty years in his dish, even as I have. We were at school together, the Viking and I, a century ago, you know."

"No, I didn't know," Faith answered with genuine surprise, for she could scarcely imagine two more unlikely schoolmates. Envisioning Lord Deal as a boy might be amusing, but she discovered such a stretch of imagination impossible in the earl's case. "And," she asked, "is that where he got his nickname?" before she wondered at whether it was a politic question, since such names were often affectionate tributes given by one's peers, and the earl evidently had none.

"Lud, no." The earl laughed, showing his long white teeth in genuine mirth, causing several fellow strollers to swing their heads around to look enviously at the fellow who seemed to be wringing some enjoyment from the day. "That came afterward. He had to earn his name in adulthood."

"It's not because of his ancestors?" Faith asked, confused at how her question provided her escort with so much merriment.

"Oh no, my dear," the earl replied with pleasure, "it's nothing to do with ancestors, but rather with descendants. It's the sort of tale I'd ordinarily be loathe to tell such a young creature," he confided, his gray eyes sparkling, "but then, I imagine it's the type of thing you already understand, since you took such care to assure me you knew all about unicorns and other horned beasts the other day. Why child, don't look so puzzled." He laughed before he dropped his voice and his head low to impart the rest of his delicious tale. "After all, if you look at a Viking, you shouldn't be surprised to find a fellow wearing horns."

Barnabas Stratton rode back along the beech avenue to the road, and though this time he wasn't distracted by the sight of his neighbor's houseguests strewn across the grassy banks, he imagined he could hear the conversation being made by the Earl of Methley and the American girl in his wake, even though they were entirely out of hearing distance and completely out of sight. It was too much to expect that Methley would hold his peace now. The earl doted on gossip even more than he disliked his former schoolmate, and that, Lord Deal thought wryly, was a very great deal to dote on indeed.

And Methley was a clever fellow, always had been, and entirely amusing when he bent himself to be so. Doubtless Miss Hamilton would be savoring the tasty whole of it by now, with the sprightly seasonings of conjecture and inference to dress it for her table. Still, for all his crimes, Methley was not a liar, Lord Deal thought; then too, he reminded himself, he wouldn't have to embellish this particular tale to make it savory either. As it was, even after all these years it stank of all the rich redolent odors of scandal, sin, and shame that gossipmongers brewed and their customers loved so well.

Lord Deal shrugged, causing his mount to pick up his paces, and this, though inadvertent, suited him, since there were many long miles between Marchbanks and Stonecrop Hall, its nearest, though happily for its owner, sufficiently distant, stately neighbor. At worst, he thought as his horse trotted down the long, treed drive, the young American girl would think him a bloody fool, and since deficient in some wise, a fellow easy to gull. As it was information, not admiration, he wanted from her, that in itself would not be detrimental to his purposes. A fellow one considered an easy mark was a chap one could let down barriers for. On that head, he thought with a smile, remembering Miss Hamilton's grace and style, a few barriers removed might provide very pleasant diversion in an evening's work.

At the best, he decided as he finally reached the entrance to Marchbanks and waved a farewell to the gatekeeper who saw him off down the long road to home, after hearing his story she'd be so sympathetic to him that she'd grant him whatever he asked, out of pity. And where he would consider that a worst response if it were true affection he were seeking from her, for the purposes of information-gathering, it would be perfect. A few years ago, perhaps, he would have disliked that reaction for any reason, he would have been sensitive about it on any score. But the years blunt one's sensibilities, he mused, which was why old people could speak so casually of death, and why he could now look back upon the incident that had changed his life with no more than a shrug which only moved his horse along.

"I lost my fiancée," he'd told the American girl. So he had, yet it made so little matter to him now that he could speak it almost as a jest, though those years ago it had been the reason he'd fled his own land to travel so far abroad that when he'd done with the parts of Europe Napoleon permitted him, he'd run all the way to the Americas. For he had lost his fiancée, and at least no one in the New World had known that, though it seemed that everyone in England and on the Continent had. But he thought, frowning now, he ought at least be honest as

Methley and not take liberties with the language. Because
he hadn't really lost her. He could have found her easily
enough if he'd wished to, and still could, in the church-
yard at Little Sutton. For actually, he'd buried her.

She'd been a lively, clever little puss, more of a friend
than a lover. But then, in those green years, he'd thought
it very good to take himself a wife who'd be his closest
friend. It would have been enough. Perhaps it might have
grown to more, no telling, he'd never known great love,
perhaps, he'd thought, it eventually grew from just the sort
of warm affection he'd felt for her. He'd liked her very
well. Tiny and plump, never a great beauty but with no
pretentions to being one, the Honorable Miss Antonia
Wilson had made her way with wit and charm, and had
done very well with that. Twelve offers, her father had
boasted, an even dozen lads turned down so that she could
make her match with you, young Deal, he'd laughed as
they downed a toast to future happiness together. And one
of those rejected fellows was the Earl of Methley, then
only a viscount, but just as witty, just as long and thin and
aching with envy. And clever. And unfortunately, he'd
been at the house party when poor Nettie had fallen ill.

Had he felt betrayed? Lord Deal wondered again. Had
Methley been as shocked as he had been when the doctor,
a garrulous old fellow called from the local village, had
come downstairs, forgetting in his perturbation that his
patient was an unwed young noblewoman, and so an-
nouncing to all, with a sad shake of his gray head, that the
poor lass was definitely going to lose her child before-
times, and because of the unexplained hemorraging, perhaps her own life as well.

Had Methley begun to truly hate him then, before he'd
known the whole of it, that hatred piling up on the dislike
they'd felt for each other as competitors at school? He,
Lord Deal thought, as his horse paced the lonely leagues
back to his home, had been in too much distress himself to
ponder it then. Not at poor Nettie's diminishing life, damn
that former self for his youthful arrogance, but because
even with all the shock and frantic whispering going on at
the house party, at first no one save himself knew that it
had not been his babe and could never have been.

But to save her soul, and perhaps in some mistaken

attempt to save her affianced's reputation, poor Nettie had told everyone, up to the moment, a week later, of her dying breath, that it had not been dear Barnabas that had given her her deadly burden, but a neighbor. A farmer. A married farmer, who was a neighbor. And one whom she had loved since she'd been a girl, and who'd been helpless in his love himself, and so had helped her from her innocence when they'd both realized she must wed, and wed away from him forever.

Poor misguided girl, he thought now. She might have saved her soul, but her confession, rather than absolving him, had ruined him completely. It was one of the oddities of society that he would have been scandalous, but absolved, if he'd been the one to jump the preacher's starting gun. But as it was, poor Nettie, even as she'd sunk into the grave, had crowned him not with a halo of respectability, but with a pair of horns. And bereaved, and totally cuckolded in his own way as well, it had been Methley who'd said, even as he'd left the funeral with stony eyes, "How odd. For here was a case where an English girl was carried off by a farmer from her Viking. Well," he'd laughed bitterly, "if you look for a Viking, you'll find a fellow wearing horns, won't you?"

It was the color of his hair, he supposed, his athleticism, and the cruel aptness of the title that did it. The name clung, though a decade's time transmuted its meaning from scorn to a weird sort of admiration. It hardly mattered. Contemptuous of its rules and depredations, he'd avoided "society" assiduously since then, and had not felt one whit deprived.

There were, he'd discovered, a great many beautiful, clever females outside the gilded ranks of those select few hundred, women who were pleased to help him transform Methley's biting epithet into a fitting compliment on his appetites and prowess in matters that his own society had used the name to mock him for. His daring and his adventuresome spirit had caused male companions to further alter the label Methley had tagged him with. They also came from all levels of society, for he'd found the term "gentleman" was not necessarily automatically suitable to any man simply by reason of birth, just as all of the odd Miss Hamilton's countrymen claimed.

He'd attended to her the moment he'd heard her speak, because her accents had reminded him of her nation and he'd enjoyed the casual way of life in her new world. He'd made friends of enemies, the task being made that much easier when both sides realized neither wanted more bloodshed in the war no one seemed to want to take credit for. He made lovers of enemies too, and there was one amusing female he particularly regretted leaving there, even though she assured him she'd not be lonely, for as soon as he departed from the wars, her husband would return to continue their private one. But for all he'd pleased himself in various ways, he'd left with all his heart, for all the while he knew his name and his place were in his native land.

He'd exiled himself from the society he was born to, but he couldn't abandon his birthright. When he finally returned, as an onlooker he could see even more clearly how bizarre it was for anyone to live by such narrow precepts, or die for them, as poor Nettie had done, or be hurt by such random, meaningless cruelty, as he had been. He became almost a crusader in the matter.

When his young cousin tarried with a hesitant suitor of her choice too long and some cruel wit dubbed her "the shelf-ish Miss Stratton," though he'd entreated her to ignore it, she'd turned in panic to immediately marry some other more obliging fellow. Now she lived with an oaf and had the rest of her days to regret having done it. Yet, he could not dislike the fellow, who was surely as wronged as he wronged his wife. For how many other gentlemen wed ladies who accepted them from need, real or imagined, rather than love? Perhaps his own family had only been fortunate in such matters, for he had two sisters who'd married unexceptionally and a younger brother in the church who despaired at what he took to be his elder's cold-bloodedness. But it was only that if it were true that love had to be blind, then poor Nettie had opened his eyes so wide he could never close them again.

Despite gossip which grew more romantically fanciful with each year he remained a bachelor, he didn't believe she had ruined him for anything but a life as a leader of the *ton*. He hadn't been madly in love when he offered for her, he reasoned. She had only failed him as a friend, or perhaps he had failed her—he still wondered at that, that at least, still nagged at him. Methley might not have been entirely wrong, at least in his condemnation. For if they'd been such fast friends, she ought to have been able to confide in him. Now, of course, he could never know if he could have been a better friend to her. She was gone, but the question had not died with her.

Or it might be, he often thought, that he ought to have loved her more. He well may have failed her in that, he reasoned, though he couldn't see how it could have been different. Although he didn't believe he was a cold man, and certainly hadn't been that at two and twenty, he supposed it was only that he wasn't the sort of fellow to ever be leveled by sentiment. That didn't mean that he could feel nothing.

He'd experienced the bitter taste of betrayal, beginning with Nettie's and then encompassing all his friends as they contributed to the gossip. But it was nevertheless true, and whenever he searched his soul he had to admit it, that he'd never known the sort of love other men seemed to suffer from. He might regret this, but he couldn't see how he might change it. It wasn't from a lack of knowledge of females, or even experience in dealing with them. It was never necessary to feel love to know passion.

Though he'd been celibate with Nettie, as society dictated, he'd not been a stranger even then to the several delights involved in intimacy with her sex. A young nobleman attending a large university, a young gentleman who'd taken the grand tour, a young blade on the loose in London, and he'd been all of them in turn, had many chances, most of them taken, to discover, if not the meaning of "love," then what passed for it for payment.

Which was never to say that he could only purchase gratification. It hadn't taken him very long to discover that there were a great many females of all classes who looked for little more than he did, and were willing to settle for even less. There were, he found, all manner of transactions in life where prices were negotiable. In cases where payment in coin of the realm would be considered crass, he soon learned that payment in kind would often be gladly accepted.

No, the episode with Nettie may have made him doubt

himself as a friend, but it hadn't soured him on females. He wasn't such a flat. He liked them very well and needed them to make life complete. In fact, he thought defensively, as he always did when he contemplated his past and his present single state, his last mistress in town had been quite conversable, as his mistresses always were, for he found scant pleasure taking pleasure from a mere body. And if he were never constitutionally able to know what the poets considered "love," well then, he reasoned, he could regret it, but he would not miss it either, no more than a blind man misses that which he has never seen.

He'd been orphaned years before and was the eldest of his family. Naturally, then, he expected someday he'd have to make a push to preserve his name and find another pleasant young woman and raise a family. This apparent lack of an ability to love was certainly no impediment to that so far as he could see, or else there would not be so many new young women presented to society each year. And "someday," he often thought, was an excellent time to take on the responsibility of populating his nursery.

But as he hadn't one as yet to take up his time, it pleased him in these uneasy times to serve his country as best he could. Patriotism, he often thought, was not only as Mr. Johnson said, the last refuge of a scoundrel, it was the last refuge of a bored and disillusioned gentleman as well. Although, he just as often thought wryly, that might be just another way of saying exactly the same thing.

At any rate, patriotism provided enthralling sport. Things had gotten very dull since the little Emperor had been given that new distant rocky little island to rule. Despite his groans and protests, he'd not been displeased when his midnight visitor had asked him to investigate the young Americans. In this case, Miss Hamilton had already intrigued him. He'd tried to warn her about gossip and its victims from the moment he'd observed her so recklessly inviting social disaster. That day he'd come upon her unbidden she'd seemed lovely, bright, and spirited, and he'd felt concern for her rise in himself unbidden. Perhaps he'd have sought her out on his own again even if he'd not been asked to, for the sake of her vulnerability. He didn't think she was a spy. And if she weren't, she'd not only have nothing to fear from him, but a great deal to gain.

Since he was self-admittedly some strange sort of missionary, he'd already tried to save her some pain and give her good advice for negotiating society's slippery paths to acceptance, if that was what she was after. Even if it weren't and she was going to stay in England long enough to be wounded, he would not hesitate to do so again.

Remembering her and his mission, he kneed his mount to greater speed so that he'd have time to prepare for the coming evening. He doubted she was a spy, he didn't believe she was deeply involved with Methley, but since she was, however alien, only a human female, he scarcely thought her serious about her lack of interest in acquiring a husband. Since she was also undeniably beautiful, he doubted that she had been unable to find one on her side of the Atlantic as well. So whatever her motives, she was at least the best that he ever expected of any female: she was interesting.

FIVE

THE DANCE PARTY at Marchbanks was not slated to begin for an hour. Not all of the hired musicians had arrived as yet, and the household staff was still in a frenzy, with the cook shrilling that his assistants were ruining him and the footmen practically panting in their haste to get all the vases of flowers, extra chairs, dishes, and tables in their places. One young skivvy was being dosed by Nurse after her bout of hysteria brought on by the housekeeper's berating, while her sister sufferers were dashing through the house answering all the bells that all the ladies were ringing for them.

A great many ladies, of course, were involved in the furor as well. There were mamas insisting on higher or lower necklines for their defiant daughters' frocks, and wrangling with them over the question of more or less powdering, or the advisability of a dash-on, or a wipe-off, of rouge from their hostile faces. There were maids frowning over their mistresses' hairstyles that would not do their bidding, threaten as they would with combs and hot curling tongs, and sudden difficulties with slippers that seemed to have shrunken in their wrappings, since they were grown too tight for dancing, and discoveries of cracked fans and vanished ribbands and various other last-minute crises of fashion.

The gentlemen had far less to do, of course. Their valets shaved and dressed them and they now either dozed or read the papers or gossiped with each other in their rooms. Except, of course, for those fellows whose desire to cut a dash far exceeded nature's expectations. Like Lord Oglivy, whose valet struggled to wedge him into his new jacket, and Mr. Perkins, whose full cravat would not come right about his thin neck after ten tries, and Charlie Bryant, whose valet was busily padding so many parts of his wardrobe for this night that when he was finally ready to step from his room an hour later, as the exhausted valet later confided to his steady lass, my lord could have fallen from a horse and bounced for a full five minutes before he felt any pain.

Miss Faith Hamilton, however, simply bathed, dabbed on a bit of cologne water, and put on her clothes. Then she allowed her maid to brush out her hair and fasten it up with a green ribband to match her frock. She did pinch her cheeks rather severely, and it must be admitted that she bit her lips fairly often to bring their color up, and patted on a dash of powder to finish off everything to a nicety. But then she was done.

The glass showed the dress fit well; it might be a bit low in front to be sure, but though she didn't seek to attach a gentleman, Miss Hamilton was no prude and liked a compliment as well as the next person. Looking at her reflection, she thought it would do, but she wished she had someone else that she could ask. The frock, long-sleeved and high-waisted and done in figured apple green silk, would suit an evening in New York perfectly. But though she loved her home and felt no shame for it, she knew there was no comparison as to what might be acceptable in a small city like New York and what was considered fashionable to persons used to a metropolis such as London.

If Molly were here, of course, she would have known immediately. Although Molly herself always dressed simply, she had a sure eye for fashion and never guided one wrong. Perhaps, Faith thought on a sigh for her absent companion, that was precisely why she herself never dressed spectacularly. But Mrs. Molly Cabal, widow, Faith's companion for the past seven years, had taken one wrong step down from the family carriage on a shopping expedition just a week before she was to set sail for England with her charge. And though she pleaded her hardihood and begged leave to come anyway, both Faith and Grandfather had refused to allow her to cross the ocean with her poor leg in splints. She'd been writing regularly, vowing in each letter that she'd join Faith soon, even as Faith wrote back each time and told her that she'd likely be home by the time the splints were off.

But Molly, good sensible Molly, was an ocean away, and young Meggie, though an excellent maid and devoted enough to venture across the sea with her mistress, was no arbitor of fashion, being too fond of glitter and too fearful of giving insult. She liked every frock Faith put on, and if pressed to the limit, only spoke hesitantly and a bit wistfully about perhaps a feather here or a sequin just there. No, Faith needed an informed opinion so that the American girl wouldn't be considered a dowd and a disgrace to the sophistication of her country. So, catching up her fan and her wrap, she gave Meggie good evening and made her way to her new friend Lady Mary's room.

She'd been afraid of imposing, but when she was admitted to the lady's rooms, she saw several other young women guests clustered around her hostess. And since they all greeted her enthusiastically and complimented her on her high good looks immediately, she soon joined them in laughter and gossip, relieved to see that she wasn't the only one to seek reassurance from her hostess. But she was.

The only other female seeking confirmation about her appearance had been that accredited beauty, the Honorable Miss Merriman. She had been in the room not ten minutes previously. But she'd already gone, having discovered an invisible spot on her fawn silk gown after having seen what her hostess was wearing. She'd returned to her own rooms immediately to change to a dazzling white frock to take the shine out of her hostess's light blue one.

The ladies remaining in the room did not have to resort to such paltry subterfuges. Though Faith could not know it, these young females, the most amiable of those she'd met, were also the most secure. They dressed and came to see their hostess out of no desire save that for amusement. They had no more need for compliments than the ocean did for water. But by no means did this mean that these were all the most lovely and admired among the company.

Miss Fontaine was the wealthiest, and though, just as some of the crueler gentlemen said, her face had to be memorized to be remembered, even by her mother, she never worried about what she wore, since as they also put it, she could afford not to. Lady Harriet might be too tall, those same rattles whispered, but she was far too titled to care. And the Washburn twins were the quipsters' delight, in fact, it was often said the wits declared it an absolute holiday the day the two were introduced to the *ton*.

The two young ladies were identical in looks and temperament. They were jolly, easy-going creatures with not an evil thought in their heads. In fact, it was entirely possible that they would have even forgiven the jesters for what they said about them. For how precocious the pair were, one clever fellow had sighed happily, why only see how they, at the tender age of eighteen, had already managed to acquire middle-aged bodies. Oh no, another wag had called out in horror, that was wrong, it was only that the pair had originally been triplets, but from their ample conformations it was apparent that they must at some time have devoured their other unfortunate sibling.

The only daughters of an honored duke, even their friends conceded the pair were unlucky in their appearance. They were heavily built, shaped like a pair of brass doorknobs, just as the wits had it. Their hair was naturally frizzed to a fare-thee-well, and above their plump cheeks they had identically small blue eyes that peered out at their privileged world from behind their grand, imposing bulbous noses.

They were commonly known as "the oath-breakers" because, the tale was told, on the day of their presentation, a notorious rake had seen one of them cross the room in front of him and was said to have whispered, shuddering, "Gad! I'll swear I'll never see an uglier chit." And then her sister came in and proved him a liar.

But had either twin heard any of this, and it was so widespread a tale that it was entirely possible that they had, they would have put it down to railery, or gentle funning. For to the eternal credit of their family, the pair knew with an absolute certainty and a faith that few priests enjoyed, that they were entirely beautiful. Made much over since birth, treated with love and warmth, the two returned those two admirable qualities to the world in full measure, and so were, despite their looks, quite popular young ladies. They made a fellow feel at home, and knowing them for any length of time, as one chap had said in amazement, one quite forgot what they looked like and began to believe they were just as pretty as they thought they were.

They knew they were lovely, wealthy, and much sought-after, and their only aim was to wed close to each other. But being no more wise than they were beautiful, they meant this quite literally. Neither would consider any beau who was not geographically near to another gentleman who could be available to her sister. Marry they would, for marry they must, but they were determined not to let a simple thing like that separate them.

And so soon as they had done with telling Faith how nicely she looked, they returned to the discussion of their primary woe this evening.

"Mama was in alt at Lord Deal's coming this evening, and how lucky we were that he's returning to society the very Season we came out," Lady Barbara said sadly. "But though he's quite a catch and exceedingly handsome, the thing of it is that Bunny and I thought it out and there's no escaping the fact that he lives leagues away from everyone, excepting for you, of course, dear Mary."

"And we can't marry you," Lady Bernice giggled.

"Still, as Mama says, he has some land in Kent, and quite a nice holding in Scotland, as well as his London townhouse," Lady Barbara said, brightening.

"But Babs," her twin insisted, frowning, "Stonecrop is his principal seat."

"There's that," Lady Barbara sighed, and in their matching moods of dejection, the pair looked like a mirror image of despondency, despite their blush-pink gowns.

"He's got a handsome fortune too," Miss Fontaine put in, not because she was a mercenary girl, but because it was her second Season, and she had learned to look at a man's bank balance before she gazed into his eyes, so that she would know sincerity when she saw it.

"But he's half Scots," Lady Harriet put in consideringly.

"What's that to say to anything?" Miss Fontaine asked, since, unlike the other geneologically involved lady, financial matters, not familial ones, were her major concerns.

"It's not quite English," Lady Harriet said, "although, I suppose it hardly matters, not with that smile he has."

"But Harry," Lady Barbara said pettishly, "Scottish is English enough, and I tell you if he had anyone decent living nearby, we'd snap him up, it isn't as if he were ineligible because of it, it isn't as if he was *foreign* or anything, or, ah . . . ," she said, pausing as she heard her hostess's intake of breath and then realizing her gaffe and looking guiltily at Faith, she said, in an attempt at a recover, "not as though there's anything wrong with foreign, there are a great many very nice foreign people about . . ."

"And if Scottish is not precisely foreign," her sister said, in a madly merry tone, which was meant as hearty reassurance, "America is not either, even though it's far, but it's English, or was, like Scotland, do you see? And anyone might marry an American if they wished to, I suppose," she ended triumphantly, as everyone else in the room except her sister looked embarrassed.

"I do believe," Miss Fontaine said suddenly, "that I'll go to my room to get my wrap," and quite forgetting that she had it over her arm, she rose and, smiling at everyone, though most especially warmly at Faith, she left, and was soon followed by Lady Harriet. The twins, in a pelter of explanations which each one began only to have the other one hush, soon followed as well, trailing excuses and such outsize admiration for the continent of North America that it seemed to Faith that one would not be surprised if they were leaving to emigrate instead of to prepare for the party, as they'd said.

Once they had gone, there was only Lady Mary and her maid and Faith left to stare at each other. And then, to that abigail's surprise, the American girl began to smile, and her mistress began to giggle, and then the two went off into whoops of laughter.

"I suppose anyone could marry an American," Mary laughed, and then in a bit more sober tone, she asked, "Do you mind very much, Faith? It isn't as though they meant to offend, or they wouldn't have said it, for they're good-hearted girls. But they don't think very much."

"I don't mind in the least," Faith said seriously, "because I think that if they thought me very different, they'd have been more careful in my presence. It's because they forget how alien I am that they mentioned it."

"It's not that you're alien," her hostess replied in some consternation, "it's only because you're not English."

"Isn't that the same thing?" Faith asked, with an admirably straight face.

"Why yes, why no," Lady Mary stammered. "But," she insisted as Faith laughed, and even the maid had to turn her head away to bite her lip, "I certainly wouldn't mind marrying an American and I don't know anyone who would, except for Harriet, and she's not likely to say yes to anyone but a royal prince."

"Well, that's quite all right," Faith said, smiling, "because I wasn't planning on asking her."

And then even Lady Mary's maid forgot to hide her grins.

"You're in luck, lad," Faith whispered to Will Rossiter as she came up to him where he stood at the edge of the dance floor and watched the guests as they arrived.

"And why is that?" he asked, bowing over her hand just as he would to any of the other lady guests he'd met this night.

"Because," Faith said, noting with approval how very fine her old friend looked in his formal dress, "I have it first hand that the Lady Mary wouldn't mind marrying an American in the least."

Will stopped midway in his bow and looked up at her, his brown eyes so alight with sudden hope and interest that Faith said at once, feeling very small for having gotten his hopes up for the sake of a jest, "But not *which* American precisely. I'm sorry, Will, but it's only that I discovered she has no prejudice against former Colonials."

"At least that's something," he said straightening. And patting her hand before he released it he said softly, "So if you don't mind, I'll just go and make sure my name is on her dance card. And for good measure," he added, "not that I mistrust your ears, Mischief, but I think I'll just slip in a word about how I am actually English, since if you've forgotten, my Indian maiden, I have not."

Faith smiled her encouragement to him, and watched him make his way to where his hostess stood with her parents near the door to the ballroom as they received new arrivals. Then she looked about herself with interest. The duke and duchess had invited new faces to this ball. There were several new houseguests who'd arrived in the afternoon, as well as a few dozen local lights who'd been invited for the night. So though the ballroom had only been embellished by some tall vases filled with flowers and the arbor of fresh leaves concealing the musicians that Lady Mary had spoken of, still it had begun to take on a festive appearance, if only from the number of the guests arriving, and the fine clothes they all wore.

Faith had begun to wonder again at the appropriateness of her relatively simple gown when a familiar voice cut into her doubts.

"Lovely. You look fresh and original, very much a creature of the New World. Now why is it, I wonder," the earl asked as he loomed up over her and took her hand, "that you hover here at the sidelines? Is it that you are too polite to cast the other ladies in the shade?"

But as this was said in the same languid drawl that the earl affected for all his statements, she did not know whether to believe him or not. And since she'd seen other ladies in fine brocades and drifting spangle-strewn gauze, with feathers trailing from their hairdos and jewels gleaming on their fingers and breasts, she tended to doubt him. She could not know that, for once, the gray eyes held no mockery. Young and supple, her honey hair smooth and gleaming in the candlelight, she seemed, in comparison to every other lady present, so sweet-limbed and innocently beguiling in her silken green frock as to be welcome and fresh as a green young tree in spring.

And so many another young man thought, for as she stood and studied the earl's pale, impassive countenance for some hint of the sincerity of his compliment, she was unaware of the fact that several of them were edging closer to her as well.

"Well," she finally commented with a laugh, deciding it would never do to take this cool gentleman seriously in the least, "thank you, but I wonder just the same if I oughtn't to have stuck a few feathers in my hair tonight."

"As in the song your countrymen sing?" the earl asked. "Or is it that your countryman calls you his Indian maiden for some other reason?"

Does he miss nothing? she wondered even as she answered, joshing, deciding not to go into a long story about a childhood fantasy Will still teased her about, "Oh, but I'm part Red Indian, never say you didn't guess it?"

And as a few of the surrounding gentlemen laughed with her, and the earl nodded at her with approval, she felt emboldened enough to add, "Mohegan on my mother's side, you know, and Algonquin on the lefthand side."

She didn't realize the double meaning implicit in her jest, nor that now some of the laughter covered genuine shock, but as the earl continued to gaze at her with admiration, she elaborated. It was not long before she had drawn quite a collection of young gentlemen, all laughing and calling questions out about the village she had invented for her ancestors to come from and the customs of her mythical people. She was having such a great deal of fun that she never noticed that there were no other females in the circle of merry guests around her, nor that the music had struck up and that sets were already forming for the first dance.

So it was that she was a more than a little surprise when she stopped for breath as she was about to launch into another story about the beavers her family trapped to make English gentlemen's hats, and a cool voice asked her for the pleasure of a dance. She looked up to see Lord Deal standing before her, and her first thought was only that she hadn't noticed him in the crowd around her, and her second thought, even as she automatically breathed "Yes," because she didn't know how to gracefully say no in front of all these people, was that he seemed, curiously, to be annoyed with her as she agreed to dance with him.

But then, the earl looked piqued as well.

"Ah too bad," he said, even as his expression belied his words as that momentary expression of chagrin slid off his long face, leaving it as smoothly cool as ever. "Your tales of your country enthralled me so that I quite forgot to ask for the first dance with you, Miss Hamilton. Then may this tardy admirer ask for the second one?"

"And then me!" young Lord John Percy cried. "And me! I've got to hear more," Gilbert North put in, stretching up on his toes so that she'd catch sight of his face and give him the nod. "Don't forget me," another young gentleman that Faith hadn't even been introduced to yet chimed in.

Laughing agreement to everyone and shaking her head to signify her delighted confusion, Faith excused herself and let Lord Deal lead her to the dance. But as it took some time before the first sets could form, she found herself standing beside her partner, temporarily speechless. For he seemed to be studying her with some disapproval. And too, just as she hadn't been able to ignore the sudden lifting of her spirits when she had first heard his voice, she'd almost refused him then because of the equally instantaneous and unsought shiver of unease and nervousness she experienced when she first saw him. She could not seem to shake it even now as she regarded him more closely, though covertly.

He'd looked dashing and totally right upon a horse, but oddly, at one and the same time, though he appeared out of place in a ballroom, he was quite in his own style, and so was thrillingly distinctive in his formal attire. For a gentleman in a black jacket with a velvet collar ought to have a gentleman's pale complexion to go with it and not be so dazzling with his tanned pelt highlighting the absolute whiteness of his high neckcloth. And that neckcloth, though correctly draped in a *waterfall*, was meant only to show a languid gentleman's homage to fashion, as a sort of frame upholding a pallid and interesting countenance, and not for emphasizing a strong, tanned column of neck supporting a well-shaped head with a great quantity of sun-wracked hair.

In short, the gentleman, though precise to an inch of fashion, breathed vigor and vitality. It was as though someone had almost tamed some elemental creature and brought him, under the barest restraint, into the salon. It was not at all the thing, but it was, as every young lady present sighed, exactly right for him, and, as many of them also hoped, exactly right for themselves as well.

"If it would make it simpler for you," he said, a smile at last transfiguring his face, changing the threat in it to mere danger, "I'll stand behind you and address the back of your head and your left ear. Because I don't remember that you had any difficulty talking with me when we last met. But if I angle around behind you for a chat, I believe that would eventually cause more conversation than we'd make."

But now Faith had managed to bury and forget the fear she'd momentarily known, as she always did when it came to her unsought, and she answered readily enough.

"It was only that you looked as though you were more likely to drag me to the woodshed than to the dance floor," she replied, and then, remembering herself, was about to explain her reference, when he answered, "So I was Miss Hamilton. But then I remembered that it was not my responsibility to give you a sound thrashing for telling tales," and here he bent such a smile upon her that two closely observant gentlemen vowed immediately to go out the following day and lie in the sun until they smoked, if only it would make their teeth gleam so brilliantly when they smiled down at a lady. "It's not my intention to act as your relative. I might be interested in that status, but I don't wish to achieve it by pretending to have been born to it," he said, knowing that he was walking on a very thin social edge, but determined to keep his balance, "but only of attaining it by more legal recourse, perhaps someday."

Faith blinked. But the gentleman could not be serious, in fact, he was definitely laughing even as he spoke, and it might be at her. And this was only conversation, and she was very good at that.

"Are you trifling with my affections, sir?" she asked, placing one limp hand high upon her breast and opening her eyes very wide, in blatant imitation of every simpering miss she'd seen at the house party.

"Of course," he said, "only we English call it flirtation."

"But I thought you were vexed with me." She grinned, batting her eyelashes so violently in jest, it seemed she saw him through a flickering frame.

"I was," he said sternly then, "I am. But for your own sake. I can only repeat," he went on, as her smile faded at the seriousness in his voice and his long hazel eyes, "don't push them too far, Miss Hamilton. Make a May game of them now, and they will make a long winter's night of this summer for you. All of them," he said as he took her hand to lead her into the opening steps of the dance.

"And since you mentioned woodsheds, if you want a country image, think of this vast room as a great hen house. For most of these creatures are very like. Society breeds the same sort of brainless, chattering, clucking things. And like their feathered counterparts, they too grow excited at the first drop of blood, and they'll peck a hole through the heart of anything they think is weak, anything they think they've wounded. All of them," he said as he took his other hand, and indicated the entire room as he included it in his sweeping bow to begin the minuet with her. "All of this honored company, all of the hens and chicks and capons and cock-of-the-walks," he continued as his open hand stretched far and swung wide, presenting her with the assembled ladies, gentlemen, mamas, papas, and chaperones. And as he raised his hand and head, he said, "They are pretty, silly, gabbling creatures, Miss Hamilton. Beware of them."

There was no chance for Faith to reply to him, for the figures of the dance took them apart and led them together, but always within ear shot of the other dancers. But she smiled and swayed and dipped and prayed for a suitable answer to brace him with when they were done. She'd joked, she'd acted a part as though her home were in a barn, but that did not mean she truly wished anyone to believe she had no manners or upbringing. If he knew that, as she believed he did, he might well mean his criticism for her own good. Even so, it was unpleasant to be chastened, it was uncomfortable to wonder if one had been in the wrong, and it was still undeniable that he disturbed her and so must be put in his place.

The dance continued, and the elders and chaperones and timid or choosy gentlemen and unfortunate or selective ladies could only watch as the long set pranced on. The duke, as host, had opened the dance with his duchess, but that lady glowered as she paced through the dance and for the second time in her life regretted an earlier decision. She ought to have let her husband begin the ball with Mary, she decided, as she spied the young American gentleman partnering her unwed daughter. For there, down the line from her, that American female was dancing with Lord Deal. Self-doubt was new to her, and ruinous to her equanimity. And so, although she'd never given a thought to anything outside her own narrow island's borders for the whole of life, she now decided that the menace from the Americas far outweighed anything she'd ever heard in church about the masses of heathen in the Holy Land, and wondered if there were currently any crusade she could join against the threat of them.

When the dance ended, Faith had some idea of an excellent retort, but even as she drew breath to thank her partner, most correctly, and give him a stunning set-down most cold-bloodedly, he said, sweetly, "Thank you, Miss Hamilton. And now may I invite you to another dance?"

But even Faith knew this was not done, two dances with one gentleman being thought exceptional and two together extraordinary, so, forgetting the excellent riposte she'd labored over, she said, "Why, you know I've promised it to the earl, my lord, and given all the others away as well."

"I meant," he explained, "at my humble home. Won't you come, and stay the weekend and dance the time away with me?"

"I may be from America," she said furiously, now positive he was making sport of her, "and so you may have felt impelled to use barnyard images in order to communicate with me, but I assure you I have no hay in my hair. But since you like such terms, I'll tell you, sir, you may call this sort of thing flirtation in England, but at home we'd call it—"

"My dance, my dear?" the earl asked smoothly, as Faith struggled with the word that had come to her mind but never to her tongue before. As Lord Deal watched with one lifted brow, she was led mutely off into the dance again. And knowing she was watched, Faith danced the night away. And despite Will's signals, frowns, and whispers, and because of Lord Deal's observant eyes upon her, she carried the company before her like a high wind from the Americas, leveling them with howling tales told with outrageous glee. If they wanted a primitive, innocent, guileless American, she thought with a mixture of anger and foreboding, why then, they should have one.

Only at last, when the last guest had left the ballroom to servants cleaning by candlelight, and the moonlight was almost fading outside her bedroom window, did Faith hear the last joke of all. For then Lady Mary, suppressing a great and contented yawn, told her happily, "Only think, Faith! Before he left, Lord Deal invited all of us to his home for the weekend, for a ball!"

SIX

STONECROP HALL WAS not so far from Marchbanks as to make an overnight stay necessary for anyone who wished to see both great houses in one day, even if that suppositional person were forced to walk back and forth to both places. And if that conjectured person weren't titled, wealthy, and in possession of the sort of Arabian horse that noble persons give stable room to, still he could conceivably take his old nag to breakfast at Marchbanks and then take tea at Lord Deal's manor without straining himself, his mount, or anyone's credulity too far. So of course there was no real reason why the party at Marchbanks should remove its comfortable self, with all the attendant difficulties involved in such a venture, only for the purpose of staying a weekend at Stonecrop Hall. Naturally, then, that was precisely what the entire party did.

Stonecrop Hall had not been opened to the occasional visitor for over a decade, and each person at Marchbanks, from invited guest to attendant servant, knew a certain thrill at being one of the first to be asked back. Its noble owner was not much in the way of society. He had that stirring name attached to him as well as that scandalous story, but that was old days, and as such, old hat. The fellow was older now and as eligible as he could stare, the elder ladies thought, with a tender hope for their daughters. And if a lady were fool enough to cuckold such a fellow, the youngest ladies decided, then she deserved what she got. And if she'd felt she had to do such a dreadful thing, some of the more experienced ones thought, why then, it might be at the very least, interesting, to discover why.

The gentlemen were mostly happy at having a change of

scenery, and a good tale to tell when they got back to the heart of civilization, their clubs.

And Miss Faith Hamilton, as she strolled along with the other guests who were being walked around the Hall the first afternoon of their visit, could only think that had she known Lord Deal sprang from such a place when she'd first met him, she likely wouldn't have been able to say a word to him, much less defy him.

It was not that she was unacquainted with the elegancies of living. Grandfather's house on Pearl Street was near the Battery, and not only was it one of the finest on the street, but it was in the heart of the most fashionable district, very near Bowling Green. Her father's home in Virginia was a great white mansion, and Grandfather even had that charming country home in the village of Greenwich, not three miles up Broadway, in the prettiest area, past the farms and through a little wood. Marchbanks was itself grand, built about the time that European eyes first widened at the size of the shoreline of America. But withall, Stonecrop Hall was like nothing she had ever seen.

It had not been planned out with just an eye to money spent and effect created, and left to amaze and inspire visitors to covet. It had obviously been built and rebuilt and revised down through more years than Faith could imagine, and each time for the comfort or convenience of the owner. It stood in a gracious park, and was built of gray stone and ringed by stone columns, but such was its charm that its glory came from its comfort equally as much as the well-designed beauty of each spacious room. It contained fully as much gilt and statuary as did its neighbor Marchbanks, but there was art rather than artifice to it. Similarly, even the paintings which hung upon the walls, as well as the decorative moldings and panels on those walls themselves, inspired the viewer to appreciation rather than estimation of their prices.

"Gosh, golly," she whispered to Will in the thick rustic accents she affected when they joked together about their relative status here among the English gentry. "It took a nice bit of change to put up this barn, don't you think? And I'll wager a dollar to your shilling it's so old, we'll find King Arthur sleeping in the best guestbed."

But Will only strolled on, seemingly oblivious to what

she'd said. It was only when he allowed himself to fall behind the others as they walked out to the rose gardens that he replied, in so low a voice that she had to strain to hear him, "Don't start now, Faith. I mean it. If you've decided to make a cake of yourself here, please understand that I have no wish to."

"Will!" she said, stopping and staring hard at him. "How can you think that? I only wanted to joke a little with you. The place is so grand, I didn't much like myself for only staring and mumbling as if I were in church. It's very nice, to be sure, but it's only a man's home, after all. I didn't think it was sacred. And anyway, what I said was just for your ears. Of course, I'd not embarrass you, I know how you feel about Mary," she explained in a fierce whisper.

"I'm sorry," he said, looking genuinely abashed as he patted her arm even as he took it and urged her along in the trail of the others. "I expect you think me a social climber, no, I know you do. But listen," he said seriously as he spoke low and gazed at her with a rueful smile, "I came here to England to find myself a wife, and a socially acceptable one at that, it's true. But I never thought I'd find everything I ever wanted immediately, and right in the house where you'd be staying. Faith, she's wonderful.

"She's beautiful and modest and charming. I know I sound like a lovesick boy, but when I was only a boy, newly come to your country and working at whatever I could turn my hand to in your grandfather's shipyards, I dreamed of coming home again someday and finding just such a wife for myself. But I didn't believe I'd actually ever find her."

"Will, I know her very well, and everything you say of her is true, but it's early days yet. You hardly know her, not really," Faith said, hoping to at least momentarily cool his ardor for her hostess.

Since Will had met Lady Mary, he'd been a different fellow, not the easy-going, humorous companion she'd known. He had transformed himself instead into this serious, quiet, and very proper imitation of an unexceptional young Englishman. She wondered if she ought to tell him what she really thought—which was that the duchess would never allow the match, no matter what his bank account, since she'd think his breeding was no account, and too, if there was any hope for him, it would never be for this staid copy of a proper gentleman he'd lately become. Because Lady Mary herself was not the picture of absolute propriety Will thought her, not beneath the affect she had to put on for her mama's sake, not from what Faith had learned in her midnight conversations with her. The Mary she knew might well prefer the old Will, the real Will, the happy-go-lucky, relaxed, and laughing Will, just as she herself did, no matter what her mama said. But then, Will did not know that Mary, just as Mary might never know that Will. Faith wondered with a sigh if she were the only one who would ever know the truth of either of them.

"I didn't come from such a home," Will said with a sort of despair, "but I can, and I shall build just such a place for myself."

"Well, I don't know." Faith grinned. "It's a mite grand for all it's so fine. Do you really think you need a castle? Because I think they've already settled their differences with the Normans here."

"But Stonecrop Hall is not a castle, Miss Hamilton," the earl commented as he came up to the pair from behind them, "it's a country estate. However fine the Viking's home may be, if you'll note there's not a crenellation in sight, nor a decent parapet to pour boiling oil down from. No, I'm afraid even your Red Indian chaps would make easy work of it for all its splendor, not to mention what a Saracen horde could achieve in less time than it takes to tell of it. Good morning, Rossiter, Miss Hamilton."

Will flushed as he bowed, and Faith herself wondered exactly what the earl might have overheard. There was no way to tell from his habitually calm, impassive countenance. Before Will could attempt some polite conversation, the earl, in the same flat, laconic tones, drawled, "Oh dear, I believe the good duchess has discovered a pebble in her shoe, or a stitch in her side, or has invented some other sort of fly for her ointment. But then, the interior of Stonecrop interests her far more than the gardens. I quite agree; after all, one rose is much the same as another, no matter which nobleman nurtures it."

Looking ahead to where the Duchess of Marchbanks had

seated herself on a stone bench in the rose garden, it became obvious that she had decided to wait there until the tour was over and was waving the rest of the solicitous party onward. As he stared, Will seemed to forget the conversation and the company he was with as well. Recalling himself, he murmured a few words, bowed, and then was off, obviously bent on intercepting and accompanying Lady Mary now that she was released from her mama's escort.

"Not too wise, that," the earl commented as he resumed walking with Faith. "He'd do better to meet with his lady in the moonlight, when her guardian dragon is safely tucked into her lair, thinking she's sound asleep atop her treasure's bed chamber. No, the duchess is not likely to encourage that connection. Not that there's a thing wrong with young Rossiter, mind, his face, monies, and manners are admirable, save for the fact that 'Mister' is not quite the word the Duchess of Marchbanks wishes to see engraved on any invitation to nuptuals she might issue, and 'Mrs.' is not the term of address she expects anyone to ever use when speaking to her daughter."

"Yes," Faith said quietly, "I've noticed that about you English."

"Have you?" he replied with a rare, long grin stretching across his mouth. "I wonder? I haven't. For it doesn't apply to you in the least. It's one of the little advantages of your sex in our country that a lady can acquire a title quite simply. Her husband, you see, drapes it over her at the moment they are united, it comes with the wedding, like the blanket on the marriage bed. It's only the gentlemen who have to perform deeds of daring, or endow universities or lend funds to our dear Prince in order to obtain an interesting title. So never fear, we English, as you put it, are not so worried about nobility when it comes to the dear ladies."

"You have the wrong sow by the ear," Faith said, her eyes blazing, for once all out of patience with the usually circumspect nobleman, "for I wasn't afraid in the first place, and I'm not a lady in the second place. I'm an American, and if we are 'ladies,' it is only in deportment, and if we aren't, it simply isn't important."

"Well done," the earl nodded with approval, "the fire,

the spirit, and the context. But my point was only that you could be, a lady that is, in the way we mean it, and no one would object. Certainly not,'' he added, his deep voice overriding any comment she could make about her disinterest again, ''anyone in my train. For I'm fatherless, poor lad, and the head of my family. My mama positively dotes upon me and while she would not think any lady deserved me, from queen to beggarwoman, she would equally so not question any decision I ever made in the matter.''

They were walking beneath an arched trellis hung with huge pink roses, and the atmosphere seemed to be almost suffocatingly bridal to Faith. She could see nothing in the gray eyes that observed her but a faint lurking humor, and nothing but the earl's words had shown any warmer intent than friendship. But still she did not know what to say to this declaration, for it was more personal than any he'd ever addressed to her. So she reached out a finger to stroke a velvety petal, and said at once to end the unnerving silence, ''Does your mama live with you?'' And then, realizing that that might sound too much as though she were interested in the more intimate details of the gentleman's life, she added, ''Are you an only child then?''

He laughed, as though pleased that he had unsettled her, and plucking the same rose that she'd touched, he inhaled it deeply before he tucked her arm securely beneath his and paced with her down through alleyways of roses as he told her about his mama, his elder sister, and his home in the distant north.

But though he told her of Hedon Castle, and spoke of mottes and baileys and corbels and machicolations and the long stone halls that rang with the history of the Methleys, he did not speak of the dry rot and death-watch beetles and fire damage and slow but sure decay that had kept his home closed for the past years. And though he went on to sing the praises of ancestors who rode to crusades and were flattered by kings, he did not mention his grandfather, who had spent half the fortune *his* grandfather had not already lost, or his own father, who had never noticed the rest of it ebbing as he'd frittered the last of it away. And when he presented her with the head of the pink rose he'd plucked before she left him to prepare for luncheon, he saw more than a slip of a girl from across the sea in a pink frock as she left him, for he hoped he saw the salvation of his name and his home in her.

There was no money left. There was scarcely enough to keep him a step ahead of his creditors, and even that step would have to be taken in boots not yet paid for. He should, he knew, have not procrastinated, he should have taken action long before this, put it down to a family failing, he thought bitterly as he stood in the rose-scented garden deep in thought. But at least he would act now. And if by selling himself, he could preserve his inheritance, then that was a very small price to pay for such a precious legacy.

His home, every cracked flag in its courtyard, every empty hallway, each cobble in its great walls, were more to him than the bones in his own body. A man did not have to marry where he loved, he had never expected to, few noblemen did. One married where wealth was, but the conceit that kept honor intact was that it was an optional, free choice. He had not the luxury of that choice any longer, but then, he was a rational man, and didn't feel he needed the illusion half so much as he needed the money.

Had he come to that realization sooner, he imagined he might have taken the last of his funds and invested it, as so many prudent gentlemen did. But he'd never been prudent, and hadn't understood the modern way to play at being a gentleman. It was pleasant for a nobleman to pretend his money came to him unsullied by the dirty hand of trade, but now, too late, the earl knew otherwise. The Duke of Marchbanks might put it about that Miss Hamilton's grandfather was an old friend, but the fellow had no title, he had only a vast shipping empire. Where then, did the duke believe his cronies think the friendship had sprung from? The Viking, at least, freely admitted to such investments. But that made his own sojourn here no easier. It was hard for a man with no funds to sit down at an enemy's full table, no matter how hungry he was. Still, a starving man would be a fool to refuse nourishment for pride's sake, and so too, he knew he had to remain here with this party of eligible young females.

It wasn't easy to associate with these girl children and foolish youths this summer, this summer of his desperation. But he was, he conceded, fortunate in so far as he had discovered a young creature who was more than wealthy enough, intelligent, very handsome, and not an utter fool. He hadn't thought to wed such as she, no matter how charming, but then, he thought on a shrug, a penniless gentleman, no matter how titled, had not the remotest hope of wedding where he thought he might have before he'd enjoyed that final discussion with his man of business.

No matter, the earl thought, he was amazingly resilient. To survive one had to be, that was the telling test; his line had not continued for so many generations because it could not accept change. He even found things to look forward to in the decision he'd made. She was clever and appealing. Most of the women he kept company with were females well versed in erotic skills. Though he hadn't expected very much on that score from any young bride he took, this American girl was surprising on many counts, so there might well be entertainment as well as economic security in the match for him.

As for her, he could offer quite a bit. He had title, breeding, and intelligence, and though he was not quite the sort of fellow requested to pose for marble statues of the Adonis, he would do; at least he'd not shame her. He'd be an amiable companion, he'd treat her well, surely she expected no more. She'd come to England to wed such a gentleman, no matter what nonsense she spoke of wishing to remain a spinster, of wanting a chance to help arrange her grandfather's business dealings. It was, he conceded, a charming excuse, almost as good as his own for being here, and about as true as that tale of wanting to visit with his dear friends the Duke and Duchess of Marchbanks again.

It seemed very near a settled thing. If any other gentlemen had captured her interest, he didn't know of it. The Viking had burned his fingers once, God knew, and indeed, whatever his aims, he obviously alarmed her as much as he interested her. Rossiter was only a friend, there was ample evidence of that; the lad was transparent in his yearning for Lady Mary. The earl scowled for a moment and then, brightening, thought that though Miss Hamilton was every bit as attractive and attractively dowered as he thought, she had a reckless tongue, and even if another gentleman seemed on the brink of upsetting things, that in itself, with a little aid, would help him dissuade further competitors.

Soon it would be time to begin the courtship in earnest, but now, the earl thought with a grin, it was time to begin dinner in Stonecrop Hall. And so, neatly beheading another bloom similar to the one he'd presented to Miss Hamilton and breathing deeply of its perfume before discarding it, he strode off to his rooms to ready himself for dinner, and an interesting evening.

The older members of the party at Stonecrop Hall were pleased and gratified to discover that young Deal had a head on his shoulders and hadn't been swerved by the dictates of modern fashion. For he didn't have one of those skimpy, fashionable, one-remove-at-a-time dinners for his guests to pick at. No, his good country cook had done dinner in the old style, and there was a plentitude of venison and beef, veal, poultry, fish and shellfish, in cutlets and steaks and fillets, covered with a parade of sauces, accompanied by several side dishes, and all of it out all at once, for everyone to enjoy at once. Although it must be admitted that it was primarily most of the older ladies and gentlemen who took full advantage of the meal, the younger people being notoriously choosy and frenchified.

The duchess was very pleased at the dizzying array of viands that the gentleman she hoped was her prospective son-in-law put out for all the company. But, as she confided to her wistful husband after dinner when he rejoined the ladies and before she sent him off to the card room so she could get a good earful of gossip, the fellow was unwed and so, of course, could afford to waste good money on a bountiful board. And to further staunch the duke's sighs over the treats he never tasted at home, she let him know that it was her considered opinion (and as such, good as gold in the bank of wisdom), that once Lord Deal had won their Mary, he'd stop emptying the family coffers for such careless largesse and be more frugal, just as she was herself.

Never for a minute did the duchess doubt that the invitation had been issued so that Lord Deal could get their Mary to himself, and after impressing her and her family with his lavish assets of house and garden, he would doubtless press his suit for her hand. She would not have laid her nightcap upon her pillow later that night with such a gusty sigh of pleasure if she had known how far that goal or that little white hand were from that gentleman's mind.

The dinner had been served in the old style because it had been so long since he'd entertained any but a few friends at his country seat that he'd never given the old cook that dwelt there different instructions. He'd been amused at the table that had been set for the company, but less so when he'd seen the gleam in the duchess's eye. If he'd known she'd be so impressed, and so clearly, plainly, and blatantly smug about what she just as obviously saw as a bid for her approval, he'd have served the lot of them bread and water and been done with it. But it was over, and now, as the company settled in the drawing room, he resolved to stay as far from the Incomparable Lady Mary as he would from a leper, and since he was a brave and charitable gentleman, he thought he'd stay even a bit further away than he would if she were that unfortunate.

Of the two Americans, since the gentleman was never a finger's width away from Lady Mary, it made it that much easier for Lord Deal to decide guiltlessly that it was only the young lady he could speak with in order to ferret out information. However, Miss Hamilton had a court in session now. Her outspokenness had gained her some admirers, her beauty others, and clearly, since Methley remained at her side like her thrown shadow, her fortune yet others. Obviously, it would be difficult to get a word to her, much less resume an oddly begun relationship with her, without an audience as attentive as any at the theater. And so her host decided upon giving a performance.

"Alas, Miss Hamilton," he said when he greeted her, coming in to join the ladies with the last of the gentlemen he'd shared his port with, "we do not dance until tomorrow night. What poor hospitality you must think this is! Tonight we've nothing on tap except for cards for the venial, conversation for the congenial, and perhaps charades for the theatrical. I'm sorry to say that I haven't even tuned up my spinet for the musical." Ignoring both the titters and the general sigh of relief that followed these words, he went on to add, with a show of remorse, "And to think of the wonderful times I had in your own country of an evening."

As Faith gazed at him with something very akin to horror in her expression, the earl, at her elbow, looked up with great interest and immediately voiced that which she would never have had the courage to say unless she'd been provoked beyond reason. "How odd, Deal, for though I should think what you were up to in Miss Hamilton's homeland of an evening would be positively inspiring to us, I didn't believe it the sort of thing you could relate in mixed company, that is, company that included Americans."

"Oh no, Methley." Lord Deal laughed, throwing his leonine head back theatrically as he did so and treating the company to a show of gleaming white teeth. "My poor reputation! Why New York is a charming city, but just like our London, not all of it is devoted to the fleshpots. I was there for several months, and surely, whatever you think of my morals, during all that time please believe there were a great many activities I took part in that can be discussed in any company."

"Indeed?" the earl said quietly, as all the guests, and not only Faith, stood by breathlessly. It appeared that the challenge, thrust, and parry going on between the two tall gentlemen was no less noticeable for all that it was cloaked in polite language and taking place in a drawing room, than it would have been if it were out in the open, and being enacted before tall oaks at dawn.

"Ah well," the earl sighed as he shrugged helplessly, though a certain glitter of amusement shone through his cold steady stare, "if you are sure the foreign office, as well as Miss Hamilton's patriotic sensibilities, will not be disturbed by such tattle. It is only that I wondered at the advisibility of airing such matters . . ." His words drifted off as he made it apparent that he was giving up his protests for the sake of good manners, in the name of civility, and not because of his amiability toward his opponent.

But his host's next words, spoken with high good humor, erased all traces of benign tolerance from his face.

"I do remember that you always had difficulty with sums, Methley," Lord Deal said merrily, and as the double-edged statement came clear enough to cut its recipient, he added, "and it's rather too bad that age has not corrected the problem. For nearly as I recall, I was last a sojourner in the Americas just after the cessation of hostilities, a matter of some year and a half ago, and then an English gentleman, although perhaps not likely to be voted the most popular fellow, was not precisely an outcast. Nor," he said, as confusion became manifest in Miss Hamilton's large gray eyes and her lovely lips began to open on a question her host would rather she did not voice in company, "an enemy. I had been there previously, to be sure," he admitted without a blink as she continued staring at him, "but I liked the land and the people so well I returned for another, shall we say, more comprehensive visit. I stayed with Mr. Sanford in New York, as a matter of fact," he added, and Faith's eyes flew wide.

"The lawyer?" Faith blurted. "But I know him. He lives near us. But then . . . you must know Mr. DeWitt, and the Parsonses too. And if you stayed there, you must have passed our house a dozen times, for we're not far."

"But alas, I never saw you," Lord Deal said softly, "for if I had, I doubt I would ever have returned to Stonecrop Hall again. At least," he added, on a inclination of his head, as if he made a symbolic bow to her, "not alone."

Their attentive audience stirred slightly. This was gallantry, and as such permissible, but it was also very near to something more, something quotable. Trust such a dashing gentleman to step so close to the edge, one envious lady thought on a sigh, and to do it with such perilously delicate grace. But instead of coloring up nicely and dropping her gaze as she took down the delicious compliment, like a good girl, Miss Hamilton paled and looked more like she wished she could take to her heels to flee.

"Then you must have seen that Indian tribe she was telling us about," an excited Lord Greyville interrupted, "the Mohegan chaps."

"Ah, yes, the fierce, painted ones she mentioned." Lord Deal sighed. He watched Miss Hamilton very closely, and as her gaze lifted from her slippers at his words, to look straight into his own eyes with a certain mute entreaty, he smiled and said, "Of course. But they're all gathered on the outskirts of town. Luckily, I stayed in the heart of the city. And there one can safely have quite a good time in a more civilized fashion. Oh yes,'' he went on, as he saw his American guest finally exhale slowly, ''New York has such wonderful places to visit that it can quite make you forget how dangerous it can be at times. Did you know they have pleasure gardens, just like ours, and similarly named? I passed quite an enjoyable evening at their Vauxhall, for example,'' he continued, and soon was entertaining his guests with tales of the sights and spectacles of New York. Though they were less bloodcurdling than Miss Hamilton's, they were so fascinating that many of the guests decided to forego the card table to hear them out. In fact, Gilbert North could be heard commenting to his friends by the time the evening was out, that New York sounded quite lively, very like a dashed fine place to visit actually, as a change from Paris, that was to say. Though, he added reflectively, with all the dangers from the wildmen, one wouldn't actually want to live there, of course.

Though the evening had been successful, at least one guest, the Earl of Methley, did not look best pleased when he left Miss Hamilton to go up to his own room. For while she curtsied prettily to him, it was the first time in hours that she'd looked at him. Most of the night she'd watched her host more attentively than a young woman hearing the virtues of her homeland being sung might be expected to, unless she was some sort of patriotic fanatic.

But his host was very gratified with the way the first evening at his home had gone. When he'd said his good night to his American guest, he'd made sure that they were far enough from the others for her to have a private word with him if she wished, and she did, and that word was most encouraging. For she'd looked at him with great sincerity and said a heartfelt, ''Thank you. You made my country look very well, and myself as well. You could have made great sport of me, you know. I thank you.''

And then she'd grinned up at him at the last. Unexpectedly and breathlessly suddenly, she'd grinned, in that second looking so warm and genuinely charming as her nose wrinkled and a small unforeseen dimple appeared on her chin from out of nowhere to fascinate him, that he just as suddenly found himself wishful of tendering her far more than his perfect bow as she was about to leave him at the foot of the stair.

Yet, even as the thought crossed his mind, she changed again, and something very much like fear appeared in her eyes, and she stammered a less confident thank you once again, and left, no, he thought, fled, to her rooms. He was heartened by this, because he felt it could mean no other thing but that she'd taken his warnings to heart at last, and was now being so extremely circumspect that she was afraid a display of such sudden warmth might be misconstrued and gossiped about by the company.

It was quite an about-face, and he smiled to himself as he made a mental note to tell her the next day that she needn't worry, he was deft enough to see that she wouldn't be compromised by him. At least, he mused, with a bit of self-congratulation and its resultant high good humor, not publicly. Because, he thought as he straightened his face and took his leave of the last of his guests, he had definitely made a beginning, he had certainly started a friendship with her, and it wouldn't be long before he could have that private chat with her. And just perhaps, something more as well.

But at that sudden thought, he stopped himself short, even as he reached the top of the stairs. Because, he realized guiltily, it was undeniably odd, even for the undeniably eccentric Lord Deal, for a gentleman to whistle a merry tune as he made his way to his chambers in the middle of the night.

SEVEN

THERE ARE TWO times of daylight that are the most comfortable for those who suffer from homesickness. One is twilight, of course, since that gentle time presages the coming of nightfall. Night's a sentimental time and though loss is felt most acutely then, curiously it is always comforting as well, at least for those who plan on going home again someday. For in the night, one may forget one's surroundings, or pretend that time is passing quickly since no matter how it's actually passing, another day has obviously just been gotten through. And in the night, of course, one may always dream of home and revisit it in that timeless way.

Earliest morning is another blurry hour when the cover of night has only lately been lifted and the full relentless glare of day has not yet been able to point up so pitilessly how far away home actually is. There's also that sense of the possibility of rescue, since the birth of the day, like any other time of renewal, is the time for hope. And too, in that pastel hour there are more opportunities to be alone, and it becomes easier for some people to bear loneliness when they don't have to pretend to jollity and contentment.

At least, so it was for Faith. So she slipped from the house when only lower servants were stirring and she walked the dewy garden paths and breathed in the pungent first breath of honeysuckle and though it brought a pang, since in the early mist it seemed so much like home, it was a pleasant pain, not so much of longing as of sweet remembrance. Nostalgia, she thought on a long sigh, was much easier to cope with than yearning.

But as she walked on, down a steep slope, away from the manor, and noted the birdsongs and began to appreciate the way the sun was slowly melting the mists and showing the gem-clear colors of another lovely summer's morning, she realized she was enjoying herself. At that, oddly, she experienced a certain unease. For at the thought that she might be becoming more accustomed to her surroundings, that she might at last be adjusting to them, she realized in so doing she was losing a part of her identity. Even if that part was only an aching uncomfortable thing, it had defined her, and if it were leaving then she no longer knew herself as well as she once had done.

But it was hard to regret the loss of pain, and so it was a very quizzical looking young woman that Lord Deal saw standing absolutely still in the path, her head on a tilt, very much like a robin listening for a worm. Or so he told her as he drew rein and saluted her. It wasn't the most politic thing to say to a lovely young woman, he realized even as he said it, but she lost that lost expression and laughed up at him when she heard it.

"Darn. I thought I was alone," she said, "and so I was listening to a nice big fat fellow rustling in the earth over there," she went on, pointing to the side, "but now that you're here I guess I'll have to pass him up and find another breakfast." And she grinned as she said it, which made him quite forget to laugh at her sally.

When she looked at him oddly, and quickly began to explain the jest, he slipped down from his mount and, looking down at her serious face, said on a belated laugh, "Oh I understood and it was clever. But you see, you grinned at me." When she looked even more confused, he gave out a genuine laugh, and leading his mount by his reins, he began to walk the path with her.

"You see," he explained, looking down at her as she paced by his side, shredding a bit of dandelion as she did so, "English ladies do not grin. Oh no," he said seriously as she looked up from the yellow wreckage she was creating at that, "they don't. They're trained not to, I think. They laugh, of course, and giggle a great deal, and have been known to simper unmercifully. But grinning," he said thoughtfully, "that closed upturned mouth, the compressed lips, that cheek-splitting subversive sort of barely suppressed amusement, no, I'm quite sure it never occurs. I think it's supposed to bring on wrinkles. But no," he said in alarm, "please don't stop, because it's charming. Ah," he sighed, as she began to laugh, "now I've done it. You're desperate to be in fashion and look at you, falling about with laughter, and not a grin in sight."

It seemed she could not become sober. Whenever she tried, he'd say something rather wistfully about her vanished grin, and she'd start up again. It was only when they reached the bottom of the lane and had taken a few steps to the right, that she saw where they'd walked and the sight took the laughter from her.

"Oh lord," she sighed.

"Yes?" he asked. And when she grinned at him, he looked back happily and said, "I couldn't resist. It's my one advantage over all your countrymen, that one pathetic jest. I had to use it, didn't I? And it bought me that grin back again, which was worth it, wasn't it?"

She didn't answer, she just looked out at the ornamental lake they'd come to. It was nothing like Marchbanks's tailored, cement-circumscribed circular body of water. But though it was clearly artificial, no natural formation being so tamely curved, or conveniently arranged into multiple landscaped spillways and goldfish-filled shallows and quiet lily-clogged pools expressly formed for the pleasure of Japanese bridges to wander across, it improved on nature. The great willows to one side certainly thought so, and their long leafy fingers trailed across its face as if tracing their own wind-ruffled images, and there seemed to be no complaint from the wild ducks which streamed in proper family file over its deeper surfaces.

"An ancestor," he said negligently, holding back his mount, who stirred with the sudden thought of drinking too deep. "It's convenient having had thoughtful ancestors. This particular fellow was constantly shifting trees and rearranging streams. He died, like Alexander, dreaming of new land to conquer. It pleased him to play at being the Creator, and the results amuse us. But don't look at me as though I were a lily of the field, Miss Hamilton," he said at once, although she had done no more than turn her head to listen to him.

"Gad, but you Americans are still a puritanical lot," he complained, and before she could assure him she wasn't, he went on, fretfully, "I pay for my forebear's play, I assure you. Though I don't work in a shop, my funds do. I invest, Miss Hamilton, though it pains those of the *ton* when I say it, but I agree with your countrymen. If it was my ancestors' work which made this earthly paradise, it is mine to keep it up, as well as to keep it in my family.''

''But I don't blame you,'' she said at once when he paused and looked out, brooding, to the lake, ''and I wouldn't.''

But before she could enumerate the ways in which she did not blame him, he went on, an unreadable expression in his sun-dazzled eyes, ''You don't subscribe to republican revolutionary ideals, as so many of your countrymen do? As Bonaparte preached? You know the chap,'' he said smoothly, ''the one who meant no harm to your country during the late hostilities? You know, the fellow who didn't burn Washington to the ground?''

She bit her lip as he looked down at her confusion and then added lightly, ''I deplore gossip, perhaps more than any man does, and perhaps with more right. But, I confess, I hear it.''

''Lord Deal,'' she said at last, for he hadn't broken the silence again as he awaited her answer, ''my lord,'' she said seriously, raising her head and looking him in the eye, ''I said a few things about Napoleon Bonaparte, you did hear correctly. But I said them as I've said a great many things since I've come here, impetuously and, I'll admit, foolishly.

''Well,'' she cried, raising her chin, not knowing that with the morning breeze blowing her thin blue skirts about her, and with the militant look in her clear gray eyes so pronounced, she looked the very picture of revolutionary zeal. Very like, he thought admiringly, one that he'd seen in France, of Liberty at the barricades, all she needed was a white blouse, a red ribband, and a banner, and, he thought critically, a somewhat larger bosom, to complete the image perfectly. But eyeing that portion of her person as she breathed in a deep breath to blast him, he thought that he wouldn't change an inch of her anatomy even if it would then duplicate the finest artwork.

The fashionable light blue frock she wore, which draped in classical style, was designed to present the female form as though it were some sort of statuary. With that in mind, and with the light behind her, it was clear to him that putting on or taking off an inch more from any part of her person would have been sheerest vandalism. The top of her bound amberwine tresses came just to his shoulder, and he decided that every inch of her person between there and the ground suited him perfectly. But a gentleman, especially one who was supposedly goading a suspected spy to rash statements, did not stare at salient points of a lady's shapely form. Thus, Lord Deal forced himself to gaze down only into an upward-tilted pair of sparkling gray eyes and attempted to disregard all else and only listen to what was issuing from that pair of peony-tinted lips.

Yet he could not help but think she looked entrancing as she angrily spoke the most conciliatory words. "It stands to reason it's nonsense, doesn't it? I mean, my lord, if you know my countrymen at all, as you say you do, you'd know we wouldn't have gone to all that trouble to throw over your old king just so we could set up an emperor in his stead, would we?"

"Politics often don't stand to reason," he answered, leaning back against his steed's caramel hide, his arms crossed over his chest, looking so comfortable she wished she could whistle the beast to motion and send him sprawling.

"Well, do you think I'm a spy, or something like?" she asked on a laugh that turned to a gasp as he continued to stare at her blandly.

"Well, as you're fond of saying, well, it has been mentioned," he said calmly.

"Oh yes," she cried, "of course. Do have your man search my luggage. I've brought some explosive material and packed it in with my incendiary pamphlets. I just can't decide which to destroy first, Stonecrop Hall or Marchbanks, my primary aim being to decimate the ranks of all English country estates."

"Thus lowering the morale of the upper classes and making it that much easier for the rabble to take over— very clever," her interrogator mused with an admirably straight face.

"Yes," Faith admitted, quieting somewhat as the idea began to enchant her. "Will and I will then most likely take to blowing up the gentlemen's clubs of London."

"Not that!" Lord Deal gasped. "You go too far, my girl," he said threateningly.

"Absolutely," Faith replied, nodding sagely, "for then the gentlemen will have to go home and look at their wives and families again, and we feel that the shock of it will effectively eradicate a good portion of the decadent ruling classes."

"I think," Lord Deal said warningly, straightening and looking down at her, "that I will have to take steps, young woman, to disarm you."

He stood before her, booted legs apart, and uncrossed his arms even as he took that one stated step toward her. He was all in russet browns, from his light riding breeches to his toast-colored jacket, and since his shaggy mane was no darker in the shifting, dappled light than the great buff horse behind him, there was only the blue of the sky above his head for contrast. There was a look half of laughter and half of something very different in the long hazel eyes which studied Faith, and the tanned visage which had held a smile now grew serious even as the firm mouth did, as those light-flecked eyes focused on Faith's own lips.

There was a warm breeze blowing which brought the ripening scents of summer to her, mixed in with the pungent odor of the horse, as well as a new and oddly interesting scent of lemon and soap and verbena, which must have come from the gentleman as he bent closer to her. And in that fleeting second, Faith wondered, just for that passing second, what it would be like, after all that shared laughter, to be caught up in those brown arms and held captive close, against that—but in the next second the great horse shifted a step and she heard the creaking of its leathers and the jingling of its fittings, and that subtle change, changed everything. For then she looked into those profoundly serious, knowing eyes and at that slightly parting mouth as he drew near and she felt a familiar, but no less dreadful for all that, stab of sheer terror.

She stepped back immediately, almost overbalancing as she did so. And at that, Lord Deal stopped in his tracks and looked at her, no longer with that disturbing growing desire, but with real surprise and puzzlement.

"So," she asked shrilly, her voice so oddly high and

artificial she scarcely knew it, "do you really think me a spy?"

"My dear," he said slowly, dropping his hands to his sides, a troubled expression replacing the threatening avid look of concentration which had so alarmed her, "I was going to attempt to kiss you, I'll admit it. And I know it isn't done. So, I suppose you were right to deny me. But you could have said something. A word would have been sufficient. Because, my dear, I was not going to attempt anything else, I promise you. I'm . . . I'm not so wild as I look." He laughed hesitantly. "You need not fear me," he explained again, when she would not answer, but only stood and gazed at him with distress.

Then, without another word, she spun around and literally took to her heels, and ran back up the road they had descended, and rounded the curve in the path and was lost to his sight.

He stared after her a long while, not seeing anything but what had already passed between them. And that, he thought, had not been anything tangible, only a great deal of good fellowship, and sharing, and humor, and then, an unexpectedly strong attraction. He'd wanted to kiss her, to taste her, to know with his lips and his body what his mind and his senses had already promised him. But his mere intention had frightened her. No, no, he thought, not frightened, the shocking thing was that he'd obviously terrified her.

A kiss was, after all, not a very great thing. Oh, he supposed some gothic families used the evidence of one to bind a fellow to a declaration, he'd heard of it, but in truth he'd never known of anyone caught in the parson's mousetrap for such a little felony. It was generally the theft, or gift, of a great deal more than a brief embrace and two pairs of lips touching that required those holy words to be so swiftly uttered. Most knowledgeable young ladies, even of the highest birth, would exchange kisses with a great many admirers before they decided which of the lucky fellows had compromised them.

Miss Hamilton was no prude, he'd swear it, her conversation was far too lively, and whatever error he'd made, the softened speculative look she'd worn before he moved toward her was unmistakable. Neither was she remotely what anyone might consider sheltered or gothic. But it was undeniable. He'd felt like some sort of great slobbering brute in that instant when he'd looked into her eyes just before he was about to embrace her. Because she'd stared at him with absolute horror. It had killed his desire immediately.

She was decidedly not a spy. The idea was ludicrous. He would post a letter to that effect to certain persons in London, he'd swear to it on any holy writ. Now he had no real reason to pursue the relationship. But, he thought as he swung up into the saddle and set his horse to a meaningful pace to ride far and wide to order his own reasonings, whatever else it had done, Miss Hamilton's outsized reaction to him had definitely not killed his curiosity. And that, he thought on a bemused chuckle as he rode away, despite her obvious fears, was the largest part of him that she ought to beware of.

This evening Faith did not seek Lady Mary's opinion of her gown. It wasn't because she was so sure that it was the correct thing, it was because she was so totally convinced that she'd done the wrong thing. She was so thoroughly embarrassed that she not only had avoided her host all the day, she'd also neatly managed to stay far from Lady Mary, and by so doing, Will too, of course. All three of those persons were either too observant or knew her too well for her present comfort. Instead, she'd passed the day distractedly, making aimless conversation at luncheon with the earl, or foolish chatter with assorted young gentlemen and ladies of the house party wherever she'd encountered them as she'd tried to hide herself in the house or on the grounds.

Now she sat at her dressing table and took a dispirited look at her image in the glass. There was nothing wrong with the frock, except for the fact that its silk was as yellow as the dandelion she'd held as she'd spoken with her host this morning; there wasn't a thing wrong with its cut, save for the fact that it was so form-fitting and low in front as to show the cleft between her breasts, and yet not low or transparent enough to show what a cheat was wearing it.

What else should he think she was? she wondered. Yet

how could she explain to him what she'd never been able to reason out for herself? She'd kissed other gentlemen. There had been other attractive young men she'd known at home, and she'd been very curious as well as a bit frightened at the thought of intimacies with them, as she imagined all young girls were. But, she sighed, though she'd never asked, she was quite sure that other, more fortunate females lost their fear once they'd experienced their first kiss. She had not. It had grown, rather, to the point that she imagined her fifth embrace was even more terrifying than her first imagined one, no matter how comely, clever, or kind her suitors had been.

The moment a gentleman's lips touched her own and she felt his arms go around her, she began to feel her pulses race, but not with healthy excitement. Instead, she always felt the same sudden, sickening threat of entrapment, and a need for fresh, free air. Always, in the heart-pounding, unreasoning terror, her partner, rapt, unreachable, totally lost in the embrace, lost all his identity as well to her, and became only a creature to flee.

She'd looked into Lord Deal's eyes, and had been drawn to him and had wanted that fascinating, firm mouth upon her own. But then, this time, even before he touched her it was as though he had already done so, the panic had loomed so large. Above all else, above all her own fear, she had feared for him. She'd not wanted him to experience her shameful rebuff. So instead, she groaned to herself, she'd insulted him more by refusing the advance he hadn't even made. After, she emphasized, since she didn't want to spare herself a jot of deserved pain, she'd practically invited him by special letter to make love to her.

There was no one she could tell about it. There never had been. When she'd been younger, she'd tried to hint at it with close friends, but their lack of understanding, or sometimes their outright amusement, had caused her confession to die even as it was born on her lips, and she'd laughed it away pretending it was a jest. It wasn't a matter to take up with a physician, although she felt it must be unhealthy, because after all, an unwed young woman wasn't supposed to allow a gentleman to make love to her at all. Similarly, it had never seemed to be the right time or place to bring it up with her dear companion, Molly. Theirs was a warm but professional relationship, and such things were never mentioned except briefly, in gentle jest, Molly being careful of her young charge's sensibilities, Faith being too embarrassed at her own sensitivities.

She often thought that Grandfather would have understood, since he was wise enough to comprehend anything. But it certainly wasn't the sort of topic she could discuss with him. She'd kissed Will the once, a long while ago, to see if she could please Grandfather by forming an alliance with him, and because he was a friend. But that kiss hadn't lasted long enough to begin to discomfort her. No sooner had it begun than they'd pulled away from each other and laughed at their own folly. Still, just because Will was more a brother than a lover didn't mean she could discuss her reaction to other men with him.

Seeking counsel from Mother, of course, was out of the question. Though she lived in a wing of the same house, it was as though they inhabited separate planets. On the infrequent occasions when she spoke with Mama, as that lady was on her way out to the theater or coming home from an assignation with some friend, or young man, they spoke of little but fashion, in the fashion of cool acquaintances. Mama didn't like having such a grown-up daughter. But then, Faith shrugged, she herself did not care for having such a childlike mama. Then too, there was the evidence she'd gotten with her own eyes of Mama's opinion in such matters. So, Faith thought, rising to her feet at once, it was obvious that as always, further thought was futile.

She'd have to steel herself to take action. Someday she'd have to force herself to remain in a man's embrace longer, and so conquer irrational fear. Yes, certainly someday, she thought, as she went out of the room and downstairs to the dancing party.

There was no doubt that her host was a tactful gentleman. Just as he'd greeted her at luncheon without a blink or a hint or a word to show that they'd ever met and spoken at dawn, he welcomed her to his dance party and complimented her on her appearance in proper, unremarkable fashion. He only seemed taken aback when she returned the compliment, and though he recovered his countenance quickly, she realized that she'd trampled upon another English custom. But he'd looked so fine in his black jacket and pantaloons, with a showing of white lace at his neck, that she'd told him so, only to realize belatedly that not only was that not done, but from the quickly repressed glint in his eye, that with her apparent admiration as well as her words, she'd thrown out another invitation to him.

Lady Mary was all in white, and with her golden hair and rose complexion she was so lovely that Faith felt a pang for Will when the Earl of Methley had the first dance with her.

"But really," Faith explained quietly and patiently to an impatient Will as he looked daggers at the pair dancing across the floor, "with the English, it is precedence, friend, that comes first. That's why he's come first. It's an honor, don't you see? He's the highest-born single fellow around. Well, just look, dear idiot, Lord Deal's opened the ball with the duchess, now aren't they a sweet pair? And do you think he's got designs on her, blockhead?"

Will only glowered, and stuck his hands into his pockets, no matter how fiercely Faith whispered that it wasn't done, as he waited for the dance to be done. The earl, regal in his usual black, and Lady Mary, delicate in white, were both graceful and noble looking. Faith had to admit they were a striking pair, though she'd rather lose her tongue permanently than confide that to Will for fear he'd rush at the earl with the most convenient killing instrument to hand.

When Lady Mary returned to the sidelines and the earl took his bow over her hand, she was flushed, her blue eyes sparkled, and Faith had reason to be very glad after all that Will had his hands in his pockets when she saw that one of those pockets now contained the unfashionable shape of a definitely clenched fist. But she relaxed when he turned to speak with Lady Mary and she smiled back at him, and that offending hand left its confines and promptly led the lady back into the dance.

The earl gazed down at Faith, and just as she was about to agree to the dance he was obviously going to ask her to, their host appeared before them. Having just left the duchess to frown at the sight of her daughter back in foreign clutches, he caused that lady another pang as he immediately invited the other treacherous American into his own arms. Worse luck, thought the duchess as both pairs took the floor, for this was a waltz, and the two Americans that were separating the most eligible, logical, best-matched pair at the dance, were now twined about them as well.

The music of the waltz by itself was usually enough to sweep all of Faith's cares away, but this evening she was held in the arms of a gentleman whose arms she had run from hours before. Yet now there was no place she'd rather be. So in confusion, she kept her eyes downcast as they danced. But she noted how well their steps matched, she experienced at last how very strong those arms actually were, and when he spoke, low enough not to be overheard, but close enough so that his breath tickled her ear, she realized that the susurration of his words alone couldn't account for the way she felt her skin tingle as he spoke.

"Miss Hamilton," he said, "or Faith if I may?" He paused, and at her nervous, abrupt, nod he offered, "You might call me Barnabas as well, or even Barnaby."

"Thank you," she replied at once, though from the way her lips snapped shut after the words, he realized it might be some time before she made free with his given name.

But, "Barnabas!" she thought with pleasure, just as he went on to muse, "Although 'Faith' makes me sound as though I were speaking with an exclamation point each time I say your name—we'll have to think of a better one. I know you weren't feeling quite the thing this morning and hope you've recovered. Your faith in me, if nothing else. Now there's a tantalizing concept I've just misspoken. You see why your name's so troublesome?" He laughed, but then said very low and very seriously, "I mean you no harm, please believe me, and so shall we still be friends?"

But he had spoken so many sibilants—even his given name had its fair share, she despaired—each of which from such close quarters sent thrills along her wretchedly sensitive ear, she could scarcely speak, but only nodded her agreement as they danced. This seemed enough for him for now, and they whirled on in silence. Then she chanced to glance up at him, and observed his bronzed face from closer than she had this morning. Even in the candlelight she saw the small green glints in his golden eyes, and hastily dropping her gaze, encountered that gently smiling mouth again, and again, though he hadn't so much as rested those sun-blushed lips upon hers, not once, she knew unreasonable fear.

She didn't show it this time. She'd swear he could not have known it, even in her hurried thank you when the dance was done. But it was too much, she was angry and hurt and confused with herself, so that might have been why, when he turned to take another partner, she allowed herself to be immediately led into the dance by a foppish young fribble she'd taken pains to avoid all week.

It might well have also accounted for the reason she then danced with everyone who asked her. And when she became alarmingly overheated, why she drank anything they brought her. Which in turn might have explained why she obliged Lord Greyville with the uproarious tale about the frozen Indian, or why Gilbert North never forgot her story of the Independence Day picnic, and why the earl laughed so heartily when she regaled him with the slightly naughty saga of the inebriated French trapper. And perhaps accounted for the reason why she laughed so merrily at every jest every jolly gentleman whispered to her, no matter how warm.

Will, of course, chided her when he danced with her, but she was really feeling very nicely at that point, and so there wasn't any difficulty in nodding and agreeing with him absolutely, whatever it was he said, although she wasn't too sure she even heard it. And yes, she assured Lady Mary, she was feeling very well indeed. To prove it, she went dancing into the earl's arms with a dreamy smile, and only lost it when she saw her host glance at her from over his own partner's shoulder with a deep concern clearly written, clear enough for her to see even in her present state, even in the distortion of candlelight, in his observant, damnably watchful, brilliant eyes.

It was late in the night, and as was usual at such an hour, the floor was very crowded. Picky ladies who'd declined dances through choice all evening danced out of boredom now. Gentlemen who'd had to load up on drink to stoke up their courage to ask that certain unattainable one for the pleasure of a spin about the floor, now bravely stumbled through dances with two such prizes in a row.

Elder couples and older singles all mingled and danced as if they never would have such a chance again, and as it was almost the last of the night, who knew for which of them this might not, sadly, be true?

So in all the crush and rush of madly capering couples, it was no great feat for the earl, unremarked, to lead a dangerously flushed and giddy Miss Hamilton to the cooler regions of the portico. There, beneath an arbor heavily hung with wisteria, she ceased dancing and murmuring something on a laugh, something to do with her enchanted red slippers that had not given her feet rest, and then looking down, giggling and saying, no, yellow ones actually, she came at last to a sort of standstill.

"You drank a very great deal," the earl said with a certain amount of amusement, from somewhere very high above her.

"Did I?" she marveled.

"You did," he verified. "I was watching."

"I wasn't," she giggled.

"Don't worry," he said coolly, "we'll stay here a while, and then we'll see you climb the stair, with assistance, when most of the others have already gone up."

"I won't worry," she said gravely, and then asked him very nicely, she thought, if she might not have something to drink as she was very thirsty.

"No, no," he said consideringly, "not even water, not now. You've had enough."

"I'm not tipsy!" she cried, stung, and thought that it was very true, for she still knew everything that was going on about her, not at all like when she'd drained all the guests glasses after one of Grandfather's parties when she'd been fifteen. It was only that she was, just as he'd said, not worried any longer, not worried at all now.

"Really?" he asked with some interest.

She looked up at him steadily, to show she was sober as a judge, thinking only that it was rather too bad that she knew so many very tall gentlemen, one could get a stiff neck from so much peering upward as she'd been doing. Then she thought with a sudden sadness, that it was only two tall gentlemen after all, and one of them made her very unhappy. But not the earl, not this long-faced, lean-faced, white-faced gentleman smiling down so benignly upon her.

He in turn saw a wistful little grin replace the sorrow she'd suddenly shown, which had immediately followed her original good humor. Her smooth amber hair had come loose from its band, and he stroked it back against her warm brow and felt its silkiness cool beneath his hand, even as he saw her lift her chin at that and look, with what must have been yearning, up to him. No, he thought, she was not that disguised by drink. And so he bent his head and kissed her.

How odd, she thought at first, how very strange that the cool and sexless earl was actually kissing her. She felt nothing else but surprise at his actions when his long, cool mouth touched hers, and so didn't react when he gathered her closer to his thin body. Except that a small, very sober voice told her to stay as she was, to remain quiescent, whatever came, as he pressed his lips against hers. Because if she was lucky enough to feel no fear even now, and if she could remain there long enough, perhaps then she could banish all her fear for all time, so that another time she could stand so for another gentleman.

But then she felt his body grow warm against hers, and noted a new tension there, as well as a new urgency in his grasp. Now, he seemed to become as lost to reason as the others had been when they'd kissed her, and it was as if he quite forgot her, even as he pulled her closer. Then she felt him pressing against her and though she was not afraid, she began to resist. But even as she began to pull back, she felt, incredibly enough, a hot moist tongue wedged against her closed lips.

"No!" she cried in alarm, and before that unwelcome unpleasantness could intrude further because of her utterance, she cried, "No!" again, and the noise of it in the quiet of the night caused the earl to release her quickly.

She gave him one disbelieving stare, picked up her skirts in one hand, and backed away from him until her back hit the long french door through which they'd left the ballroom. Then, turning around at once, she pushed open the door and soon lost herself in the prancing throng within.

The earl composed himself as he waited long enough for

the young woman to collect herself and take herself off to her room. He rested his hands on the balcony rail and stared up at the soft night sky, and didn't seem as discomposed as a recently rejected gentleman perhaps ought to be. In fact, he smiled to himself in the dark. Poor child, he thought magnanimously, he couldn't blame her. She'd gotten more than she'd bargained for. She'd wanted him, he knew that. She'd come here with him without a murmur and then gazed up at him with a world of invitation in her eyes. And she'd enjoyed the embrace, her passive acceptance showed that. It was only that she lacked the experience to contribute more, and he'd gone on too fast and frightened her away.

It would be better next time, he thought with pleasure. After all, after tonight they would have all the time in the world.

Lord Deal slowly stepped back into the house. There had been no need to rescue her, she'd broken away even as he'd angrily thrust the door wide and drawn breath to demand her immediate release. Fortunately, he realized belatedly, she'd managed better than he would have done; she'd extricated herself before he'd made a scene. There'd been quite enough damage done to her reputation this night already without his adding his mite. For he'd been about to commit mayhem the moment he saw her clasped in Methley's embrace, and then, he hadn't even known whether she'd gone there willingly or not.

He drew the door closed quietly. If she wasn't in her rooms when he returned to his guests, at least he knew she'd not likely follow the earl out into the moonlight again. He'd seen her expression as she'd left Methley. But then he sighed, the enigma bedeviled him. He remembered her face just as clearly when she'd pulled away from him this very morning. It had been fear he'd seen, both times. And he'd not even touched her.

Miss Faith Hamilton, after ordering her maid to bring a basin of cold water and sending her to her own bed immediately thereafter, immersed her heated face in the basin and counted until ten and then didn't pull up until her lungs demanded a new breath. Then she set about scrubbing her face until the pain of it penetrated her still foggy senses.

No more experiments, she told herself angrily, as she dashed the water over her cheeks. No more tests, she pleaded with her better self as she lay her washcloth down. For if her aim was to feel something other than fear when a gentleman attempted to make love to her, then she'd already been successful.

Then the brash young American Miss Hamilton, more coldly sober than she ever wished to be, and totally alone, as she now knew she would always be, sank down to the side of her bed and wept, tears and water intermingling as they ran down her streaming face. Because all she had learned was that there was yet another emotion she could now experience in a man's embrace. And that was scarcely an improvement, for it was only disgust.

EIGHT

THE YOUNG MAN paused in his pacing, wheeled about, and faced the other gentleman who was sitting at his ease, quietly, in a tall-backed brocade chair, his legs crossed and fingers steepled, watching him expressionlessly.

"Of course I understand," the young gentleman said angrily. "Good grief, Deal, don't you realize I've thought of little else? Or at least," he said, the back of his neck becoming a little red even as his earnest young face flushed, "I've thought a great deal about it. I've had other concerns, I'll admit. But Faith's behavior is directly tied up in that as well. Blast," he sighed, dropping down into a nearby chair as though suddenly shot as he accepted the hard truth of his defeat. "Thinking about it is about all I've been able to do, too. She pays me no mind at all, but then she never listened to anyone but Mr. Godfrey, and he's an ocean away right now."

"And he sent her here to marry?" Lord Deal asked thoughtfully.

"God no," Will Rossiter answered wearily, "he's no tyrant, and he wouldn't order her to her wedding even if he could. And," he said more forcefully, "I doubt if even he could do that."

"She's no intention of wedding anyone?" Lord Deal asked gently, with only a hint of disbelief, and then when there was no immediate reply, he sighed, rose, and went to look out a window.

This Sunday morning it was drizzling. There was little to see but mists floating over his wide rolling lawns outside the library window. The guests were abed, the trace of rain having given the older ones a convenient excuse for missing church, and the younger ones, another good reason for sleeping in. Most of them would be departing in

the afternoon, so their servants were already busily pack-
ing and preparing for the remove. But young Mr. Rossiter,
like his host, was in the habit of an early morning ride, no
matter the climate, and so it had been an easy thing for
Lord Deal to wait about the stable on some trifling pretext
and then casually request a word with him alone when
he'd come back from his morning exercise.

But having a "word" didn't necessarily mean receiving
the ones he wished to hear in return, so Lord Deal thought
for a moment more before he said, without turning his
head from the dampened landscape, speaking as much to
the window pane as to his guest, "You don't have
to answer me. It goes beyond politeness to one's host
to tell tales about one's friends and employers, I know.
Please understand that I don't ask out of love for a
good gossip. But it's precisely because of gossip that
I do ask. Speaking of which, if you've had your ear
to the ground at all, you ought to know that I'm rather
an authority on the subject, having been the subject of
so much of it for so long."

Mr. Rossiter left off his hopeless, abject aspect and sat
up sharply, only to shift in his seat uncomfortably. His
host could see this very easily in the reflection in the glass
through which he seemingly was looking out over the long
green lawns of Stonecrop Hall. There were certain unfair
advantages a chap had over his fellow man after having
worked for his country in foreign lands, but Lord Deal
didn't feel in the least guilty about this as he appeared to
continue to gaze ahead. Then he permitted himself an
audible sigh before he went on to muse aloud, "There
would be talk about Miss Hamilton even if she only sat
in a corner and sewed a fine seam. She's American,
which would be exotic and interesting to us no matter
where we encountered her. She's an heiress, or so it's
said. She's very lovely as well. And she just happens to be
the house guest of a highly visible, socially active duke of
the realm, and his family, which just happens to include
the acknowledged beauty of the Season, to boot."

He noted that the young gentleman sat bolt upright at
that, and nodding, as though to himself, he then went on,
"Of course, she'd occasion comment. And you have as
well, Mr. Rossiter. Because, to the tattles' delight, it

appears that you've both set your sights on making highly eligible connections, and as such, are fair game for all sorts of speculation, not to mention outright fabrications. Even with all that, Miss Hamilton's behavior of late gives rise to a great deal more talk, and none of it beneficial to her. Or to you. Believe me, Rossiter,'' Lord Deal said as he spun around to see the young man looking at him with the worried expression he'd been carefully watching for in the window so that he'd know precisely when the time was ripe to turn and finally confront his guest, ''she, at least, can come to harm through it, yes, even if, as you refused to say, she doesn't choose to marry here.

''I'd like to prevent that. I'd like to help her. And that's why I ask personal questions of you, since you're the only chap here who really knows her circumstances. Perhaps there's something you might say in passing, something that you're too close to see for yourself, that might help alleviate matters. Telling me about her grandfather, her family, her aims, and her background would not be betrayal, or just to your own benefit, never think it. She must be made to stop, you agree?''

''Oh aye, I agree.'' Will shrugged, but then, as unexpectedly as if he had dropped off an item of clothing, he gazed at his host with a face suddenly neither so young nor so open as it usually was, and with his brown eyes serious and hard as stones, he said, ''All true, my lord. But why should you concern yourself so much about it?''

Barnabas Stratton smiled and sat himself opposite the young man again. He liked him much better now, and told him so before he said as honestly as he was able, ''Because I make it my business to confound gossips wherever I can. Because I am not so fond of the Earl of Methley that I should wish to see your friend Miss Hamilton have no other choice but to confer her fortune upon him if she is indeed seeking a mate here. Even if she is not, say then, because she interests me. And I like her. Good enough?''

Will Rossiter sat still and considered for a moment. Then he sat back. ''Good enough,'' he said.

''Now, Franklin Godfrey is a fair man and a good man,'' Will then said slowly, ''and if Faith dotes on him, she's every reason to. If he hadn't taken her from her mother's care, God knows what sort of life she would have led. Not that the lovely Mrs. Hamilton would have abused her daughter, it's more likely that she just would have forgotten which room she'd put the brat in, and maybe she'd not have remembered until a few years later. Unless, of course, that room had one of her favorite mirrors in it too.''

Barnabas Stratton grinned and settled back in his chair. "And the father?" he asked.

Will made a face. "Have you any experience with southern gentlemen of the worst sort, my lord?" he asked.

"Ah yes," Lord Deal nodded. "But please, call me Barnaby, as my friends do. But that bad, eh?" he asked.

"Worse," Will sighed, though he smiled when he shook his head, "because, Barnaby, aside from the insincerity, and the weak character, and the poor treatment of his slaves, there's the women, you know."

"No, I don't, Mr. Rossiter," his host said with interest.

"Oh yes," Will replied, "but then, that's only another excuse for the unhappy couple's living apart, and their constant wrangling when they do get together. And, oh, it's Will, Barnaby."

"Then Will, is it claret, ale, lager, or port for you?" Lord Deal asked, as he rang for refreshments, since it now looked as though it would be a long and interesting rainy Sunday morning.

"The roses, for the red, of course," Lady Mary said thoughtfully as she gnawed at the end of her pen, "and the white's simple enough, since that can be roses as well, and there are lilies and stock available and loads of meadowsweet, too, if you don't mind them, although the gardeners might, since they're weeds actually, but that's of no account, because it's the blue that's the real problem."

"It isn't that important, honestly Mary," Faith said at once. "There's not the slightest reason to trouble yourself—"

"But of course it is." The other girl looked up from the list she was compiling. "Certainly it is," she repeated at once, with as much surprise as if her guest had just denied the existence of the supreme being, rather than questioning the need for another party. "It's your birthday, and you're so far from home, and since it is, why it's an excellent reason to have a bang-up party. Even Mama says so,'' she added triumphantly, as though that there could be no further word of argument after that fact had been clearly stated.

As that shot caused her guest to pause in her denials, Lady Mary was relieved that she didn't have to go on to add the precise reason why Mama had been so amicable about having a party to salute her troublesome guest's natal day.

''We've got to have some sort of do,'' the duchess had announced soon after they'd returned to Marchbanks, ''in order to get Deal back here again, and repair any damage that dreadful girl did to our name at his home. *She* might not care that she's made a spectacle of herself, with her uncouth tales and her hoydenish behavior with all the gentlemen, but as we are sponsoring her, as your father insists we sponsor her,'' she amended bitterly, grimacing and sitting up in her bed, staring fixedly at her daughter, ''it is of primary importance that we remain unfazed by her attitude. That is not to say that we should signal to the world that we tolerate it, mind, but rather that we make it clear that we have no choice but to harbor her, because of your father. If we have a party for her, we demonstrate that. If she scandalizes herself again, we can continue to distance ourselves from her. But if we hide here, we give credibility to the notion that we are in some way responsible for all her dreadful behavior.''

But Lady Mary liked Faith very well, though she'd never dare to let slip a word of that to Mama. Although she felt the reason for the celebration might not be what she would wish, she reasoned her new friend would never have to know of it. A party or a present could be a joyous thing whatever the spirit it was given in, if that spirit didn't show through, and she resolved to see to it that it did not. She'd gotten permission to decorate the premises more lavishly than she had for her own ball not a week before, since this one was to be given in the manner of reparations. Fortunately, Lady Mary thought, valuing money so much, Mama had reasoned that a generous expenditure of it would impress the world as much as it did herself.

Of course the guest list would be much the same. All of their houseguests had hung on, London being in the doldrums at this time, and few of them were willing to leave for greener pastures at other country estates so long as the wild American girl was here to enliven things and contribute to chat that would spice dinners at those other tables when they eventually did move on. As any practiced houseguest knew, the gift of a fine, rare, polished bit of gossip was always the best hostess present.

"Deal will come," her mama had prophesied, "because if he does not, he shows that he is insulted or angry with us for what transpired at his home. Unconventional he may be, but he is not so farouche, I think. So, Mary, see you spare no effort to convince him of your amiability when he does appear. Attempt to keep that rude American creature away, she's done enough. Leave her to her countryman, he must have some experience with savages. Or to Methley, he doesn't seem to mind, as well he should not. She may be as wild as an Indian if she's got the amount of money your father says she has coming to her. And that's more to his purposes than manners or morals now."

Lady Mary swallowed hard and sighed, remembering her mama's words, and then because of her training, was able to shake unhappy thoughts away and bend her head to work again.

"Columbines then, I think," she said emphatically, raising her fair head from contemplation of her list, "and larkspur, or even perhaps, if the gardener is willing to seek them out, bluebells and harebells. You don't mind common weeds if they're the right color, do you?"

"Oh Mary," Faith said, smiling, and looking down into a pair of worried eyes of exactly the same hue as was being discussed. "It's charming of you to think of decorating your house with the colors of our flag in my honor, whatever sort of blooms you use. And I don't even think of them as weeds, they're wildflowers, which means to me that they're flowers in someone's garden, if only God's. I don't stand much on ceremony, as you well know," she said ruefully.

A brief silence followed her words. Neither girl had spoken of the events at Lord Deal's party two days before, and both knew that it must eventually be spoken of.

"Faith," Lady Mary said, lowering her lashes over her mild cornflower blue eyes, "ah, there's been a bit of talk about what happened Saturday night. That is to say, some of the stories you told, though amusing and very clever, in fact, were a bit, if not precisely warm, then . . . unconventional. And the way . . . Faith, did you know that here, in order to be popular with the gentlemen, and the ladies as well, it is important not to be *too* popular with the gentlemen?'' she blurted.

''Oh,'' Faith said slowly, a bit of color rising in her cheeks as she turned aside, ''so someone saw something and said something about me and Methley? But that was a misunderstanding, I promise you. I'd had a bit too much of the punch and when we walked outside I thought he only wanted to help me clear my head, and I never expected—Oh Mary,'' she groaned, turning to the other girl, her eyes becoming dangerously damp as she tried to blink her apparent emotion away, ''I promise you I never thought of anything more, no, nor wanted anything more either.''

But now her hostess appeared to be just as distressed as she herself was. ''You, and the earl, outside?'' she asked weakly, one hand going to her heart so rapidly that the pen she still clutched in it left black tracks upon the breast of her pristine white morning dress.

''Oh damnation,'' Faith wailed, ''you didn't know.''

The two overwrought young ladies stared at each other.

''You and the earl?'' Lady Mary asked again, shocked.

''Me and my rash tongue,'' Faith muttered miserably.

Then the two, in silence, eyed each other's reactions. Then they began tremulously to smile at each other, and then to laugh, and then they fell upon each other's necks laughing in outright, if somewhat overwrought, fashion.

''I didn't want his advances,'' Faith said at length, drawing back, and looking at Lady Mary with evident sincerity, ''and I didn't mean to make a fool of myself with the other gentlemen either. I do know better, good breeding and good manners are the same, I think, on both sides of the ocean. It was only that, ah, I don't really know,'' she lied unintentionally to herself and to her new friend, blinding herself to how her reaction to her host had influenced her every action that night, ''but it was badly done of me, and I'll never do it again, and not just to save my reputation, but because I don't like being fuddled with wine any more than I enjoy making a spectacle of myself, I promise you.''

"I'm quite sure that the earl will do the right thing," Lady Mary said staunchly.

When Faith looked at her curiously, she went on quietly, "He'll doubtless offer for you if he compromised you, he is a gentleman."

"Oh I hope not," Faith gasped, "no, not that he's not a gentleman," she laughed nervously, "but that he doesn't think he has to offer, for he doesn't. Nobody knows, nobody saw, it was only a kiss." As her companion took in a quick breath, Faith added hurriedly, "And I didn't like it in the least, and I'm sure he didn't either. He'll put it down to the punch and the moonlight, and if he doesn't, be sure I shall."

"But he's very witty, and so very well read, and handsome in an unusual way. You could do far worse," Lady Mary said, but she turned her head as she said it, so, Faith thought, her guest should not see her lack of enthusiasm for what she felt she ought to say.

"I'm sure he's all those things," Faith insisted, "but nonetheless, he's not for me."

"But your grandfather, I'm sure, would welcome just such a match," Lady Mary persisted before Faith cut her off by saying forcefully, and at once, "But Mary, Grandfather would not be marrying him, now would he? And so much as I love him, Grandfather that is,—see how even the subject of wedlock with the earl scatters my wits so that I can't even express myself?—but so much as I love Grandfather, as I said, I cannot sacrifice my life to him, nor would he, I think, expect me to do so. He is my relative, and not some demanding pagan god," she said with a nervous little laugh.

"After all, Mary," she continued reasonably, "no matter what a catch Grandfather thinks him to be, when the minister departs and the wedding guests have drunk their fill and staggered off to their own comfortable beds, and all the envious relatives have exited, sighing, it would only be myself who would have that night and all the other nights of my life left to live with the lucky fellow I wed. Only me, alone. And so I think it's only myself who has the right to choose the fellow, don't you?"

This was so contrary to everything that Lady Mary had ever been taught about love and marriage that she could not frame an immediate reply. For all it came from the innocent lips of her young friend, it was almost, she thought dazedly, like the devil himself quoting scripture, and just as seductive and tempting an insidious notion as that scaly fellow could be expected to broach as well.

"At any rate," Faith sighed, "I'm grateful that you're giving this party for my birthday. And not just because I need cheering up now that I'm about to achieve the great age of one and twenty, still unwed. But because at least this way I'll have a chance to right my wrongs. Just because I don't fancy a fancy gentleman for my wedded husband," she explained on a grin, as much to herself as to Lady Mary, "it doesn't follow that I ought disgrace myself and my entire country does it? So let's plan your red, white, and blue party for me, your Yankee Doodle lady, and I'll promise you I'll be such a proper young miss at it that I'll make everyone think we're the most boring nation on earth."

"Oh no," Lady Mary sighed, her eyes wide with admiration for her spirited, fiery friend. "Whatever else they might think, Faith, I promise you, it will never be that."

"Now that would please Will if he heard it," Faith laughed happily, and as Lady Mary ducked her head at that, Faith smiled to herself before she sat and began to debate the order of refreshments. Yes, she thought, on a grin that had nothing to do with lobster patties, that would please Will very much indeed.

As it turned out, Faith had even more good reason to be glad for the forthcoming party. Since it was to be given a week to the night after her personal disaster at the festivities at Lord Deal's house, and as it was to be a party with an American theme, she insisted on helping Lady Mary with every detail and there was no way she could be denied, since, as she claimed, she was clearly the resident expert. Thus, she had very little time to spare for any of the other company at Marchbanks that week.

She saw the earl at dinnertimes, of course, there was no eluding that. She could, and did, plead weariness each night after that meal in order to make an early retreat to her rooms. But had she announced any infirmity that might keep her from communal dining, not only would she have been dosed by her solicitous hosts, she'd be forced to give up her part in planning the forthcoming party. Faith weighed the disadvantages of her present situation against the possible drawbacks which might arise if she avoided the company entirely, and found herself willing to swallow some of her pride along with her dinner opposite the earl each night. There was, after all, only so much that could politely be spoken at a crowded dining room table, and whatever that might be, it would surely never be an offer.

Thus, while Faith thought that the earl looked each night as though he dined on canaries rather than mutton, he only whispered jests and gossip into her apprehensive ears. She was relieved that he was clearly vastly amused, rather than insulted, by her sudden shyness and reticence in his presence. She supposed he'd taken her rejection in the proper spirit, but then he was known to be a sophisticated gentleman, and, she imagined, found an insignificant foreign miss's distaste for his passionate embraces about as important as he'd discovered those same embraces to have been. Which was to say, she decided, if his reactions had been anything like her own, that he'd found the incident to be almost as pleasant as finding half a worm in one's half-eaten apple. She was only grateful that it seemed not to have affected his pleasure in her company as a dinner partner, at least.

She managed to avoid the other gentlemen even more completely, but since she was making her presence a rare sight to the ladies as well, they none of them could take her absence at their entertainments each evening as a personal affront. Instead, they were all heard to say at various times, and with various underlying meanings, that they could scarcely wait until Saturday night, for it was clear that this birthday party of Miss Hamilton's promised to be the capstone of their stay at Marchbanks.

No one scolded Faith for her total involvement in the coming party except for Lady Mary, who complained now and again that her friend ought not to work so hard for her own celebration. It was, she said with concern, not fitting that the recipient of honors should have to slave so hard for them. Still, her mama was pleased that the unpredictable chit was no longer under foot, and even Will, while displeased that he could not so frequently see Lady Mary, was more than happy with things as they stood, though he would rather have died ablaze at a stake than admit to being so much of a mind with the duchess. But then, in all honesty, he was more concerned with matters having to do with the unpredictable chit's open mouth than he was with anything to do with feet.

So Faith involved herself with gardener and housekeeper and butler, coordinating and planning as well as ruling on all matters American, although she had never given such a party before and by the end of the week had decided never to do so again. For no, she'd told the musicians, reels and squares were well enough, but Americans also waltzed, and yes, she'd informed the housekeeper for the fourth time, Americans did use cutlery as well as knives when they sat down to eat, and napery as well, and, she explained to cook with great patience, their food was comprised of more than pumpkins.

With all her tribulations, she also realized glumly that all of them, from lowest maid to highest guest, itinerant musician to resident staff, believed her to be laboring, like an ancient pharaoh, only for her own greater glory. Not one of them suspected that it was only that she'd have gladly flung herself headfirst into any project in order to avoid, as well as to avoid thinking about, all those she'd so soundly embarrassed herself among: her hosts, the company, and the earl. And most particularly, of course, Lord Deal. Although now, from the safe vantage point of a week's time passed, she could begin to vaguely understand that in his case it was not so much that she'd embarrassed herself before him as it was that his mere presence had the uncanny power to embarrass her.

Thus it was with extremely mixed feelings that she went to meet him when she was told he'd come to call upon her the afternoon of her party. Doubtless the duchess would have come running to the small salon as well, not so much to play chaperone as to ensure that not a word passed between them escaped her. But that lady was off on a visit this afternoon assuring herself as to the perfection of the ensemble she planned to wear for the gala tonight by passing judgment on her old friend Lady Moore's outfit for the evening. Lady Mary hung back with the housekeeper and waved Faith on, telling her she'd continue to see to the floral arrangements. And so Faith had to face the gentleman alone.

That wasn't why she hesitated before entering the room where he awaited her. It wasn't any proprieties that she feared she'd overset by meeting with him alone. Even as she turned the knob in her suddenly cold fingers, she became aware that it was her own equanimity she didn't wish to upset. But nevertheless, she didn't hesitate to enter, because though in some strange fashion he always alarmed her, he never failed to be the person she found herself enjoying conversation with the most since she'd arrived in his country. There had been, despite her trepidations, many innocent chats shared when she'd been at his house, even after that disastrous ball. All of them always, of course, in a room filled with people, always, of course, on innocuous subjects, but just the same always fascinating and enlivening as well.

And too, though she hadn't laid eyes on him for a week, it seemed she often thought of him in the night. Then she discovered herself, all unbidden and unplanned, suddenly envisioning him, both face and form, where he didn't belong. For she often saw him right along with the omnipresent pictures of floral arrangements and table plans that seemed to have branded themselves on her brain so that they came to her as patterns printed on the underside of her lids when she closed them to sleep, as such things tend to do after so much long and concentrated study of them.

It was curious how it was the small things she most often recalled in those unguarded flashes of recognition, minute details of his vivid face she scarcely remembered noting were those that most frequently sprang to her mind. It was not so much his white-toothed smile she envisioned, for example, as it was the three arced parallel lines that etched themselves in his lean bronzed cheek just to the left side of his mouth whenever he smiled at her. Nor was it so much any picture of his tall athletic person she often found herself imagining, but rather the long, strong shapely hands that mutely spoke so eloquently of the rest of his graceful form. Then always, she would force herself to other thoughts, even to longing for home, since those reveries, although far more painful, were somehow less disturbing than those odd, unsought images of him were.

Now, as she entered the room, she noticed the differences between the real and imagined man very much as an artist might, seeing that the shaggy, sun-burnished locks had been trimmed back a bit, and the tanned vital visage was just perhaps a shade more golden, as was the hand that took her own. She fought back the strange joy she felt at his action by forcing herself to note, prosaically, that it was only natural that this should be so, for he passed so much time out of doors and it was high summer now.

He gave her no reminder of her past folly. There was no censure in his admiring glance, no undercurrent of malice in his voice, as he said, with a smile to grace his graceful bow, "I've come to bid you the happiest of birthdays, Miss Hamilton, and to present you with a little token of my esteem for the occasion, because since I'm not a guest at Marchbanks, I couldn't give it to you this morning when you awoke, and didn't wish to hand it to you in all the confusion tonight."

Faith accepted the slim parcel he handed her, along with a sudden realization of a quandary, for she was wondering whether she ought to tell him that so far no one had given her so much as a bit of rat cheese for her birthday, even as she just as suddenly recalled she hadn't expected to receive any presents either.

Since she said nothing in that moment, but only held the parcel limply and looked back at him, amazed, he went on pleasantly, "Perhaps you think it's odd in me to rush my fences, but there's nothing so belittling to a fellow's taste as to have his gift admired in the midst of evidence of everyone else's better taste and better-thought-out tributes, and I suspect, nothing more difficult for a lady than to have to feign ecstasy at each and every one she dutifully unwraps. For both our sakes, I've brought mine to you now, so that you can open it in private. It is rather private in here, isn't it?" he observed, looking about the otherwise empty room.

"Can it be that my recent spate of sociability has so exonerated me socially as to make my hosts trust me completely?" he asked bemusedly. "Not that I planned to molest you, mind, not that that's such a terrible idea," he added quickly on a smile, "but it's singular to find that such correct persons as my hosts have decided to trust me not to do so. There isn't another person in sight," he mused, clearly not altogether pleased at this freedom he was supposedly extolling, "and we're not even on horseback."

But now Faith's wits had returned to her. "I think," she said wryly, "that it might be more that they don't care a jot anymore. No, no," she corrected herself hastily as she saw the quick sympathy spring to his eyes, "that's not strictly true either. It's only coincidence, I suppose. The duchess is away just now, and Lady Mary has last-minute party arrangements in hand, and everyone else is off primping or some such, I expect. I don't know, really," she admitted, a little hurt, now that she thought about it, by the notion that they thought her so disgraceful or believed her reputation so defiled that there was no further need of protecting it, so that she went on to say boldly, "And I really don't care, not really. I expect you've better things to do with your afternoon than molesting me, anyway. But thank you very much," she said sincerely, looking down at his present and so missing the wicked grin he'd put on at her words, as well as the step closer that he'd taken to her.

She had only begun to take off the wrappings, finding herself almost as a child again in her eagerness to see the present, feeling the same juvenile wonderment and pleasure at knowing that whatever it was, it was something that he'd thought about and brought expressly for her when she hadn't even been thinking of him, when their privacy was ended.

The butler appeared at the doorway to the salon, bearing a large, gaily wrapped parcel. "Excuse me, my lord, Miss Hamilton," he said after he saw that he'd gained their attention. "Lady Mary said that I might find you here, Miss Hamilton, as it appears that this package has just been delivered by a messenger, and is addressed to you."

"No, no," Lord Deal said at once, taking his own package from her hands so she could receive the one the butler handed to her. "Now I insist you open up the other first. It might be," he jested, "that mine will be so diminished by this one that I'll want to hide it in the coal bin. It's only fair," he protested, holding his present behind his back and sidestepping her as she laughingly attempted to take it back again. "You have to give me the opportunity to snatch mine back and get you a better one if I have to."

By the very way he said it, Faith was sure his gift was unique and wonderful and she was doubly anxious to see it. But obediently, she turned her attention to the other one first.

"It's not signed," she said in puzzlement, turning the white card over in her hand before she set it down and began to unwrap the box. "It only wishes me the happiest returns of the day."

Her attention was so fixed on what she was doing that she didn't see his smile slip at her words. It was only when she'd opened the box and drawn the tissue paper back that she at last looked up at him. But then she was in no condition to note what expression he wore. Her face had grown paper white, and her hands trembled almost as much as her lips did when she broke from her immobility and at last lifted the present out from the box. Even then, she only held it out to him at arm's length, and very quietly, her head shaking unbelievingly from side to side, asked him only, "Why?"

It was a large and cumbersome mass of feathers she held out to him. For a bizarre moment, he believed, in his confusion, that it was some sort of large dead bird. The barnyard scent of it was repellent enough for that. But then he made out its apparent shape and form. It was obviously a clumsy attempt at a representation of a feathered head-dress, fashioned of rudely cobbled together chicken and turkey feathers, all still with bits of clotted ingrained filth of the henhouse still clinging to them, the whole bound by a profusion of bright red, white, and blue ribbons.

Another white card fluttered down from the mass of it as she held it out with shaking hands. He automatically stooped to retrieve it, and saw the bold, large, printed words, "For our Indian Maiden," inscribed there.

"Why?" she asked again. And for all his supposed glibness and quickness of mind, in that moment, though he thought he knew only too well, there was no sane answer he could give her in reply.

NINE

THE GENTLEMAN MOVED swiftly. He was a guest within this house, and yet despite social dictates he did not hesitate to go immediately to the door and close it almost all the way. Then he went to the young woman who stood before him and took the loathesome bundle of ragged noisome feathers from her nerveless hands and dropped them back within the box they'd come from. As he closed that box and retied it securely, he said curtly, throwing the remark over his shoulder, "Sit down at once, before you fall down. This shall not trouble you again, you shall not see it again."

When he'd done, he turned and saw that the young woman had seated herself as he had bidden her, but that she still held her shaking hands out, fingers parted as though they dripped gore and she could not bear to acknowledge them as her own. "But why?" she repeated, in a shocked whisper.

He gave her his handkerchief for reply and she absently took it and unconsciously began scrubbing motions with it, twisting it and her hands together, though she never took her eyes from his face, nor did the question leave those wide, dazed gray eyes.

He stood before her, looking down at her, considering what he should say, for all at once she seemed very young. Her creamy skin had gone so dead white that only a few faint previously undetectable light fawn freckles lent color to it high on her cheekbones, and with her long light straight hair worn back and down against her neck as it was, she seemed very vulnerable. But as her eyes searched his, some of their bright intelligence already returning, he sighed and knew that there was no other answer he could give her but the truth.

"Someone thought it was amusing," he said coldly, and then realizing that the harshness in his voice startled her as much as his words had done, he explained more gently, for his anger was never at her, "I'd like to get my hands on whoever it was, but I doubt we'll ever know."

But he did know that though it might have been anyone, there were, in fact, several he instantly suspected, and more whose loose talk doubtless had provoked the incident. Not the least of the vindictive gossips was doubtless her own hostess, but as she had to remain within this house for a while longer, and as his fury was tempered with each passing moment, he was grateful that he'd always followed the dictum that what he could not prove, was best forgotten.

"Be assured," he went on angrily, "that it was someone's idea of high good humor. No," he said gruffly, "never that, there wasn't anything good in it. It was sheer cruelty, but, you see, in certain circles, that is considered the highest sort of humor."

She watched him closely, as a good student might attend a tutor the day before an examination, so he paused to marshal his thoughts and find a way of explaining it to her without adding, as he'd just caught himself about to do, that it was precisely what he'd warned her about. Whatever else she needed now, he thought, it was not to have him tell her righteously that he had told her so. And then, too, he realized, for all he'd known the possible consequences of her behavior, since she'd never before associated with any ornaments of the *ton*, there really had been no way she could possibly have anticipated the sort of cruelty she'd invited. She could never have encountered it at home. Only an extremely sophisticated, weary, and blasé society could breed such a concept of humor. And so he tried to tell her.

"You see, Faith," he went on to explain, as he leaned against a desk near to her, "anything that can be done and then later amusingly related to others to while away a dull hour is considered capital fun. If it's outrageous enough to then merit being passed on by yet others, it becomes even better. The stuff of anecdotes is the stuff of fame, and fame is the goal; whatever pain it causes is of no account. No one's immune. High rank only enhances it—just look at Prinny. You could paper a palace with the cruel caricatures of him. The stories about his foolish deeds are too commonplace to even raise a chuckle anymore, and insults given to him behind his back are the prime meat at every *ton* dinner. And he is our Prince, our Regent.

"Brummel's ruined himself because of one of his jibes about 'his fat friend,' but since the quote's become so famous, I'm not at all sure he still doesn't believe it was all worth it. After all, if you've spent your life in pursuit of the one devastating, quintessential shocking statement, how can you regret finally having made it?

"No," Lord Deal sighed, "it isn't done just in the name of princes either. Nor is it only coxcombs who indulge in the sport. Everyone, everywhere in society, loves to hear the latest *on-dit*, and will be in ecstacies if there is a good quotable, vicious jest in it. You wouldn't know most of the parties involved, but you may have heard of our playwright Sheridan? His name comes to mind because he's lately fallen gravely ill and so everyone's been reminiscing about him. And as they still delight in remembering, when his son married a dowerless girl and he lamented it, young Tom told his father not to worry, for, as he said, though the lady was poor, her parents were industrious in that her father was allowed by everybody to be the greatest swindler in England. Perhaps it was that quip alone which reconciled old Sheridan to the marriage, for a good mean tale is coin and currency in our world. And the young man was talking about his own wife's family!"

Lord Deal shook his head in sorrowing wonderment.

"What merriment those sorts of stories elicit! Even I've heard scores of them, most not half so clever, and still that's not a fraction of them, since tattle-bearing tongues usually still in my presence."

But, he noted, his own tales seemed to be having some good effect on his audience, for the girl had regained her natural color, and when he smiled at her and asked meekly, gesturing to her, "Is it such a damned spot, or is it the part of Lady Macbeth you're after?" she laughed briefly, but left off twisting her hands and wringing his handkerchief.

"You warned me," she said at last, softly, and then raising her eyes to his, she said so quietly that he had to bend forward to hear her, "but I thought you were exaggerating, only spoiling sport, just trying to make me behave according to your own code, and because I thought I was only staying on for a little while I thought it made no matter. But it does," she said wonderingly, like someone who has examined herself after an accident and is amazed and disbelieving at finding a bleeding wound.

"It was a nasty thing to do, because it more than poked fun at me. Because believe me," she said with a bit more spirit, "we make sport of foolish folks at home too. But this was more than that, it was more than unkind, it was as though by sending me those dirty feathers they were dirtying me. The worst part of it is that now I feel as though everyone has been mocking me, all along. How shall I know whom to believe now?" she asked as much to herself as to him, blinking in surprise at the query and paling again, as though that question was far worse than the incident which had prompted it.

But as it was a question which he suddenly realized that he had never successfully answered for himself, he fell silent for a moment. Then, forgetting his own struggles with the problem, he said that which he supposed was the right thing to comfort her with. Yet even as he spoke it, he began to understand that he did mean every word of it, that he must have resolved it, after all.

"You must believe in yourself, Faith," he said seriously, "because you know you're not a fool. You must continue to trust those people you feel comfortable trusting. Never give up the trusting. The worst that can befall you is that you will have been wrong in your judgment and might invite more insult, and lose a little more faith in the general run of mankind. But insult was invented the same day praise was. And disillusion's only part of growing up. Bruising your pride is as common an experience in that process as skinning your knee is. You Americans do take a little tumble every so often when you learn to walk, just as we do, don't you?" he asked gently.

"I think," he went on, knowing from the ease with which the words came to him that what he was saying was more than exactly right for cheering her, it was precisely true for him as well, "that just as it would be absurd to give up learning to walk because of a misstep, it would be folly to give up on all mankind because of such injuries. Because then you'd be crippled in some wise as well. Likely then you'd find it that much simpler to become just as small and cruel as those you shun. No, far better to trust and be betrayed, than lose faith forever. Now, not only am I convinced that I might have put that better,'' he paused to consider, ''but it also illustrates what trouble that name of yours gives me. It wouldn't have felt awkward in the least,'' he complained, ''if I had said, 'lose Mary or Henrietta' forever. But, then too, I don't think I'd mind so much if I lost them, it's Faith I'm concerned with,'' he said, in hopes of seeing her smile.

But she sat quite still, her head cocked a little to one side as she pondered his words. He found that he was tempted to laugh and mention her characteristic pose to her as he had once before. He found that he was tempted to do far more. Then, because she remained silent, he knew that too many emotions were tangled in her mind right now. So he said lightly, ''I know just how you feel.''

And to show her that he was not just mouthing an idle cliché, he went on to tell her why he'd said it.

It took quite some time for the duchess to convince her best friend that the exquisite gown she'd planned to wear tonight was unsuitable, because the only real reason (though if the duchess were persuasive enough her friend would never know it) was that it was far superior to her hostess's own frock. The gardener and Lady Mary were horrified to discover that the columbines were past their best bloom and the stock in little better case, since both flowers insisted on shedding their tiny bells as soon as they were nicely settled into their arrangements. And so Lord Deal had time and to spare to tell Faith how he'd acquired his nickname, and discovered he needed every minute of it.

He carefully told her the entire story, leaving out only that part of it where he placed the blame upon Methley. That omission was not so much because he was noble or raised as a gentleman, as he'd halfway convinced himself that it was, but because, he came to realize in the midst of his story, he wasn't sure of her feelings for Methley and didn't know if it would displease her. And he discovered that he very much wished to please her.

He told her about Nettie's painful ending and beyond.

To prevent Faith from imagining her ugly birthday surprise present that unique, he told her about all the gifts of horns, of antlers and rams' horns, drinking horns and musical ones, all and every physical embodiment of the plays on words about the cuckold's emblem that had ever been thought of, that had found their way anonymously to his doorstep in those bleak months that followed his having been given the name Viking. All of them, he assured her, had been long forgotten, but the name would be with him forever.

"So you see," he said at length, "a foolishness of feathers, which no one saw but us, and which can and will be easily disposed of, is not the worst that can befall one by far."

"But I never thought your name insulting," she protested. "Indeed, it's very dashing. Whatever it was meant to signify at first, you've turned it into a neat compliment by the way that you live up to the better meaning of it. Well," she said, as he gave her an ironic smile, "it's very much like what Mr. Kensington, who's quite an old man and lives with his daughter down the street from us at home, said. You see, he told me that originally you English thought calling us 'Yankee Doodle Dandies' was the worst sort of slap. You meant it to mean bumpkins. We took it differently, and we've cause to be proud of it now. Truly."

"Surely not 'we' English—I wasn't even conceivable at that time. I mean," he explained as she looked at him oddly, unsure of his point, "while forty years might be just a drop in the bucket for your Mr. Kensington, my parents hadn't even been wed at that time. No," he corrected himself as she began to color up, at last understanding his pun, "I lie. I was, for at least they had already been introduced by then."

She thought he might be trying to get her off a painful topic with his jests and appreciated the gesture, if not the mode of it, but also knew there was one other thing she must say before he left the subject completely. It was remarkable how he'd sat and spoken with her and in the space of an afternoon made her feel she'd found a true friend. It might be, she thought, that he'd only done so to save her from self-pity, or to cushion some of the pain she'd experienced when she'd seen that ghastly "present." It might all have been no more on his part than the courteous act of a gentleman who'd unwittingly witnessed a female's distress. Whatever the spur for his gallantry and friendship, it was possible that they might never speak that way together again. He'd spoken of trust, but she could already feel that virtue ebbing away within herself. Still, there was a thing she wanted to make clear to him, so she battled with her misgivings and said all in a rush, "But I was trying to say that whatever the name originally meant in your case, there's no shame to it. For you couldn't help what your fiancée did."

"Yet, I might have," he said slowly, "if she'd confided in me."

"Yes and then what?" she argued, as always forgetting both embarrassment and her place in the cause of justice. "Would you have married her? Would you have accepted another man's child as your own? And speaking of trust, you might well lecture to me about it, but could you ever have trusted her again? Her . . . her lover was still available to her. But what if, justly shocked, you'd refused her then? Why, there's no guarantee she would have lived longer, but then you would have had much more cause for feeling guilt."

This was so reasonable that he had no answer, but only gazed at her in dawning wonder at that entirely new and comforting rationale she'd given him, as she rushed on, "I think it wasn't the sort of situation where you could've done anything right, even if you'd have had a chance to do anything at all. She was a weak creature of unseemly passions, and you certainly couldn't help that."

He'd been listening quietly to all she said, and his eyes had never left her face until the very last. Then he stiffened somewhat and an expression of disbelief came across his face.

"But no," he said, shaking his head, "surely you don't believe she was ever that? She loved the fellow, though perhaps she shouldn't have, for a number of excellent reasons. He'd never have been able to court her honestly, nor ever had the slightest chance of winning her legally, and he'd wed another because he'd known it, besides. She may well have been weak. But 'unseemly passions,' Faith? What is a 'seemly' passion?''

"Why, I don't believe there are any." She laughed, and was puzzled when he did not laugh along with her.

"Well," she said nervously, rising and shaking out her skirts, "now may I see what present you've brought me? Although you've eased my mind so much about that other wretched one, I think that alone is present enough for me."

But he did not rise to her remark, instead he raised himself from where he'd been leaning, watching her, and came to stand in front of her. He seemed very tall now, she thought anxiously, for he looked down at her from what appeared to be a great distance and for once there was no laughter in the clear eyes, and his face was unnaturally somber.

"Faith," he breathed so softly that she thought she'd never heard her name spoken so much like a sigh, "do you think passion itself unseemly? It isn't, you know."

And then very gently, very carefully, and with great tenderness, he bent his head and kissed her lightly on the lips. She stood absolutely still, and when he'd lifted his mouth from hers, she opened her eyes to find him looking at her strangely. He seemed more perturbed than impassioned as he said softly, curiously, "You lock your lips against me when I touch them, does that mean you withhold yourself from me as well? It's only a little thing, a kiss. Are your lips so cold because you disapprove of me, or of my actions?"

There was nothing of the ardor she dreaded in his voice, and he didn't seem as if he were about to touch her again either. Still, she was taken aback. Never before had any man asked her about her reaction to his kiss, not even after she'd bolted and run away from them. If anything, they'd always signified they disliked the lack of kisses from her, rather than finding a lack within her kiss. But she'd never discussed such things with any man, not even with Will. All they had done together was to laugh when the embrace ended. Now all she could say in her great astonishment at his question was, "No, I like you very well. Really."

"Ah well then," he said with a smile, "we'll put it down to surprise. And try again."

But this time he didn't so much as brush his mouth against her lips as she stood frozen in surprise, for when he came close enough to do so, he drew back and said chidingly, "Faith, now what sort of new American craze is this? Kissing with the lips closed? I can't think that it will become the rage here."

She drew breath to argue his mistaken impudence, and as she opened her lips to tell him of it, he chuckled and then even as he breathed, "Yes, just so," he kissed her again. His mouth was warm and extraordinarily sweet against her own, and she discovered herself leaning in toward him, relaxing in his arms as they held her with gentle comfort. Yet even as she felt herself stirring, she felt the familiar thrill of blind terror arising along with the excitement he began to make her experience. But thankfully, before it could overwhelm her, he drew back and looked at her again with something more than desire and less than passion in his searching gaze.

"Ah yes," he said, and she thought his voice was a bit uneven, although his face had become unreadable. But in the next second there was no trace of anything but amusement as he said, "You're right, it's bad enough they send you feathers, but if I continue and someone spies us, they'll be sending you little caps with Viking's horns sewn on to tease you with. I only closed the door," he said as he left her and went to open it wide again, "so that not even a servant could get a glimpse of that vile jest they presented you with. I meant it to go into the fire unremarked by human eye as well as tongue. And if you were good enough not to accuse me of closeting us together so that I might begin a seduction, the least I can do is to honor that trust, so much as I'm loathe to.

"But," he said brightly, taking the large package and placing the slimmer one he'd originally given her atop it, "I think I shall be an Indian giver, after all," and he paused to smile before he explained, "I find there's quite a different gift I want you to have tonight. So I must go and see to it. I'll study this barnyard joke before I consign it to flames, but I doubt I'll discover more than how badly it's been put together. Don't trouble yourself about it. Whoever sent it won't confess, and there's little point of suspecting everyone. Let's think of it as its author or authors doubtless will, as a bad joke spoiled further. I'll see you this evening—nothing short of violent death will prevent me. Good afternoon, Miss Hamilton,'' he then said as went into the hall. He bowed for the oncoming butler's benefit, before he smiled for hers, and then he left her.

There's nothing like a party with a theme to bring out the child in all the invited guests. Let a group of people already bored to bits by each other's company discover themselves asked to the same masquerade and they will inevitably be in uproarious spirits and perfect charity with each other within the first hour of their arrival. This is because all the same old faces and places will have been transformed by masks and costumes and decorations to the point where the guests can deceive themselves into thinking every bit of it new and exciting. It's the same principle used in the theater, where a length of rippling blue fabric can invoke an ocean, and a few bright spangles and a dash of kohl can create a Cleopatra from the stage manager's maiden auntie. For there is scarcely a human who does not react to a bit of applied fantasy. And so the guests at Marchbanks entered the ballroom to discover themselves enchanted.

The flowers announced themselves even before the eye could take them all in. Lady Mary and the gardener had worked prodigies. Great vases, huge urns, even enormous cooking vessels had been pressed into service and filled to overflowing with blooms. Where Marchbanks had failed them, the village had met the challenge. A great many bees in the locale might find the next few weeks' work netted meager pickings, but tonight the ballroom at Marchbanks was transformed into a bower of red, white, and blue blossoms.

The duchess's wooden trellis, which was dutifully trotted out every season to decorate her every party, had not been neglected either. But this time, it had been swathed in streamers of red, white, and blue fabric and similarly colored blooms had been affixed to its well-worn railings. The punch bowl had been enlivened with cherry and strawberry syrups, a pale lemon ice melted into the center of it, while a few blue blossoms floated on its surface. It might not, as one gentleman sadly noted, have tasted like much, but it was at least a stirring sight.

All the ladies wore frocks that were in keeping with the theme, save for the chaperones and several mamas who never participated in anything but the gossip and eating at such affairs. Lady Mary wore white, with ribbons of red and blue affixed to her hems and sleeves. The perennially Incomparable Miss Merriman was dashing as ever in a flowing blue frock with a vivid scarlet overskirt. The Washburn twins plunged into the spirit of the evening in bold fashion by donning different outfits for once, one of them daring to wear a blue frock and the other, white. But this was unfortunate, since it left an opening for some wags to recall that old scurrilous story, and wonder aloud in whispers and snickers as to whatever had happened to the poor Washburn chit in the red dress.

And Miss Hamilton, the guest of honor, stood in the center of the ballroom to receive her guests in a low-cut blue gown with a narrow panel of white which began just below her high breasts, and then gradually drew further open to disclose more white fabric as it widened to the hem. Lines of small red bows beginning modestly with only two bows in the first row, a few more in the one beneath that, then increased in number as the rows descended in orderly fashion, stretching across the gathered white material as the panel grew wider, clinging to the front of the frock like butterflies alighting. Her long sleeves were slashed open to show more glimpses of white satin held together by tiny red bows. The local dressmaker had earned herself more than commendations for her efforts.

Although Faith might be gratified at how the house had been transformed in her honor, it soon became apparent to her that not all the guests knew precisely why this should be so. Gilbert North congratulated her roundly on her birthday and then told her that he thought it was devilish good and neighborly of her to get herself up in the colors of the Union Jack for the occasion. But when the Earl of Methley unbent from his great height to reassure her by mentioning that the lad could have as easily been insulted by the fact that she and the room were gotten up in the French tricolor, she laughed and agreed that it didn't matter in the least. The room was lovely, her gown much admired, and try as she might, she could detect no malice in any voice that congratulated her, nor see anything but smiles upon all of the surrounding faces.

Thus it was very natural, she told herself later, that when Lord Deal was announced she should feel her stomach contract with anxiety. And when she watched his graceful figure making its way to her through the crowd, it was only to be expected that she should feel her fingertips grow cold and her heart pick up its errant beat. For, as she convinced herself when she found herself so unexpectedly frightened by his appearance, it was only that the sight of him brought back the nightmare incident of the afternoon. Perhaps it was the artificial glamour of the night that accounted for it, but if it hadn't been for his presence she wondered if she would have believed the shameful thing to have happened at all. So when he bowed over her hand and looked up into her eyes, Lord Deal found no welcome in those grave gray depths, but only doubt and confusion.

There was to be dancing, there was to be a late dinner given, but all of that, everyone decided, should wait upon Miss Hamilton's receiving and opening her presents. It was not that anyone expected to see anything very extravagant or unduly impressive given. This was not only because Miss Hamilton was a virtual stranger to most of them. After all, here in the countryside the guests had been cut off from all their favorite shops, and a party given on a mere week's notice was considered to be impromptu in any event. But there was, as always in such cases, a great deal of curiosity about how creative or foolhardy one's fellow guests had been, since half the fun of giving gifts at such affairs was in seeing what the other fellow had brought.

But evidently such was not the custom in the Americas, since Miss Hamilton seemed unwilling to open any of her gifts. It wasn't until Lord Deal suggested making a merry ceremony of it, he reading out the cards, Mr. Rossiter passing the parcels to her, and she then opening them, that she agreed to the plan. And so in due course, the party was enlivened by the appearance of several combs, quantities of ribbons, two pairs of gloves—one short, one long—a few fans, a gilt brooch, a pair of paste buckles, a small scent bottle, three ink wells (for foreign correspondence, the assorted doners explained), several packages of french soaps (for domestic baths, a wag volunteered), and seven different handkerchiefs, each successive one greeted with a louder groan. There were some more substantial tributes from her closer friends, who'd evidently ranged farther afield in their efforts to please her: a pretty brocade fabric-covered lady's notebook from the earl, a fringed Chinese sunshade with a silver knob from Will Rossiter, a handsome little beetle with golden wings and ruby eyes from the duke and duchess, and an enameled sewing case, all over miniature roses, from Lady Mary.

At the end of the spontaneous gift ceremony, Lord Deal suggested that the musicians strike up. As several of the gentlemen began immediately to edge or elbow their way to the ladies of their choice so that they could have first call on the first dance, one of the guests noted that there were still three unopened gifts on the table that had held them all.

"Here," Lord Greyville called, snatching one of the large ones up. "What's the matter with this lot?"

There was a certain grieved note in his demand, since the young gentleman himself had given what he deemed a perfectly nice handkerchief and was still smarting over the way everyone had greeted it with catcalls.

Lord Deal coolly divested him of the package and placing it back upon the table gently said, "Why, these two arrived with no signatures on them, and so not knowing what to announce, I simply didn't announce them. Then too, as it turns out, since everyone's present is accounted for, I didn't think it necessary."

While quicker wits groaned at his statement and Lord Deal bowed at their unwilling acclaim, Lord Greyville continued to eye the parcels suspiciously.

"Didn't see yours anywhere neither," he muttered.

This was undeniably badly done of Lord Greyville, since it was the height of rudeness to point up another fellow's omission. But several eyes opened wider at this declaration and a general mumbling followed it, none of it so much in condemnation of the rash statement so much as it was in acknowledgment of the truth of it. Faith, of course, had realized it long before Lord Greyville's unkind comment, since she'd been looking for the parcel she'd almost opened earlier in the day, and not seeing it, had found herself unable to stop wondering about what it had been replaced with, even as she'd been unmasking all the fans and handkerchiefs.

"I had hoped to present this more privately," Lord Deal sighed as he picked one small box from the table, and several ears almost visibly picked up at the intimate nature of his admission, "if only so that my exquisite taste wouldn't embarrass everyone else." As charmed ladies sighed along with Lord Deal, and the wiser gentlemen smiled at the deft way he handled abuse, and still smaller-spirited ones grudgingly thought it was only because he'd had to learn to do so, the gentleman presented the box to Miss Hamilton.

He did not read the card aloud this time, but she saw it and read it to herself and didn't know whether to laugh or weep at it. But he'd said "trust" this afternoon, he'd specifically recommended it, so she slipped the card saying "For our Indian Maiden" into her skirts and, taking one deep breath, brought out his present into the candlelight.

At first, she only saw feathers, and it seemed that her heart and her breath stopped together. But then as she heard the other ladies coo and comment with delight, she saw it was far more than that. It was a stiffened blue silk headband, set at intervals with small light trembling aquamarine, rose, and crystal pendants. And there were indeed three feathers on it, three soft, silky curling plumes, set in ascending height from front to back. The first was dyed in graduated shades of red, and that plume swept back into the second which was purest white, which in turn drifted into the last, of clearest blue. If the band were affixed correctly, the plumes would sit above a lady's right ear, and seem to grow back into her hairdo in the latest, most fashionable manner.

Lady Mary played abigail and immediately set the band into place for Faith. No sooner was that done than Lord Deal took her astonished thanks and asked for the first dance in return. And as he led her into the set, he lowered his head and whispered so softly that the rest of the company, even those in the same dance set, only saw the plumes tremble from the weight of his breath upon them—but then, they would not have understood what he said anyway. "Use," he whispered, setting the plumes to dancing, "that which cannot be ignored."

And then he led the American lady, her head held very high, into the dance.

She had cause later, to hold her head so high for so long that it caused her neck to ache. For even as she stepped into that first set, the disgruntled Lord Greyville, assisted by a few bored, mischievous friends, opened the remaining unclaimed parcels and unearthed another feathery tribute, this one so unhygenic, not to mention unaesthetic, that the butler eventually had to set a footman to take it between two fingers to the trash. The other was only a long pipe of the sort that Dutch burghers favored, but it had been wrapped around with tricolored ribbons and annointed with various feathers as well, these however, looking as though they'd been pillaged from a pillow. In both cases the gifts were addressed to "The Wild Indian."

When the Duke of Marchbanks finally arrived at his bedroom late that night, he was shocked to find a note from his duchess awaiting him, requesting his presence in her chambers immediately. A hurried consultation with his valet assured him that it was only the first week of the month, and as he had already dutifully asserted his husbandly rights toward the end of the previous month, he could not imagine why his lady required him in her rooms so soon again at such an hour. But he was never one to doubt her wisdom.

Even so, he said "London?" with such great surprise evident upon his usually bland round face a few moments later that his lady fixed him with a look of great annoyance. "But no one is there now," he exclaimed, consigning some ninety thousand unfashionable souls to oblivion.

"Just so," the duchess agreed, sitting back against her propped pillows contentedly. "And as someone is attempting to smear your trading partner's granddaughter's name here, it is best that she go there."

At that, the duke looked about himself furtively, though he ought to have remembered there could be no one in the rooms with the couple, otherwise his lady would never have made the ugly reference to the reason why Marchbanks and all their personal treasury was still in such good heart.

"It can't hurt Mary, she's already got her pick of the cream of the crop. But tonight's whispering and snickering about those hideous 'gifts' and the American creature's reputation can do no one any good. It might well begin to rub off on even such a faultless girl as our Mary if it persists," she said threateningly. "Slander smears everyone. At least in London there'll be no one to notice, and since the American chit did stay here for some weeks, if she isn't exposed to the *ton* for the rest of the summer, no one can say you haven't tried. Then too," she said slyly, "by autumn Mary may well be settled better than we'd hoped. Yes," she said with great pleasure, "it was none other than Deal himself who suggested the plan."

"Ah," the duke said.

"And, he assured me he will be there in London too."

"Aha," the duke replied.

He gave his consent to the plan, and more. For his lady was in an excellent mood that night and willing to put up with a great deal from him. Because, as she thought later, when she had to think of something to keep her mind occupied while the rest of her person was being otherwise employed, the plan was both practical and pleasing. Mr. Rossiter would have to find himself rooms apart from them, a guest in town being quite a different matter than one accommodated at a country estate, since in the city a gentleman was expected to secure his own lodgings. Miss Hamilton would be in social seclusion, and Lord Deal, available.

The plan was an excellent one, she sighed, inadvertently encouraging the duke to excesses she didn't mind, as she didn't notice them, being too busy contemplating the remove which would relieve her of two Americans, and perhaps, with luck, in time, even a daughter.

TEN

*T*HE REMOVE TO London was only marred twice by the American girl. Although her compatriot had the decency to blush for her, and her host and hostess retained their civility, however barely they did so, her younger hostess had abetted her to the point where she let herself in for a good scold when her mama finally got her alone in Town. For the journey, which ought to have been accomplished by dinnertime, was delayed so long by Miss Hamilton's whims that it was darkest night when the family carriages finally pulled into view of Piccadilly.

Then, of course, it was too late to send Mr. Rossiter scrambling to see to his new rooms, and it was only Lord Deal's kind last-minute offer that kept the Duchess of Marchbanks from doing, out of sheer courtesy, that which she had no wish to do in cold reality, which was having to offer the chap accommodations in her own townhouse.

The earl, who had accompanied them to town as well, had made no such generous gesture. But a glimpse at his face, even in the dim gaslight outside of the Duke and Duchess of Marchbanks' townhouse, would have told an acute observer that the omission might well have been caused by physical constraints as profound as the mental ones the duchess experienced. Everyone knew that the earl's own townhouse was let out each season for a fee to other families. He made do with rented rooms in a respectable, but less exalted part of town with the excuse that one man did not need so much dwelling space. That hypothetical thoughtful observer might also have realized that it could have been that he had neither the extra servants, funds, nor rooms to afford such generosity. But for once, the sin of insolvency did not lower the earl in the duchess's esteem, since she preferred to think his lack of hospitality was due to a laudable disinclination to fraternatize with Americans any more than he had to do, poor fellow, in order to wed his fortune.

Not that she truly feared Mr. Rossiter's attentions would turn Mary's head; Mary was too well trained for that. The duchess had already firmly ruled the fellow ineligible, no matter how pleasant his person or personality, or more importantly, how full his pockets, since he had neither family nor background. There was no real immediate cause for alarm despite his obvious interest, since he hadn't approached the duke with any offer. Still, it was better to be safe than sorry, forewarned was forearmed, the duchess thought, and a great many other adages she'd seen on samplers besides, because there was no question that the annoying young man had been monopolizing Mary's time since he'd come to England.

But, as the outraged duchess later fumed to Mary when she'd gotten her safe to her rooms, even Mr. Rossiter had been embarrassed for his countrywoman's inexcusable behavior. And rightly so. Imagine, having to halt a remove to Town simply to get out and stroll about goggling at castles? And ruins of them too, rather than proper ones. Because neither of the attractions that Miss Hamilton had gasped at had a smidge of fine art, furniture, or treasures to be seen, and not surprisingly so, because neither of them had any roofs either. The only old families in residence in those ruins had been those of mice and daws, and still the girl wasted time on them, as she stood and gaped like a ninny.

Deal and Methley had displayed the most exquisite manners, of course, both accompanying the chit so she wouldn't turn her ankle or plunge off a battlement in her wanderings. And Mr. Rossiter had, of course, followed Mary everywhere, as constant as the shadow she cast on the cracked pavings. As the duke had dozed, and the servants snickered, the duchess had sat and fumed in her carriage. Bad enough that she had to put up with such behavior, worse that it had been her own daughter who'd ordered the procession to stop each time. Shocking as she was, the American girl would have had neither the authority or the temerity to do so, the duchess now howled, so loudly that her own maid, accustomed to outbursts, forgot herself so much as to visibly wince.

"But Mama," Lady Mary protested, "it meant so much to her. In fact, when I told Faith that we'd lived near to Old Sarum Castle forever, and had never so much as stopped there, not once, nor knew anyone who'd ever even roamed around the place, she was staggered. For Mama, there aren't *any* castles in the Americas, not one."

This information silenced the duchess for a moment, but Lady Mary didn't know that it was contemplation of her daughter as well as of the barbarous nature of America that stilled her mama's tongue. Never had her daughter disputed with her before. It wasn't much of an argument, indeed, it might not have seemed precisely to be one to anyone else, but it was so unheard of for Mary to protest a good scolding that it was as if she'd raised her voice and shouted her mama down and out of the room.

The duchess had borne four children, three of them now grown, and those three, as she thanked her creator daily, males. So she had known her share of opposition in her time, however blunted it had been by years of dealing with a firm parent such as herself. Thus, she realized that the worst thing she could do would be to further vilify Miss Hamilton. The duchess knew very well that a child might do more mischief in defense of a friend, than that friend, however dangerous, could ever do to the child. She dropped the subject suddenly, refusing to utter another word. Then, stiff with insult and seemingly stung nearly to tears, the obviously wounded mother sent her daughter directly to bed.

The duchess refused to smile as she wished to when she saw the frightened glance her daughter gave her as she slunk off to her rooms. Only when she was alone did she indulge herself, because she believed the specter of guilt would make a good bedmate for her daughter this night. And then, thinking of beds and mates, she resolved to summon Methley to her house the next day to have a good long coze with him. And then again on the next day, to invite him to dinner, and the following day to tea and dinner, as well. It was obvious now that the more accessible he was to Miss Hamilton, the sooner he'd be able to take her off their hands. Only then, with her gone, would

Mary return, chastened and obedient, to herself and to her mama again.

But at an indecently early hour of the morning, before such a fashionable fellow as the Earl of Methley had even been shaved, Lord Deal and Will Rossiter paid a call upon the noble Boltons at their new London lodgings. It was then that the duchess realized that one ought to be quite specific in one's wishes, since even the most well-meaning acts of providence could get the spirit of the thing right and the mechanics of it all wrong. For though it was true that Mr. Rossiter was now off her hands and safely snugged away elsewhere, at least for the meanwhile that *somewhere* was Lord Deal's townhouse, and thus if the nobleman was to be allowed to pay court to Lady Mary, Mr. Rossiter would have to be admitted each and every time as well.

The ladies' riding horses having not arrived from the country as yet, and Lord Deal's handsome sport curricle not really being suitable for four, the quartet decided to go for an early morning promenade to show Miss Hamilton her first glimpses of London. The duchess watched from her window as they set out, the two couples deep in animated conversation, Lord Deal and Miss Hamilton first, then Mary and Mr. Rossiter, with two maids following a few paces behind. Of course, the duchess admitted, the sidewalks were too narrow for them to walk four abreast, and of course, Lord Deal, as a native and a gentleman, would understandably be expected to partner Miss Hamilton and point out the sights to her, just as in all propriety, Mary would do the same for Mr. Rossiter. But they walked at so slow and stately a pace that the strange parade had an eerie uncannily processional air to it, and the duchess's hand flew to her heart as she thought for one mad moment that she detected the distinct scent of orange blossoms hanging in the air.

She was not a superstitious woman, so she did not spit or make signs as a peasant might, to ward off imminent evil. She was a lady, so she only flew into a vile temper and then proceded to reduce every female in her employ to tears that morning, and every male to thoughts of murder, with the exception of her husband, as that gentleman, under cover of the general distress, crept off, gratefully, to his club.

Lord Deal, just as the duchess imagined, was busy explaining the myriad sights and sounds of his city to Miss Hamilton. She, in turn, said not a word, but only walked at his side, wide-eyed as a child, so overawed that she didn't even notice that she kept to an unusual complete unbroken silence. Some weeks ago she'd gone directly from the docks to the countryside and then to Marchbanks, and in her weariness and gratitude at being on dry, unmoving land at last, had noticed very little about the actual lands she traveled through. But now, though she somewhat absently realized she was dumbstruck as a country girl, she couldn't as yet cope with her amazement at this great city.

There were easily ten times more people thronging the streets here than she'd ever seen upon the pavements of New York, even during the great invasion scare when the militia had come to swell the ranks of the city. The traffic, the horses and carriages, the people of all classes and kind, and the noise they created was something quite out of her experience, although coming from New York, she'd previously considered herself a sophisticate.

But as she did come from a great port city, she was used to the atmosphere of an Oriental bazaar that typified such commercial centers. So she scarcely blinked when they strolled past emporiums that vended everything from ribbons to carriages to great works of art. It was the manner and the ease with which these Londoners could fill their leisure hours which staggered her, as well as their actual numbers. There were museums here, and art gallerys, as well as historic monuments at every turn. New York boasted one great theater that was the pride of the city, but here, evidently, there were as many to choose from as there were days to fill with amusement. Her escort spoke casually of concert halls and opera houses, ballet theaters, theaters for the drama, and still more that were solely music halls. He even mentioned one he might take her to some day, since, as he grinned, it was always a great favorite with the children, being specifically designed for productions featuring horses and equestrian displays.

Her escort did not press her to speak, nor, she dimly perceived, did he, for the first time since she'd met him, seem to expect any reply to his comments. From time to time, he'd look down into her face, and had she been gazing back at him instead of at the sights around her, she would have seen his own expression soften. Yes, he thought, watching her drink in his city, he had made the right decision after all. Let her first sight of London be at this unfashionable hour, on these unfashionable streets, so that when she at last encountered those of the *ton*, she would already be acquainted with the scope of Town, and would not cause anyone to mock her as a rustic for her genuine confusion and amazement. There was enough talk about her, let her not be pilloried for her honest reaction to their world.

Will had seen London when he'd been a youth, and yet he too remained quiet as his gentle guide pointed out interesting sites to him, and so she never knew that all that enchanted and amazed him to silence was her own soft voice and lovely face.

It was when they had done with touring a great many streets of the city that Faith at last found her tongue. "It's a lucky thing," she said after Lord Deal had not commented on anything for a few moments, "that my enemies can't see me now. Lord—and I don't mean you," she giggled, before he could say a word, "what an absolute bumpkin I'm being. But I swear, I've never seen the like!"

"And you haven't seen half of it as yet. Wait until nightfall, then I'll show you how my city puts on all its airs and graces," he replied, smiling, and before she could answer, he added gently, "Don't fly up, I do know you've a theater at home—in fact, I attended some fine performances at the Strand there—but I look forward to showing you our theaters and Opera. Not so that I may belittle what you have, please believe me, but only so that I can brag a bit too. After all," he explained, "I don't have one savage tribe or fierce bear to impress you with, so I have to do the best that I can with our landmarks and history and entertainments."

"Oh dear," she said ruefully, "you don't understand—I do understand. That is," she murmured in unease, ducking her head as she spoke, "I never tried to pull your leg, and not only because you've been to my country, but because there was never a need to. But I don't think I'll ever do it again, to anyone. You see," she said, and from the way she stopped walking, drew in a breath, and then looked at him squarely, he knew that this was very difficult for her, "I'm very sorry I began the whole foolish thing. I think it was only because I felt so homesick and heartsick and out of place, and—ah, it doesn't merit even discussing further. I apologized to Mary last night, and now, if I may, to you. Please, believe me, that's all over with, I'm sorry for it, you were right. And if I was treated badly by those anonymous gift-givers, then I suppose I deserved no better."

Then she could say no more, but only looked down at the pavements again. Lady Mary and Will, seeing the other couple come to a halt, engaged in serious conversation, busied themselves by looking with exaggerated interest into a shop window filled with toys. The two maids were too preoccupied with gossiping about the housekeeper to try to listen, but even if they had, Lord Deal's low-pitched tones would have gone no further than the straw margins of Faith's downcast bonnet, as he intended.

He was glad she'd given up the games she'd played and yet oddly displeased with himself for giving her advice, however good, that had eventually cast her down so low. She was a creature of spirit, to him she seemed very much a creation of the New World that had impressed him with all its vigor and promise. Had she been an obedient little miss, he doubted he would have passed an extra hour with her beyond that which the foreign office deemed absolutely necessary. As it was, he no longer cared that he no longer had any real reason to pursue an acquaintance with her, the fact that she never failed to engage his interest entirely was now reason enough.

"Oh come," he said softly, placing his hand lightly upon her cheek and waiting until she lifted that bent head and her clear gray eyes met his, "you were never meant to be a penitent, even if you had good cause. Which you don't, you know. The house party is ended and so is all the talk along with it. It's over and done and soon forgotten. Other, better scandals will come along to sweep your little peccadillos into a dusty corner. You don't believe me?" He shook his shaggy head in mock sorrow and then said with determination, "Then come along and I'll show you how minor your crimes are on society's balance scales."

He tucked her arm firmly beneath his and then signaled

to the others to follow. "It's only a few streets from here. We'll have a look in, and then we'll have a leisurely stroll back before the sun gets too high. You didn't bring a sunshade," he said critically. "Now that is a far worse sin in the eyes of the *ton* than inventing tales to terrify their impressionable young people with. We're off to Humphry's," he paused to tell Lady Mary as she approached with a question apparent in her eye, "to show Faith that there are even more infamous folk in London than herself."

"Oh yes, what a splendid idea," Lady Mary cried. "It's the very thing."

Faith wondered whether Lord Deal was going to lead her to someplace like Newgate Prison, which she'd read about in all the tour books before she'd even set foot upon the ship, but when she asked him that, he laughed so heartily that she flushed.

"Oh no," he answered after a pause in which he admired the way the pink tint mounted high along her cheekbones, before he felt ashamed of himself for putting that beautiful but doubtless painful cosmetic there, "not Newgate. This is a gallery of rogues far worse than that." But he intoned this last so mysteriously she knew he was jesting.

Even Faith knew when they approached their goal, for there were a few passersby paused in front of one shop, hands in pockets, or clasped behind backs, or in some cases lifting quizzing glass to the eye to better study all the bright prints on display in the huge bow window. Later in the afternoon, Lord Deal knew, there'd be a larger crowd, but he had counted on the fact that the day was too young for there to be very many of the *ton* collected on the sidewalk perusing the latest crop of caricatures offered for sale in the window.

There were at least two dozen on display, and though he knew some of them would be rude, or crude, and possibly unfit for a young female's inspection, he also knew there were few young females who somehow didn't get a glimpse at most of them anyway. Still, he didn't plan to give Faith enough time to inspect them in detail, it would be enough that she saw how many famous folk were villified in them, and how others of them were persons she'd never heard of, nor would ever hear of again, though their names currently enjoyed a passing notoriety in London and its environs.

He felt it would be salutary for her to see just how fleeting both fame and infamy were in the fashionable world. Because the Bourbon, Bonaparte, and Hanoverian gentlemen and each of their respective mistresses were by no means the only ones portrayed as fops and fools, and sold, gaily colored, for a few pence. The list of those ridiculed changed often and was a daily source of amusement to the public and a reliable register of the political mood of the nation, as well as a true chronicler of the gossip of the *ton*.

The quartet drew near the window, and soon Faith was entranced by a vivid picture of the Regent at his play, and was so shocked and yet enormously titillated that she could scarcely tear her eyes from the depiction of his excesses. Will was grinning at a political cartoon, and Lord Deal was only watching Faith with vast amusement, and so when Lady Mary gasped, Faith was not the only one to pay no attention to her. But then, when Lord Deal said abruptly, "Come Faith, we must go," she ignored him. When he tugged at her arm, she looked up at him in very real annoyance at the tone of his voice and his imperious treatment of her as well as at the way he interrupted her contemplation of the picture.

"Really," she complained, "you dragged me all the way here . . ."

But then she saw his expression and knew there was something very much amiss. His tanned face seemed more yellowed than golden now and white lines were visible beside his tightly compressed mouth, though it seemed his eyes blazed. She looked quickly to Mary, but Mary was staring horrified, gloved hand to mouth, at a caricature to the left side of the window, even as Will attempted to guide her away. And then of course, Faith saw it.

An immediate silence fell even as her gaze fell upon the picture, though at that moment Faith would not have been able to hear anything above the singing of her blood in her ears, just as she could not feel Lord Deal's grip loosen on her arm. It was only after a long moment's shame that would last the rest of her life, if only in her nightmares, that she could at last admit she could hear him and the world again.

"Faith," he said hesitantly. "Faith," he repeated in

sorrow, "I am so sorry. I did not know, I swear it. Come away. Come away now."

There was no further word said as he called a hackney coach. But after he helped Faith into it, he had brief, low words with Will before he leaned into the coach and said very simply, "I'll follow soon. Wait for me. I must speak with you." And no one asked to whom he spoke, for no one spoke again until the hackney reached the Duke and Duchess of Marchbanks' townhouse once again.

For, Faith thought on a repressed, choked laugh that had nothing to do with humor, what was there to say, after all? She could not even complain that it was a poor likeness. Of course, the naked breasts had been absurdly exaggerated—she was well, but not quite so blatantly, endowed. And she'd never worn the feathered headdresses that had been delivered to her, or even owned a breechclout, and certainly she would not have advanced upon Methley, the duke, Lord Deal, or any of the other gentlemen who'd been at Marchbanks with a wicked carving knife. And even if she had, they would not have quivered and cowered away from her as they did in the caricature, but then, it was titled, "The Wild Indian Takes Marchbanks by Storming It," so she supposed it held to its own mad rationale. Oh, Faith sighed, now, she would go home now, it was enough.

"But you cannot run now," Lord Deal told her only a little while later as he paced in front of her in the morning room.

There were some small things to be grateful for, Faith thought as she watched him rove the room, as a drowning woman might be relieved that it was warm and not cold waters she perished in. For the duchess hadn't been home when she'd returned to the house, and now both Lady Mary and Will had flown in the face of convention and let Lord Deal speak with her alone. But then, she sighed, it might well also be that the pair, both more astute than she (as who, she corrected herself, was not?), had decided that it was impossible to sully her reputation any further and so knew that it hardly mattered if she were left alone with Lord Deal or a gang of riotously drunken convicts at this point. Her sigh was not unnoticed and the gentleman ceased his agitated pacing and spoke sharply to her.

"Oh, I imagine you can go home, there's no law against it, there are ships leaving weekly. Of course, you can go home. But I should think that if you ever want to be able to live comfortably with yourself, why then, you cannot. Of course," he said caustically, coming to a halt in front of her, "it may be that things like honor and self-respect are not important to young females, I could scarcely be expected to know that, and it may also be that only we here in Britain place such a high premium of those qualities for either males or females."

"You know that is not so!" she cried, stung from wilting with sorrow in her chair to shoot up to her feet in fury.

"Of course I do," he said calmly, looking down at her and smiling, "but I thought I would remind you of it. I've found that shame and self-pity and misery are all very well in their place, but if you ever want to leave that dismal place, the first step is to get angry enough to move on. No doubt, in time you'd discover that for yourself—I did, in my turn. But I don't believe you have that time to waste now, and as I've traveled the same road you're on, it's only fair for me to draw you a map of it.

"Faith," he said seriously, taking her two hands in his and gazing down at her, all humor gone from his face, "I suffered a great deal once because of other people's unkindness. It took me a long while to understand that I had to make my own happiness, and disregard the rest. Tongues will wag and tales will be carried for so long as there is idleness, cruelty, and boredom in the world, and I don't doubt that will be as near to forever as one can get. Likely someone spread nasty rumors about the saints in their day and probably, in a future so far ahead that we cannot conceive of it, gossip will still maintain the status of high art in certain circles. It will always be with us. I believe it goes with the human condition, like head colds or fleas."

When she grinned reluctantly, he smiled back at her and said soothingly, "It scarcely mattered if you'd been circumspect or not, you know. There would have been talk in any event. You just made it a bit louder and increased its volume in other ways. But no one with any sense will heed it for long, if you are not heedless yourself in future. After all," he mused, freeing one hand to raise it and gently trace the countours along the top of her cheekbone, "it's an obvious lie. Whoever heard of an Indian with freckles?"

She stared into his long hazel eyes and whatever she imagined she saw there robbed his words of all their comfort and she drew back sharply.

"Indeed," she said brusquely, "I wondered at the name myself. I should have thought they'd call me a barbarian or a savage instead."

"Oh," he said casually, though he looked at her very keenly, "but they already have a barbarian, the poor lady is a Russian princess who made the mistake of befriending a young lording of ours. And as for savage, they have no less than two of those. When one, a young woman from Yorkshire, wed and settled into obscurity, they appointed another, some benighted young chit from the dales whose crime, like her predecessor's, was that she had more money than documented ancestry.

"Oh yes, there are a quantity of amusing names. We have a dozen 'Naughty Sir Thises,' and a score of 'Dirty Lady Thats,' as well as Popes and Priests, and one of my associates rejoices in the name Vicar simply because he's known for having been extremely ungodly in his youth. There's a Black Duke of the fairest complexion, whose recent history has been even fairer, though he'll never shake the name, even as I shall be a Viking forever, though no ancestor of mine I know of ever did anything but run madly for cover the instant he spied the long boats coming. So too, Wild Indian in time can come to signify nothing. But why are you so very afraid of me?" he asked in exactly the same tone of voice that he'd used for all his reasonable discourse.

That was why it took her a space of a few blinks to understand the question, and even then, she could not frame an immediate coherent reply.

"You are, you know," he persisted softly, "and it's far more important, to me at least, than this matter of foolish names idle fools invent. I've thought about it and can't believe it's merely a question of propriety because I attempted to make love to you once, and looked as though I meant to more often than that. You ought to be used to reading such desires in a gentleman's eye. And although a young woman may worry about a gentleman's overstepping the bounds, in those cases, I've found she's either apt to avoid him altogether, or to let him know in no uncertain terms that his next embrace will be tantamount to a declaration. But you make it a point to tell everyone you want no romantic ties, and until now you've made it clear you don't give a fig for society's conventions. So you see, if it's neither your heart or your reputation you fear I'll harm, your behavior's rather puzzling, not to say outright insulting to me.

"At first I thought it was because I was English, but I've come to know you better and you're never so provincial. As it's not a matter of nationality, or politics, is it my appearance? Am I repulsive? But then surely someone, sometime, would have been honest enough to be brutally frank with me. To be honest with you, it's never been a problem to me before.

"I don't believe I'm vainer than most fellows," he said, looking at her thoughtfully, "but I don't think it's my personality either, for I believe you enjoy my company as much as I do yours, and that is to say, quite a lot. And yet, even with all this, when I come close enough—ah there, you see?—you step away. And that look, oh that expression you put on, Faith. What is it? Can you enlighten me? I cannot be so fearsome a fellow or I'd send children screaming down the street when they caught sight of me."

"You're not, no, no, absolutely not," she stammered, "and I don't fear you, not at all," she lied, knowing only when he came closer to her and carefully placed his hands upon her and gazed at her searchingly before his lips slowly covered over her own, that it was really no lie. For then, even as she returned his kiss, she understood, in the moment that was given to her before the fear grew too strong to ignore, that it was true that it was never him that she feared. It was only herself.

He released her immediately, dropping his arms and lifting his head the moment that he felt her mouth tense and her body stiffen against his. But the look in his eyes was so sympathetic, there was such sorrow and kindness and reflective, pitying consideration apparent in his grave, handsome face that she could not bear it. It horrified her far more than passion ever had done. And so at last it did send her running from the room, just like a child, just as though he were every bit as fearsome as he jested that he might be.

Long after Lord Deal had left the Boltons' townhouse, long after he'd stood arrested and amazed as Faith had fled from him, and after Will had gone with him to luncheon at his club as his guest, the duchess returned and received the Earl of Methley as her own, only invited guest. Lady Mary was not asked to join them, as neither was Miss Hamilton, but if the earl found this singular, he gave no hint of it when his hostess received him in private.

Nor did he seem to have found it either an uncomfortable or stressful afternoon, since he stayed in conversation with the duchess for two long hours, which was longer, in fact, than most gentlemen of her acquaintance could have borne without some visible signs of distress. Yet when the interview was over, and she gave him her hand to bow over, her guest wore almost the identical small pleased smile that his hostess did. For he had promised her he would return the following day, and she had promised him far more.

ELEVEN

IT WAS THE ODD quirked smile that the earl wore that Faith noted first when they were left alone in the room. They'd been at tea, she and Mary settled opposite the earl and the duchess, the two pairs at either side of a small table in the salon, exactly as they'd seated themselves each day this week at teatime when the earl had joined them, which had been every day this week at teatime. But this time, the duchess's cup had slipped in the middle of a macaroon and the midst of a high point in one of the earl's bright bits of tattle. She'd immediately risen and sailed off to her rooms to change her stained skirts, with Mary in tow to supervise the procedure.

Faith waited politely for the earl to go on with his story, but he seemed disinclined to continue it once his hostess had left. Which was, Faith supposed, only polite and only proper, but lord, she was weary to death with both polite and proper after this interminable week of behaving in so strict and circumspect a fashion. The duchess had taken charge of her socialization completely since that morning she'd toured the city with Lord Deal and Will. There had been teas and tours and seats at the theater, but always with the earl, and often with the duke, and save for Lady Mary, of course, no one else and no one more youthful.

There were a few good things about her present circumstances, and Faith had consoled herself by reciting them in her head each night as she lay abed, sleepless to the point of pain due to lack of exercise of mind and body. One was that the condition was sure to be transient, since surely, she thought, her hosts would want their daughter to see other gentlemen, even during this thin season in Town. And the other was that due to the present circumstances there was, of course, no way for her to cover herself with ignomy again, since it was almost as impossible to scandalize oneself amid the decrepid dowagers and soundly married middle-aged gentlemen friends of the duke that she consorted with each evening, as it was to ruin her reputation when she was entirely alone in her bath. For at least, as she reasoned glumly, although untoward thoughts and longings might well eventually take one down the road to perdition, one only had to pay the toll if the journey was taken in actuality rather than imagination.

Her imagination had been the most active part of her for all this week, she sighed each night. Lady Mary, oddly enough, did not seem to mind the way they occupied themselves these days, but Faith found that she missed Will enormously, and had to admit that despite all the confusion it caused her, she'd longed for a glimpse of Lord Deal as well. But all she saw of either of them was their calling cards on the butler's tray each day when she'd returned from yet another lifeless junket.

Lord Deal had asked her why she feared him, and she thought she knew, but the question that kept her startlingly awake each midnight was her own. And that was why, if she feared him or her reactions to him, which she had to admit she did, did she then still wish to see him? It wasn't only his lively conversation or humor she missed, most peculiarly, she discovered herself missing the threat of him.

As she lay in her darkened bed, unwillingly conjuring up images of his face and form, her skin even tingling at the unsought memory of his touch, for the first time in her life, she began to wonder at whether those few moments of unadulterated pleasure she'd found in his lips weren't well worth the subsequent feelings of panic she experienced. Perhaps, she'd allow herself to think at last in those irrational dark and private hours when her better judgment slept as she did not, perhaps paying the piper would be worth the dance he'd lead her. These terrifying yet exciting thoughts would, strangely enough, buy her a night's slumber. Then morning would come, and sane reason would awaken with it. Unfortunately, boredom must have shared the same bed, for it arose with the dawn as well.

Perhaps she was becoming like a child who goes on nightly crusades and battles midnight pirates to enliven a lackluster life, she'd think upon arising each dull dawn. By the clear morning she could see that these new night fantasies were only pillow-bred things, grown between safe, snug coverlets, since they evaporated at first light. Still, during the past week, she sometimes wondered on an interior giggle if it might not be long until she retired at noon, just to have time for all those strange fantasies she dared at last to dream with her eyes wide open. But she was grateful for them; they were rapidly becoming some of the most interesting things in her waking or sleeping life.

The Earl of Methley was one of society's best known raconteurs, yet Faith never found herself looking forward to their daily meetings as Lady Mary did, though she agreed that they provided the only real patches of enjoyment in their present lives. The lanky earl had been with her each day, and yet never in her thoughts any night. He was charming and clever and very amusing company. Yet even though he'd once embraced her, she felt no danger emanating from him, just as she sensed no warmth either. In fact, she found it difficult to understand why he'd been so constant a visitor of late. If she didn't know better, she'd think it might be Lady Mary he'd fixed his attentions on, since he was equally as pleasant and attentive a companion to both young women.

Still, she'd been sure to see she'd never found herself alone with him again. It was never his person she feared, it was his words. For though his advances at Stonecrop Hall had been midnight ones, likely spurred on more by bottled spirits than lustful ones, she recalled that he'd begun that first sober afternoon to say things that were a few hundred percent too serious to suit her.

Now at last circumstances had left them alone together again, and as though he read her thoughts, he said, with that same odd smile on his lips, "An unlikely cupid, our duchess, but a competent one. I've wanted some time alone with you, Faith, and although I'm not best pleased to have a tea table and plates of cakes as witnesses to my declaration, I'll not quibble at my good fortune. In short— for I don't believe you wish me to go down upon one knee, do you? I'm far too tall to do the thing with any panache, and don't want to lose you to a fit of mirth, before I win you—I'd like to tell you that I propose to go to the duke with an offer for you. I assume he's acting *in loco parentis*? If not, then please give me your grandfather's direction, for I'm in earnest about this, Faith, I very much wish to marry you.''

"You can't mean it," she gasped, coming to her feet as though he'd spilled hot tea instead of cool words over her.

"Is it so sudden?" he asked. "Hardly," he said, rising as well and stepping around the small table to capture her hand as though he knew she'd flee if he didn't anchor her in some physical way. "You didn't imagine I'd conceived of a yearning for the good duchess, did you? You may not have enjoyed our first embrace, but I assure you I don't cultivate unnatural passions. I certainly wouldn't have subjected myself to such company for all this while unless I'd been serious about getting to know you better. I did, and I cannot help but feel we will deal very well together."

It would have been undignified, if not impossible, to drag herself away from the earl, so Faith only said, in what she hoped were casual accents, "But my lord, I've told you I don't wish to wed, though naturally I'm very flattered and appreciative of the honor you do me."

But he laughed at that and only said, "Oh yes, indeed. Very appreciative, which is why you've snapped me up so fast, I suppose. I suppose then too, from your hesitancy, that you're about to insist that you intend to stay on only a little while longer before you return to New York to begin your career as a merchant?"

He awaited her reply with an ironic grin upon his long face and she knew then, from the mocking way he'd put it, that he'd never understand that that was precisely what she wished to do.

"Look here, Faith," he said, turning her bodily so that she faced him, and then lifting her chin in his hand so that cool gray eyes met an angry gray gaze directly, "we haven't much time, I'll put it bluntly. We could learn to get on very well together. So far as material matters stand, I've no funds at all, as you must know—none. Still, don't denigrate what I do have to offer you, which are several impressive holdings, including the most precious ones of all—an old respected title and a firm place in society. Although on the face of it, you have far more—youth, beauty, wit, and riches—still, it's time you faced the truth of it. You'll not do better, I assure you. Have you, for example, seen this?" he asked, releasing her chin and reaching into his jacket to draw forth some folded papers.

When he began to spread them out, she began to say, angrily, "Oh, no, I've seen that—" before she caught her breath as she caught sight of the first one he opened.

The picture showed a Red Indian girl clad in little but weird patterns of paint, with scalps dangling at her waist, labeled variously, "L-rd D-l," "The E-l of M-thl-y," "L-rd Gr-yv-le," and others she did not bother to try to read when her gaze fell upon the second caricature. This one depicted several gentlemen drowning in a pool, and an Indian girl in the act of rescuing them by tossing pound notes and coins to them as lifelines, while two terrified and terrifying plump maidens, obviously the Washburn twins, tried to cower in ludicrously unsuccessful fashion behind a single slim tree. Which explained, Faith thought dazedly, why even those two kind-hearted girls had never attempted to contact her again. And the last showed a foolishly long-limbed, obviously passionate gentleman embracing an unclad Indian girl, and before she dropped her gaze, unable to further study the obscene details that were rife in the illustration, she read the title: "The Earl Attempts (to Tame) a Wild Indian."

"I understand there were yet others," the earl said, as he folded the papers again, "but someone was quicker than I, and had already bought them up by the time I got to the shop. I relieved the sellers of all these that were left and made sure that they got my logs to burning brightly this morning before I came here. But my point is that they have been printed, and will continue to be printed, with worse to keep them company, until the situation is altered for good. If you go home, it's possible they'll be discontinued," he said, watching her closely, "but then, I shouldn't count on the dear duchess not informing your family of their existence anyway. For all her civility, she's a marplot and a dreadful gossip. While I, of course," he said, showing his white teeth in a wide smile, "am far superior, for I am a wonderful gossip."

Faith said nothing as he tucked the papers back in his jacket. Noting that she'd not smiled at his sally, and seeing clearly how feverishly she was thinking, he went on,

"Marriage to a respectable gentleman would erase these slurs more quickly and certainly more quietly than any lawsuit would do. But I fear that their very existence has already warned off any respectable gentlemen. And as for Deal," he said, aware of how she froze at the mention of that name, "he's been the featured subject of such endeavors often enough in the past, I believe, to paper over the whole of the ballroom at Stonecrop Hall with only the poorer examples. I doubt he'd be delighted at acquiring more, even if he were inclined to be in the least serious about an American female, or indeed, even if he were to seriously entertain the notion of wedlock again. Not that he's prejudiced—about Americans, that is to say—but I think he'd welcome some serenity in his life. Indeed, I think he deserves some now," the earl said comfortably, "don't you?"

"And you?" Faith asked angrily, wanting to lash out at someone for all the distress she felt. "I suppose you don't mind being the target of such gossip. How kind of you."

"Not in the least," he said with evident amusement. "I mind quite a bit, to be sure. But I can weather this, as can you, if we are married."

"If," Faith said, holding her head high and giving him a look of blazing contempt, "you have my money to build you a shelter from those inclement weathers, you mean to say."

As he didn't answer, but only gazed at her contemplatively, and since as always, she immediately regretted her outburst of temper, she sought words to heal whatever hurt she'd dealt him, and in so doing, tried for honesty. "Ah, it's not that," she admitted on a sigh. "And I don't blame you if it is. I do come from merchant stock, and I do understand the value of money. But my lord, you don't love me, never pretend I'm your heart's desire. So it would be foolishness itself to wed me, for I'll bet there are heaps of girls here in England with more money than I who'd find your title more desirable than I do, since they were bred and raised to instant respect of it."

"Love?" the earl asked, his thin eyebrows going up. "But I don't expect to find that in marriage, my dear, and no one of my class does. I wouldn't insult you by suggesting it. And no one I know," he said, with the first real hint of emotion he'd shown, though she could not make out just what it was before it was gone again, "gets to wed their heart's desire. 'Heart's desires' fade, my dear; they change with every beat of those fickle organs. But mutual respect can remain forever. I didn't know you looked for love in marriage, but I believe we'd do well together, anyway. You might not 'love' me precisely right now, but I think," he said on a smile that grew to something more, something that got her to back up as he came nearer to her, "you oughtn't to worry. I do believe we can amuse each other very well, and who knows what that can grow to become? And since, as you've seen, I've already been characterized as your ardent lover, I think it only fair that you let me demonstrate how pleasant that can be for us as well."

"But that's just it," Faith blurted, driven to the wall in actuality as well as imagery now as he advanced upon her. "I don't like to do such things. I don't, I never have. Ah," she hesitated, in her extremity finding the truth and bringing it forth at last, but trimming it to fit the occasion and her need, "you remember what happened when you kissed me the once? Well, it wasn't you, it's always been that way for me. I just don't like lovemaking."

He became still. He didn't wish to insult her, and so he could scarcely tell her that he'd never expect a true lady to care for the idea of lovemaking, for she wasn't a true lady, after all. But she'd mentioned her inability to respond to other gentlemen in the past, and mentioned it with considerable regret. He realized, with a jolt of surprise, that Americans must have very different morals than were expected from well-brought-up females of his own land. Small wonder then that she'd not responded to his cool, tentative, patient courtship. But win her he must, and whatever her morals. He felt he was very close to his goal, whatever her protests, and the duchess had assured him that he was not far wrong. It was only that he now must tread very carefully.

He was neither a stupid nor an uneducated man, and so after a moment, he thought he'd hit upon the answer.

"Of course," he said smiling as soothing and placating as a draper assuring a valued customer of the excellence of her choice, "but it's never your fault, either. It's different in your country than it is for us. It was the puritans who founded the place, wasn't it? They'd jail a man for complimenting a woman on the sabbath, and drape their females in armor if they could to keep appreciative eyes from her. We're far more liberal about such natural things as relations between the sexes here.''

"Liberal?" Faith hooted, her amazement conquering her fear, especially since it now seemed that the tall gentleman had no intention of sweeping her up in his arms. "All I've heard is 'proper' and 'meet' and 'fit' and 'acceptable' and 'unexceptional' since I've come here! Liberal, indeed," she scoffed.

"You've only seen the duchess's England," the earl said smugly, "and that is like seeing the Pope's Rome. Impressive, but hardly typical. Don't worry, now that I see the difficulty, I'll be sure to enlighten you as to the truth of the freedom of our society."

Then, hearing voices in the hall, he grimaced. "So, can we say then, Faith, that we've at least reached a tentative understanding?" he asked.

"Oh no," she gasped, "for I never said yes."

"But," he bent to whisper as the duchess entered in a new, dry gown, "you never said no either." And then, grinning, he greeted the duchess, the Lady Mary, and resumed his merry tale.

"I don't like it," Will said, putting down his fork with the slice of beefsteak still impaled on its tines, untasted. "If it's not by chance, it's by choice, and I know it's not chance. We've called every day, and they're never there. And we never run into them at night neither."

"The duchess travels in circles we circumvent," Barnabas Stratton said after swallowing a mouthful of wine, and when he realized his young friend was too disgruntled to see humor in his neatly turned phrase, he explained, "We've been at the music halls when they go to the Opera, when we frequent the Opera, it's not a night you'll find paragons like the Duchess of Marchbanks in attendance. I didn't think you pined at not being invited to the sort of socials the duchess finds thrilling, but no power on earth would move me to wheedle an invitation to one of the teas or socials she delights in. Well," he amended, smiling gently at the association that one word instantly brought to his mind, "very few powers on earth, that is to say. But I promise, if we don't encounter them in a few more days, we'll beard them in one of their dens of propriety, even if it means I have to grovel and scrape more than a man of my advanced years ought be expected to."

"Methley's there, and every day too," Will grumbled, biting into his beefsteak as though it were the earl and not just his name, who was being grinded up so savagely.

"Methely," Barnabas said, contemplating a bit of potato, "hasn't a prayer. She's amused by him, but only that."

"Only that?" Will cried, abandoning his beefsteak again. "But he's got a title and blood as blue as ink, and the duchess lets him run tame in the house."

"Do you seriously think that any of that will influence Faith in the least?" his host asked casually, smiling more broadly as he saw his guest's face grow ruddy.

"Not Faith," Will admitted then, as contrite as a young boy might be, "but I wasn't thinking of Faith at all. You knew that, didn't you? I suppose," he said, a rueful smile replacing the embarrassment on his face, "you think I'm a pretty paltry fellow, forgetting all about Faith and her problems. It doesn't matter if you deny it," he sighed, pushing his plate away, "because I accept it's true. I was charged with looking after her, and all I can do is think of Mary. Of course, Faith won't care a rap about titles and coats of arms and what all. She's got a head on her shoulders, and no family pushing her to marry nobility, and she's older too," Will said defensively.

"Three long years the Lady Mary's senior, an ancient in fact, you're quite right," Barnabas agreed, and attended to a pickled onion before he asked, ruminatively, "But Will, my lad, if you believe the lady is light-headed enough to be swayed by such things as blood and titles and her mama's importuning, why have you laid your heart at her feet? It's no secret, and I think we're friends enough so that I can admit that I'm surprised to see you so smitten with a lady who possesses a face more attractive than her mind."

"You don't know her!" Will shouted, and brought both hands down upon the tabletop until the relishes did a jig on their silver tray. Lord Deal remained still, only his eyes widened. But this was as good as a sharp rebuke, for Will calmed himself with a visible effort and then appealed to his host's reason by saying, "I'm sorry, it's very bad of me to shout at you. You were kind enough to put me up here, and have been my friend in all ways—you deserve far better. But she's sweet, and bright and gentle, aye, and clever too. It's clear you can't know her if you say such things."

"And you know her so well?" Barnabas asked quietly, but Will scarcely attended to him as he went on to explain earnestly, "I never thought to actually meet someone like her, I always thought such a lady would remain a dream. But Barnaby, when I was very young, I came to London to try my hand at work here before I eventually shipped out to America to make my fortune. For a little while, I delivered packages. One day, one freezing winter's day, I brought some frock, or shawl or some such, I scarce remember now, to an address not so far from here. My hands were blue with cold, as blue as Methley's blood I'd say, that is, where the chillblains hadn't cracked open to show my own common red blood.

"I'd come in through the servants' entrance and the housekeeper allowed me to warm my hands by the fire while the mistress of the house inspected the parcel and its contents. As it happened, there was something amiss with it, something not included, and the lady was so agitated she came down to the kitchens to quiz me about the delivery.

"I was very young, Barnaby, but I'll never forget her, I believe she changed my life. I'd never seen such a beautiful female before. She was all gold and pink and she looked—ah how can I say it? She looked as though she'd been cared for and watched over tenderly for all her life. I could hardly answer her questions, the perfumed scent of her made me drunk, I think. I remained mute, so eventually she gave up and tried to give me some coins for my troubles.

"I drew back, I was horrified, and I put my hands behind my back. She insisted on giving me a gratuity, and when I insisted on refusing, her cook, a great fearsome female," he laughed now, in reminiscence, "threatened me with a carving knife if I wouldn't take the coins and be done with it. I think I almost wept then, Barnaby, I was very young indeed. But I did finally manage to explain it was that my hands were bleeding now that they'd warmed up, and I didn't want to get the nice lady's hands dirtied with my blood.

"She wept, Barnaby," Will said, shaking his head in an amazement that had lasted for more than a decade. "Then she bade the housekeeper bandage my hands, and insisted the cook give me some cakes and a warm nog, and then she sent me home with a scarf she'd had her maid take from her own husband's wardrobe. She became my ideal of a lady, Barnaby, don't you see? And I vowed that I'd work, I'd spare no effort, and someday if fate was kind, I'd have such a wife, and I'd raise such daughters.

"Only twice in my life have I been silenced by a woman's beauty. That time, and the moment when I first laid eyes upon Mary. She's the exact picture of the lady I thought of, and longed for, and worked to deserve, for all those years. I can take care of her, and I can bring her to want me too, if only I'm given time and opportunity. I've already got the energy and ability, and always believed you can achieve anything you work hard enough for. It's how I've gotten this far. But you think I'm a sentimental fool, don't you?" he asked his host, his sincerity as well as his longing clear in his open, honest face and guileless, steady dark brown eyes.

"No, Will, there's nothing wrong with sentiment or hard work," Barnabas answered at length. "A man's the worse without a balance of each. But I only wonder if you're being quite fair to Lady Mary. I wonder if she knows who she's supposed to be for you?"

"Only herself," Will replied fervently.

"Ah yes," Barnabas Stratton sighed, and then he shrugged. "Then I think you ought to finish that lot of food up before my cook comes after you with a carving knife. He's sensitive as a mayflower on the subject of his dinners. And then, we'll take ourselves off to confront the duchess and her charges. It's time, high time we did more than leave our cards with them."

"We'll call on them again?" Will asked, laying his fork down again in his excitement.

"My dear fellow," Lord Deal exclaimed, laughing, "you'll make that bit of roast dizzy if you keep waving it about. No, we won't. We shall happen upon them quite by accident at the Cumberland Gardens this evening, where they're going to hear a concert. Yes," he laughed, "of course, I know, and have known everywhere they've been for all this past week. Not everyone in London puts their hands behind their backs when coins are offered to them," he explained, as his guest, grinning broadly, dutifully put the bit of roast away and out of sight forever.

The night air was warm and sweet, made far warmer by all the torches blazing light down upon the press of people they illuminated, and made more pungent by all the perfumes that had been liberally splashed on by both the ladies and the gentlemen promenading in the Vauxhall Gardens this night. Faith said nothing as she walked along the narrow paths that hopscotched from stretches of dim night to patches of leaping light, but as she'd explained briefly when the earl quizzed her about her continuing silence, "nothing can come out, when so much is going in."

Their coach had gone first to Vauxhall, rather than to Cumberland Gardens as the duchess had announced at teatime, because the earl had said reasonably enough when they'd set out that Faith should see an assortment of such gardens and have the opportunity to judge for herself which one would be her favorite among them. Some, of course, she could not see at all, since their clientelle was deemed too low to brush shoulders with, but Vauxhall and Cumberland, at least, had patrons from elevated as well as lower classes. Those of the loftier set who were pent in the City this summer due to family dramas or other cruel circumstances, might often be found passing sweet evenings at such places, and so, as the duchess ruled, their party was unexceptional.

There was a feeling of playfulness and vacation in the very air. The gardens were informal enough so that the gentlemen could be dressed comfortably, and yet festive enough so that the ladies could put on summer finery. Faith wore a light blue gown that drifted deliciously about her body each time a small night breeze whispered by its gauzy skirts. She could understand why the duchess had said the gardens were so popular with all the citizens of Town, even those of the *ton*.

There was the open air to be taken, there was music and dancing and fireworks and light refreshments to be indulged in. The duchess didn't mention that there was also sport for naughty gentlemen and errant ladies to be flushed from the shadows in such places, sport that couldn't be discussed with innocent young misses. But then, in all fairness, though it was doubtful she didn't know of it, it was very possible that like most society matrons, she didn't choose to know of it, which amounted to the same thing.

Lady Mary remained close-mouthed as they explored the gardens as well. But since the paths were too narrow for them all to stroll abreast and since she had to walk with her mama (her papa had begged off from the engagement), her quietude was understandable. She'd been unusually morose at dinner as well, but protested when Faith got her alone before they came down to join the earl that it was only the merest headache which was unsettling her. She was such a fragile creature, or at least, she behaved with such delicacy that Faith imagined it might only be something so simple as the time of the month that had cast her friend into the sullens tonight.

The music played and in the distant pavilion, people danced to it. The far-off tunes mingled with the sighing of the trees, their rustling leaves adding winds, and the crickets, counterpoint, to the melodies. The entertainment took on the enchantment that a soft summer's night adds to all diversions. The stars shone brighter than the trinkets upon the breasts and wrists of the ladies who stood in the pools of rippling gas and torchlight. And when suddenly the cold blue stars exploded into flying comets and expanding flowers and pennants and snakes and flung themselves across the night sky, dribbling fire down to the treetops, Faith was as thrilled as a child and breathed "oh" and "ah" at each burst of the fireworks display along with everyone else in the crowd.

"The lights obscure the best," the earl said, and so he urged Faith on and she went with him, oblivious to him, stumbling blindly, until she felt grass beneath her slippers, for all the while her head was thrown back so as not to miss a second of the spectacle. He chuckled as he steered her past obstacles, and moved her out of the path of collisions with other gaping spectators. But he'd been right, and when she came to a halt, the sky was clearer, purer, untainted by man's homemade and off-colored lights. Now she could even make out how the fireworks climbed upward, seeing the racing dark shapes that remained a secret against the darker sky until they attained their ripest moment, and then blossomed forth to decorate the night. Now that she knew their secret they lost some of their magic, but nothing could lessen their effect.

When the explosions of color stopped, and nothing was left of them but a pale gunmetal blue wind and the smell of sulphur drifting across the stars, Faith sighed. "That was wonderful," she said contentedly.

She looked around to see the duchess's and Mary's reactions, suddenly wondering if she'd been too enthused for their idea of propriety. Yet surely, she thought, there could be nothing gauche about gaping at such wonders, surely they remained breathtaking no matter how often they were seen. But now that she looked earthward again, she saw that she stood upon a grassy lawn, not far from the pavements and crowds, but it was only herself and the earl who stood there. The duchess and Mary were nowhere to be seen.

Before she could ask him where they were, he spoke. He towered above her, and she had to hold her head back almost as far as she'd done when she watched the display of incendiary devices as she tried to read his expression. But that she couldn't do, for his pale face was indistinct, outlined against the black sky. Only the white of his neckcloth and shirt and cuffs shone out blue-white from the mass of the dim shape before her, as did the gleam from the surround of his eyes.

"They've gone on," he said, the white of his teeth now showing as well as he smiled down at her. "They've left us to the night. Don't worry, we've the duchess's approval; even she realizes a courting couple must have a bit of privacy. And it's easy enough to explain that we became separated in the crowds. As long as we make relatively fast work of it, we can escape censure."

"And Mary?" was all that Faith could think to say, while she thought furiously of the possible merits of running from him. She was wondering about the advisability of attempting to get back to the townhouse alone, when he replied, "Ah, but Mary is a perfect lady. Thus, Mary does what Mama wants, didn't you know that? But don't fret, I'm not a barbarian, my dear, and this is Britain, not the wilderness, and I want you for my bride, not my captive. I'm not kidnapping you.

"Oh no," he said, smiling again, "it's not to be ravishment, unfortunately. It's only that it's time for a little surgery. A small operation, and a painless one. I'm just going to remove the scales from your eyes. Come along, my dear," he said, taking her hand fast in his. "You're famous for your intrepid spirit. You should be pleased. It's time for a little adventure."

TWELVE

THERE WERE, the Earl of Methley believed, only two ways to conquer dread or distaste: either by being forced to repeated exposure to the threat, or by understanding the exact nature of it. Sometimes both methods together served the purpose, since both bred familiarity, and familiarity was the enemy of any strong emotion, as it numbed both pleasures and fears.

If one was thrown by a horse, one got back on the beast until all fear was gone, that was the accepted and effective manner of teaching horsemanship. And if one feared something more ephemeral, like crowds, or public speaking, or even, as in this case, lovemaking, why then, if one could be made see that it was both commonplace and survivable, the sting could be removed from it. Hadn't he himself been taught oratory by being forced to recite in front of the rest of his form? Hadn't he himself been able to court foolish, wealthy young girl children once he'd been made to see the sheer necessity of it?

Now it was time to begin his companion's schooling. He wasn't fool enough to believe one brief evening's encounter with the reality of adult life would remove all her hesitancies and fears. But such a drastic instant cure was scarcely necessary either. There'd be time enough for that in marriage, he mused, as he studied the contours of Miss Hamilton's profile shown in silhouette against the dark square of the carriage window in a wash of lamplight, and he noted with abstract approval the purity and grace of it from the downward sweep of her lush eyelashes to the gentle upthrust swelling of her breasts. Yes, it would be a pleasant duty to undertake.

Had she been a gently bred English girl, he'd never have brought her so far. But had she been a gently bred

English girl, there would have been no impediment to their union; she'd not have expected enjoyment in marital relations, or if she did, then she'd rather have perished than admit it to him. And if his chosen bride had been a fearful young lady of the *ton*, he'd have instructed her as to her marital duties very differently too, by whispers, gentle touching, and careful teaching, all and only in the legally wedded night.

But then, he realized, such supposition was pointless, had she come from his world, she'd have accepted his offer when it was made. For, as he'd noted and the duchess herself had confirmed, the chit liked him very well. In any event, the only other gentleman she showed a care for, however she attempted to conceal it from him, was Deal, and the Viking, the earl thought on a grimace, showed no signs of needing either of the things she could offer him: a wife or a fortune.

But the earl badly needed the one benefit she held out, and though he'd lately had different dreams of his own, he was committed to realism now, and so was hourly growing more reconciled to the other aspect of her dower as well. He was determined to have her, in any event. Which was why he'd taken this bold step this evening. There was little time left to do else. This candid young woman would have to be shown the truth of the matter outright before there could ever be a union between them, and that union would have to be accomplished soon. His creditors were growing more vocal with each passing week, even as she spoke more frequently each day of returning to her home, and so of passing beyond his reach.

As yet, there was no need for anything so drastic as an abduction or a forced lesson in marital technique of a more physical sort. He was glad of this; he wasn't the sort of gentleman who'd instantly enjoy employing such tactics, nor did he think there'd ever be a chance for any real pleasure between them if they began in such a manner, even though the duchess assured him that due to her upbringing the American girl both expected and would appreciate such a spirited courtship.

The duchess was a tough old bit of mutton, and as it became apparent that she disliked her American visitor prodigiously, the earl found himself beginning to doubt the lady when she told him the time of day. No, he wouldn't employ such crass methods of bringing the young woman to heel. He was a thoughtful gentleman. But he'd never had a similar experience to guide him and could only deduce the extent of her, and perforce his, problem. For all his worldliness, desirable females had always fallen into only four categories: unwed and thus untouchable, married and either willing or unwilling, and professional. Of all of them, of course, he'd had the least to do with the first group.

Although he knew nothing about young unmarried chits, he believed all females must share a commonality and so he'd thought he'd hit upon the answer the night she'd fled his arms. The rightness of his supposition had been borne out when she'd readily admitted her sorrow at her lack of passionate response. It was clear to him that only Miss Hamilton's shame for her secret desires could account for her fear of his, or any man's, embraces.

This night, much in the fashion of an impatient gardener who brings winter-barren branches into a hothouse, he would attempt to force her to an earlier bloom than expected, in order to meet his own schedule. He would try to bring her to adulthood all in a night, and in so doing, inflame all the hidden sensuality he believed her capable of as well. If he could achieve these aims, indeed, if he could do no more than remove her fear of him, he'd remove her last objection from his path in far more civilized and equitable fashion than the duchess suggested.

But if it were not possible to arouse her, it would be an unfortunate, but not a devastating circumstance. Nature was kind in that respect, and wise as well. A female didn't have to love the business of making love to produce an heir for her husband; if that were so then it would be, he thought on a chuckle, leaning back in the carriage, a lonely old world indeed. Tonight's errand would be enough to remove her objections to the match, of this he was sure. For it would illustrate the foolishness of her trepidations to her by showing her that all the world, and the fashionable world as well, commonly partook of such pleasures. A child learned by observation, he rationalized, and so he would see to it then that she had a great deal to observe this night.

He told her none of this. She was, after all, very young, and as he was a great deal older in many ways, he decided he knew better than to engage in a debate with her. Moreover, he believed if she knew what she faced she'd find a way of defending herself from the truth of it, as all prejudiced people do when confronted with an anticipated argument against their cherished beliefs. Yet even if she were intractable and if she learned nothing from this evening's efforts, the circumstances alone, apart from the duchess's kind cooperation, would ensure her future acquiescense. He'd rather she welcomed the match, but it was being made even as they traveled onward, nonetheless. There was little for him to do now but wait upon events. Thus, they rode in complete silence until he recognized the street the coach entered. Then he reached into his pocket to withdraw a gift for her. But as he handed it across to where she sat huddled in the furthest corner of the carriage, she shrank back from him.

"Oh come, my dear Miss Hamilton," he drawled, "look before you cower. It's only a demi-mask. It's got holes for the eyes, and no teeth at all. Put it on, my dear, and like the youth in the fairy tales with his cape of invisibility, you shall be able to see without being seen. And that's rather important where we're going tonight."

Faith sat straight up at his words as though he were a strict governess threatening her with a backboard, rather than an abductor menacing her with the unimaginable.

"I am not cowering," she said staunchly, though she felt like trying to creep beneath the floorboards as she spoke, and had been attempting to judge the speed of the coach for some time now, wondering when she might be able to leap from it without breaking her neck.

"And I don't want to go with you anywhere," she went on, trying very hard not to sound like the frightened child she felt, "and I'm appalled at your behavior, my lord. I am, I really am. What you're doing is no more than kidnapping, pure and simple, and I'm not at all entertained by it, and I wish you'd forget whatever bad joke this is, and if you do, I promise I'll forget all of this as well," she said in a rush, as the coach slowed to a halt and she realized she didn't want to get out any more than she wished to remain within it with this man who was suddenly a stranger to her.

"But I don't want you to forget it," he said pleasantly. "My whole aim is that you'll remember every moment of it. Now, if I wished to use you for my foul purposes, I promise you I would have done so already and not wasted all this time traveling across town. I don't know what you do in the Americas, but here, at least, a comfortable bed is not necessary for such sport, an uncomfortable carriage will do just as nicely for us," he smiled, even as she wondered from the amiability of his words and the incongruity of his actions, which one of them had run mad.

"I want you to like me, Faith," he said sincerely as she gazed down at the proffered bit of velvet and buckram he held out to her, "and so I don't mean to hurt you, and here is my pledge that I'll keep you from harm, but only *if* you stay by my side, and *if* you say not one word, whatever you see, and *if* you keep this over your face. Only your eyes will be open to insult, my dear, and at that, you may well discover as many another has, that it's less of an offense than it is a rare treat. But don't fret," he said, laughing, "I'll never ask you to admit as much to me.

"But I do insist that you put on that mask, and that you leave the carriage with me now," he said in less conciliatory tones, sounding more like a harsh schoolmaster than the friend he claimed to be. "We'll only pass a little time within this house, and then we're off to another even more interesting one for a short while, and then, alas, our time is up and I'll have to take you home again. By then, of course, you will understand why it would be in your better interest to claim we'd passed all the time at Vauxhall together tonight, attempting to locate the duchess and Lady Mary, and to never breathe a word of this excursion to anyone else."

She managed to tie the mask on, if only to prevent him from coming close enough to do it himself as he began to indicate he meant to do, and as she fumbled with the strings, he added, "Because you understand, my dear, that with your reputation, no one, absolutely no one, will believe that you were forced to it."

The house was a stately white townhouse, with gilded railings and a burly footman on guard at the door. He was gotten up in the gorgeous fashion of another era, clad all in green silks with a powdered periwig. And so Faith thought that for some bizarre reason her companion was making a game of taking her to a masquerade. But the earl wore no mask of any sort; in fact, she noted, the footman seemed to recognize and acknowledge him as he bowed them into the house.

The huge main salon was overwarm, and overfurnished, and overly gilded, and too many candles, inadequately grouped, gave insufficient light to the scene. It was over-crowded as well within, and so it took several moments for Faith's eyes to adjust to the areas of golden light contrasted with deep shadow, as well as to the sting of scent which lay heavy in the air, along with the almost visible aromas of tallow and snuff, and smoke from cheroots. All the while that she blinked and sniffed at the air, the earl propeled her further into the room.

A sweet-faced elderly woman swam into her circle of vision, and Faith was able to focus upon her as she came directly up to the earl. She found herself comforted merely at the sight of the dignified lady in her purple turban as she came forward to greet the earl, and began to at last take a lively interest in whatever odd jest the earl was playing on her with all his theatrics. But even as the lady said, with evident delight in her cultured tones, "Ah, my lord, how good to see you again. But I see you've brought your own entertainment tonight—no matter, we welcome you," Faith began to take more careful note of her surroundings, and began to believe her senses entirely disordered.

There were groups of gentlemen everywhere within the room, chatting, laughing, drinking, and standing together. None of them wore masks, as none of the ladies present did. And in each group of gentlemen there were several ladies included. Although at first it had appeared that these ladies were as magnificently attired as the doorman had been, as Faith grew accustomed to the inconstant light, she saw what she could scarcely believe she saw, that these females wore less than all their costumes.

Some stood in what appeared to be their shifts, some wore even less, some had only the bottom portion of their persons draped with any fabric at all. Perhaps because such seminudity was commonplace, everywhere, Faith now perceived, as her eyes accommodated themselves to their new surroundings enough to take note of detail, gentlemen openly fondled those portions of the females that were uncovered, some so casually and absently that it appeared as if they toyed with an adjacent breast or buttock as other men might finger a fob or a quizzing glass when they were speaking.

The earl had warned her not to speak, but at that moment Faith could not have uttered a word even if that word could have freed her from this nightmare world, as she inchoately wished someone could. For then the elderly lady smiled at them again and sailed across the room to greet another arrival, as the earl guided Faith to another, less frequented corner of the room.

"You are safe," he whispered, lowering his cool lips to speak directly into her ear, "for you see," he gestured, indicating another masked lady, who stood with a gentleman silently watching a couple entwined on the cushions on a settee, "real ladies," he went on so softly that no one save Faith heard him, "generally only come here to watch the gentlemen and the hired help. Some, I'm told, find it inspiring. But the gentlemen! Ah my dear, that fellow so pleasantly engaged before us might be only an unknown young chap, but look about you. There are dukes as well as earls here, all sorts of peers of the realm. You might even discover someone you know. Shall we look for the Viking tonight?" he asked gaily. "It would not be something wonderful to find him here, you know. Some nights even royalty visits Mother Carey's establishment to play with her chicks; it's quite the established thing to do."

But Faith stared with incredulity as the couple on the settee became more entangled and she at last remembered exactly what they were about to do with each other. Then she, forgetting all else, and trembling so that the earl looked at her sharply, gasped all at once, in a panic, "I must go, oh I must go, only let me go from here," and she pulled desperately against his hold upon her arm.

The gentleman on the settee did not look up from his endeavors at this, for he had gone too far to hear her, but his partner, who was, after all, only paid to participate, glanced up from her charade of ecstasy at the words. The masked lady and her escort were diverted enough to stare at Faith curiously as well. At that, the earl gripped her arm hard and dragged her away from their notice.

"Are you mad?" he demanded.

She made no answer, but did not cease trembling, and he saw even in that strange gilded light that her eyes were wide and frantic and that what he could see of her face was as white as death. He murmured something angrily beneath his breath and, still holding Faith by the arm, quickly made his way to the door again.

It was his sudden stab of terrible self-doubt, as strong as it was rare, that made him relax his hold on her as the footman opened the door for their exit. It was the concern at what had chased him from her premises so soon after he'd arrived that caused the proprietress of the establishment to rush after him. It was the fact that she was no match for his long legs that caused her to signal for her doorman to intercept him on the outer stairs just as he motioned for his carriage once again. And it was his attempt to assure them both that nothing was amiss, so that they would not study his companion too closely, that made him loose his hold on Faith completely so that he could push her toward the open door of his coach.

So it was when he had done with reassuring the pair as to their establishment's excellence and his own health's untimely failure, and had turned back to join Faith in the carriage, that as he bent double to step inside he was arrested in mid-motion when he saw that she was not there. And then he stepped out again and spun around to stare about wildly and discover that she was entirely gone from his sight.

The only sound within the room was the deep steady pulse of the clock on the mantel. It was too warm an evening to lay a fire and so there was no glow and sputter and crackle of flame to enliven the atmosphere either. The only motion in the room was that of the thin brown liquid swirled about as the gentleman turned his wrist and contemplated the depths of the goblet he held. Other than that, even he, clad in a dressing gown and sunk in the depths of a club chair, stayed as still and silent as any picture on the wall in the dimly lit room. And the only diversion the gentleman had was the thought that he'd never need hire a rat-catcher to inspect his townhouse. For if he'd had so much as mouse in the place, he thought, its steps would have rung out like hoofbeats had it ventured one paw's worth across the floor.

He didn't know, he sighed, why he expected more. It was late, his house guest was already abed, filled with so much of the liquid his host was now inspecting in his glass to ensure his rest that it was doubtful he could have opened one eye if a horse had indeed galloped across his bedchamber. The servants had retired for the evening, and it being a bachelor establishment there were few female servitors, and those few all nearly as old as the male retainers, so there wasn't even a hint of a giggle, scurry, or tip-toe issuing from their quarters either. No, Barnabas Stratton thought, staring dully at his glass, the only one awake in the entire establishment was the gent who owned the place, and he, poor wretch, sat up watching over it as sleepless as a night watchman with a bad tooth.

"But when he got there, the cupboard was bare, and so the poor lord had none," the lone gentleman whispered to himself on a scowl, and drained off the rest of the liquid in his glass rapidly in a morose toast, deciding belatedly that he really didn't care for the stuff at all.

But none of it was his fault, he argued with himself. He'd started the night with high hopes. He and Will Rossiter had gone to the Cumberland Gardens and strolled about for a fruitless hour netting just what they might on any night there, which was only greetings from several acquaintances and invitations from several strange young females who wished to make their more intimate acquaintances. They'd gone at last to make inquiries in the coach line, and discovered that the duchess's carriage was not in wait there, nor was there any hired hack engaged by the earl. It was only as they rode toward Vauxhall Gardens, thinking their informant might have gotten the letter of their destination wrong but the spirit of it right, that they saw the duchess's carriage in a line in front of the Swansons' townhouse. And while the duchess might have at the eleventh hour opted to go to one of the Swansons' musical evenings, Barabas had told his young guest firmly he did not think he'd led a wicked enough life as yet to deserve having to attend another one this side of Judgment Day.

They'd dined alone, and Will had been so despondent, and had done such an excellent imitation of a sponge, both conversationally and literally, that after Barnabas congratulated him on the imposture, he'd also promised him that they'd call on Lady Mary and her guest the very next morning. But now, Will was likely deep in woozy but happy dreams of that forthcoming meeting, and his host was wide awake to the problems the poor lad faced all unknowing, as well as to the problem he himself faced, that he had only begun to know.

It was a lonely night that capped an empty week, and the gentleman arose to refill his cup at least, when he at last heard a small noise that nevertheless intruded and pierced the bland silence. He froze at once. His senses suddenly changed from mossy introspection to preparation for combat. He waited for the next telling sound to identify the source, and had a moment to regret he was not a more conventional fellow as he pictured a chase that might erupt from this room to spill out into the street, as it once had done when he'd discovered a cracksman entering his library through a window. He was not best thrilled with the fact that as usual, he wore nothing beneath his dressing gown, wincing as he pictured what a glorious sight he'd make running the miscreant down St. James Street. He sighed; it was only another reason he'd have to hope there was only one intruder and that that one could be rendered unconscious with only a few blows.

He was not so surprised at the invasion of his solitude as he was at where the sound was emanating from, as he lowered the light and stole closer to the front door. This was, after all, London, and large cities bred thieves as frequently as they produced bad vapors, and there was little way to filter either evil phenomenon out of the best areas or the worst ones. A good thief could evade the watch like a night-born shadow, but why a good thief would be trying the front door at this empty hour was more than he could imagine. There was a gaslight directly in front, and never half so many shadowy niches as either the back entrance or that tempting library window offered. He waited with a grim smile, for whatever the fellow's reckonings, his final accounting would be the same.

So when Lord Deal, secreted in the darkness of his entry

hall, at last heard his door knocker openly, blatantly, and thunderously sounded, he almost dropped the pistol he'd collected from his desk in his startled confusion as the din at the door reverberated throughout his sleeping house. But he was a resilient gentleman, so it took only two more sharp knocks before he flung open the door wide and confronted his nocturnal visitor. And then, he let out all his indrawn breath in exasperation, for it was lowering to discover the imagined assassin or burglar was only a midnight reveler, disheveled, likely tipsy, and obviously strayed from some riotous celebration. And a woman, at that.

"My dear lady," he said in annoyance, "your comrades are not within. Try your luck elsewhere."

He was already beginning to close the door in her masked face, when he realized she stood unnaturally silent. The vague troublesome thought that she might not be merely a drunken reveler, but some lost young woman come to the sort of harm that can commonly befall a female who travels the nighttime city streets alone, by choice or chance, caused him to hesitate.

It was then that she said, in weary despair and unmistakeable accents, "Oh Lord Deal, please, please get me Will."

And before his heart stopped beating altogether, he caught her up in his arms and bore her, unresisting, inside his door.

He'd gotten her to the library and the chair he'd so recently vacated, and was lowering her gently into it when he heard Mr. Fielding, his butler, ask in quavering but game fashion, "My lord? Do you need assistance? Shall I call the watch? I've young Tredlow here," the butler went on with rising courage and authority as a few more bare running feet could be heard pounding down the hall, "and Wemberly as well now, do you require our assistance with . . . ah . . . anything?"

This last was said with a bit less certainty, since even at a distance and in the light of the one wavering candle he bore, the butler could see that his master was bending over a recumbant female. No more than that could be ascertained, since Lord Deal's own large form bent over the chair obscured most of the sight, and as one of the taller and more enterprising young footmen later remarked in chagrin, the mort was wearing a mask as well. Lord Deal was usually the most circumspect gentleman, but as Mr. Fielding was later to comment ruefully to the housekeeper, he was, withall, a young gentleman still. And though it was his usual practice to take his entertainment in more discreet fashion, there was never any doubt, his valet often confided importantly, from the sort of scent, powder, and paint that sometimes clung to his evening wear, that he took it. This time, the butler sighed, in the manner of one whose life's work was to be put upon, he obviously was taking it home. For after a pause, his master's abstracted voice came back clear and curt, "No, Fielding. Thank you all anyway. Everything is under control now. Good night."

It was a dismissal, and a dismissal was an order, so Mr. Fielding swept all in front of him, from envious footmen to curious kitchen help, back to their beds, if not their slumbers. He himself only paused a few more moments, to be sure that his master's guest, Mr. Rossiter, still slept soundly, and to ascertain with a bit more gratification that Mr. Hodges, my lord's valet, had also slept through the entire disturbance. Then the butler went off to his own room, with a dollop of importance to sweeten his sleep, secure in the knowledge that the morrow would see him king of the servants' breakfast table.

When the house had returned to its stillness, after Lord Deal had closed the door to the library and poured Faith a cordial and seen her drink it down, he at last moved to do more than wait for her to speak. For it did not seem as though she would ever speak again. She sat quite still and seemed to be in shock. He bent slowly, and carefully untied the mask and drew it away from her face. Then he saw the tearstains, then he saw the complete exhaustion and deep sorrow plain in her lovely, drawn, and white face. Then, at last, his own composure broke and he turned away for a moment so that she would not see his own face, or hear his jagged sigh.

After that lapse, he turned his attention to her again, and his dark tanned hands knotted into white knuckled fists as he asked in a tight voice, "Faith, only tell me who it was. If you know. If not, tell me where it occurred, and I will discover all. He shall not go unpunished. I'll call a doctor as well," he went on, trying to keep his voice even, "and we'll keep it close, Will and I. Only please, trust me and tell me.''

"But," Faith said, as she closed her eyes as if to deny him, "I wanted to see Will. I didn't want to bother you."

"Bother?" he said desperately. "Don't you count me as your friend as well? This changes nothing, I swear it. I only regret it with all my heart, and," he vowed, finally enclosing her small cold hands in one of his, though he longed to catch her up in his arms and rock her like a child and weep with her for the indignity and despair of it, "I want to help you through it. So tell me, who has done this thing? Or," he asked, as he started at his own thought, and understood for the first time what precisely the expression signified when someone said that their blood ran cold, "who were they who did this thing to you?"

But then she opened her eyes and at last looked beyond herself and directly at him. Something in his face, or in his troubled eyes, or in his voice, had woken her from her self-absorption at last.

"Tell you what?" she asked.

He drew a deep breath and said as unemotionally as he was able, so as not to distress her more, "Faith, I must know only because for my own sake I must make reprisal on your behalf. Or if not for that, then so that other young women will not be made to suffer as you have done. Plainly then, who was it who attacked you?"

At that she sat up and stared at him in lively terror, the little color remaining in her cheeks draining away.

"Oh lord," she gasped, "not that. Never that," she swore, as he in turn looked ill at her distress. "I mean," she said, her gray eyes luminous and wide, "no one. I haven't been attacked. I was abducted," she said angrily, "and humiliated as well, but not physically, and I did escape. But I wasn't attacked, not in the way that you mean, oh no," she said, looking very frightened now, where, he suddenly realized, she had only looked worn and wretched before. That, and the petulance that he had definitely heard creep into her voice when she'd said "abducted," convinced him as no disclaimer she could have spoken would have done.

It was a night of revelations for him. He was so relieved and yet so angry with her at the same moment that he suddenly understood now, decades after the fact, just why after he'd gotten himself lost on a shopping expedition when he was five, his governess had exclaimed that she didn't know whether to kill him or hug him first when she found him strolling homeward, unharmed and whistling to himself.

And since he liked indecision no more than any other man, and having been prepared for tragedy had instead found himself playing the fool, he tossed the leftover unnecessary tact and delicacy of feeling to the winds and glowered at his surprising guest. He rose to his feet, forgetting that they were bare, and planting his long legs apart, crossed his arms and in his bright robes, unintentionally resembling a fierce medieval warrior, he glowered down at her where she huddled in the chair he'd just so tenderly deposited her in.

"Just what in God's name are you doing here at this ungodly hour then?" he demanded.

"I thought," she said in a small voice, "that Will could help me, I think. I didn't know where else to go," she whispered even lower, as her eyes began to fill with tears for the first time since all her adventures began this evening, "and well, oh I don't know, it just seemed the only place to go. I was so confused and unhappy and I just found myself heading for here, since I knew Will was here, and you and . . ." But she didn't finish saying what naturally came next, for she couldn't bear to admit her unthinking, unhesitant reliance on someone who now looked as though he wished to murder her and cast her lifeless from his house.

"And you were right," he said, shaking his tousled head, even as her first tear doused his white-hot rage and tempered it to cool, keen reason, "this is exactly where you should have come.

"Exactly where you belong," he whispered as she at last came into his open arms with a sob, as he gently pulled her there. He held her close then, and comforted her, and only that—no matter what his butler thought as he sniffed and turned on his side in his bed, and imagined his employer doing with the young female in the library, and envied him heartily all the long way down to sleep for, as well.

THIRTEEN

SHE LOOKED VERY well there, he thought, though he couldn't utter the compliment aloud. It was an entirely inconsequential thought, anyway. But now, as she rested and sighed with relief as though she'd put down a heavy weight, the first thought that sprang to his mind was how very well she looked tucked up into his favorite chair, with a lap rug he'd ferreted out of the closet covering her. She looked like a sweetly sleepy child peeking out of her coverlets, no never a child, he corrected himself, for if she really put him in mind of one, he'd have no difficulty speaking to her now as she awaited his reply.

Her color had returned after she'd done weeping in his arms and he'd administered another cordial and wrapped her into the rug, and then sat quietly and heard out the whole of the story. Now she was pink-cheeked and shining-eyed. Her long lustrous hair spilled around her. In the dim light, the manner in which she lay back and cuddled comfortably into the rug, the disarray of her clothes and hair, all made her a delicious vision that conjured up disorderly thoughts of tumbled bedclothes, coverlets, and pillows for him, as well as a great many other untidy delights that he had to forget entirely before he spoke one more word to her.

There were yet other things that came to his mind that he would have to strictly set aside before he could speak. What Methley had done, her bedeviled listener had thought all the while that she related the abortive "adventure" she'd endured, was far worse than villainous, it was stupid. There were gentlemen who subscribed to the belief that cold women could be warmed by heated stories and pictures. That made no more sense, Barnabas thought, than believing someone terrified of dogs would become a fancier of the breed if locked in a kennel with a pack of them overnight. But he couldn't tell her this either, not yet.

Because there was one grain of pure reason that had shone through all of Methley's clouded thinking, which doubtless had spurred on the madness. She did fear men, there was no doubt she did, if he had not heard it from her lips, he had nonetheless tasted it there, it had shaped her life, it had touched his, and it would be difficult, if not impossible, for any man to win her as things were. Shyness in a well-bred young female was understandable; reluctance, or a good imitation of it, to engage in lovemaking was often encouraged, but Faith's reaction to an embrace transcended this. Her immediate response was very close to sheer terror.

That very point had been troubling him for the past days easily as much as it had evidently preyed on the earl's mind tonight. But bringing her to a bordello so that she might see the act and so put aside her fears of it? Methley might have done more damage this night, Lord Deal sighed, than even he had originally intended. Likely the earl had planned ruination for her, if only of her reputation, so that she'd have to accept his suit, and hadn't thought of any damage done to her mind or soul. Or did he even care, Barnabas thought savagely, so long as her fortune remained intact?

It was the devil of a coil, he realized, running his hand through his thick, shaggy hair for want of something more constructive to do. Here he sat with a delectable creature he liked very well, alone and at an hour past midnight, and he couldn't even tell her how lovely she looked to him. Nor did he dare touch her, certainly not after what she'd seen tonight. Nor could he admit that he understood why her abductor had treated her to the sights he had. All he could do was to be her friend, a better friend than he'd ever been to any man or maid, for whatever else transpired, he was determined that he not let her down as he'd failed Nettie all those years ago.

But even if he succeeded in that, he couldn't win. For as he was coming to see too clearly with each passing hour, what he wanted was to be far more than that to her. His instant, deep, and horrified reaction when he'd thought the worst had finally brought it home forceably to him. When he'd thought her violated, it was as though he himself had been. It was no longer any use denying it to himself, she'd crept, all unnoticed, which was perhaps the only way any female could have gotten past his guard, too deeply into his heart for him to ever pluck her out again.

He ought not to be surprised, he thought. She, after all, exemplified all that he had admired in the New World, and all that he valued in the old. She had morals (albeit it was possible she couldn't help that), manners, wit, and beauty, as well as a warm heart and high good humor. She could be a man's friend and partner, as so many of her countrywomen in the new wilderness had to be, since being decorative alone was never enough for a man there. Yet she could remain unquestionably a tempting female, as so many in his old world required a female to be. The problem was, he sighed again, it well might be that she could never be more than tempting, and would eternally appear to offer all that she could never give. And unfortunately for himself, he could never take that which was not given.

But now, it was he who must give something, and if that were only to be comfort, why then, he thought, he would try to give that in abundance. That commodity, he'd often found, came best if packaged in laughter, for the healing touch was often the lightest one.

"Would you like another cordial?" he asked pleasantly, watching the level of liquid in her glass shrink. "That way, we can float you home when the time comes, and won't have to bother to call a carriage at all."

"Oh dear," she said with a guilty start, for since she'd arrived she'd been taken up with so many things she'd never given a thought to her eventual return to her noble host and hostess's house. She'd been so glad to get here, away from the nightmarish streets she'd somehow managed to traverse, shrinking into the shadows at every coach that rattled by, running the faster for every man who'd looked to her or called to her or come near to her. Barnabas said it was a miracle she'd gotten to him safely, and so it was, and if it was, it wasn't the only thing to be grateful for. Barnabas himself had been rather a miracle too.

The moment she'd been able to wrench away from the earl and sprint down the deserted street, she'd known she couldn't go back to Lady Mary to see her guilt or return to the duchess to read the spite and deceit plain in her face. She'd thought of Will, and remembered he'd been lodging with Lord Deal. Or, she wondered only now as she sat safe and comforted, had she thought of Lord Deal, and then remembered Will might be with him? No matter, it might have been a miracle that she'd found a homeward-bound lamplighter who'd known the street and hadn't thought to taunt or terrorize an unescorted female. But the true miraculous revelation had come the moment she'd seen Barnabas open his door. Then she'd known she was saved from the night and safer than she'd ever been. Somehow she trusted him implicitly to protect her from any threat, even from herself.

But it had been odd when she'd found herself within his house, in his very chair, to see the athletic gentleman she'd always thought so vigorous and hardy turn pale with shock at her distress. She'd only managed to speak at last so that she could spare him further discomfort. His hazel eyes had been bleak with despair, his strong, long hands had shaken as he'd handed her a goblet of liquor to down. She'd never known she could affect someone so strongly, it amazed her still. Yet in a small, secret, dreadfully perverse part of her mind that she examined briefly now and then quickly hid again, she had never felt so powerful before either.

Then, of course, when he'd realized she was unhurt, she'd feared he might correct that circumstance in his rage at her. In all, she'd been through so much emotion, both hers and his, in the last hours, that she felt curiously numbed to all sensation, just as her hand felt sometimes when she'd leaned on it for too long.

Now she was safe, and it was very good to sit and talk with him in the dim quiet of the late night. It was singular for a well-bred young woman to visit a gentleman in the dead of the night and sit alone in his home, sipping strong spirits and laughing with him. It wasn't done in any country she knew of, it was shameless behavior, but it was very good, and she no longer cared a fig about all the rest. Too much had happened, there simply wasn't any emotion as strong as shame left to her. So when he mentioned her ultimate, proper destination, instead of being horrified at being reminded of her odd behavior, she pulled a face that made him laugh.

"I don't want to leave," she said childishly, snuggling down into the chair with a rebellious pout, since tonight, it seemed she could say anything to him.

"And I don't want you to either, but you shall." He smiled. "But not just yet," he added, and she sank back again with a relieved grin. "We'll think up a suitable revenge before you go," he said lazily as he seated himself on a hassock he dragged up close to her chair, and arranged his robe decorously around his legs. "Yes, absolutely, and we'll wake Will, too, to get his opinion. But in time," he reassured her and himself, "all in due time. Let's let them all stew a while longer, the duchess and Lady Mary, and Methley, too."

When her grin faded at the mention of the earl's name, he decided to pull those fangs first. And the best defense against dread, he decided, was disrespect.

"Methely," he said, "is a corkbrain. I suspect it's possible he thought you might find the view he'd exposed you to either inspiring or incriminating enough to move you to immediate wedlock. It was fortunate then, that as it happened, even less was seen of you than you saw of the activities there. Ah, yes, our illustrious longlegs is much more of a misguided clunch than a villain. Unless, of course, he was just a blameless patriotic sort of fellow who felt that Mother Carey's establishment was a must-see on any American tourist's itinerary, second only to the Tower in historic value. It might have been that he took you there to impress you with Britain's supremacy in vice as well as virtue."

"But we have such at home too, you know," she murmured over a suppressed giggle.

"Oh, really?" he replied, noting that her color had returned in force, and beginning to wonder if there wasn't a deal more in Methley's method than he'd previously supposed, since she now was recovering very nicely indeed. But then he understood that the combination of her relief, the cordials, the warmth, and the absurd hour of the night was making her giddy, and was very glad of it. So he refused to make Methley's mistake and stifled an impulse to tell her he knew the places she spoke about only too well, and said negligently instead, "But I doubt you'd take tourists there, would you?"

"Oh, no, I wouldn't have to," she said airily. "We're much more modern. We run regular tours of such places on Saturdays and holidays at home."

He rocked back in soft laughter and then smiled his approval at her. Though they sat close, the room was so still they unwittingly spoke in ever diminishing, subdued voices, and when, now and again, one of them laughed, even that sound was automatically muted in respect for their privacy and the dreaming night surrounding them. What had begun in fear was growing into a shared mood of increasingly high spirits. It wasn't long before they reached a point of night and mood where silly things seemed exquisitely clever, and the merest jest attained heights of hilarity the sober day could never equal.

He congratulated her on her homeland's superior wisdom, and began to complain at how it was just his luck that he'd missed the tour when he'd been there, and although his conversation remained within the limits of delicacy, of course, his topic could not. She suffered an onslaught of muffled giggles when he agreed that it was a splendid idea and asked her if she'd have been more comfortable this evening if Methley had gone about the thing the open, frank new American way and appointed the duchess as her guide.

"Methley said," she finally said thoughtfully, gazing down fixedly at her lap, ignoring his question as she rightly should, "that if I looked close, I might even discover you there—at Mother Carey's tonight, I mean."

"Oh," Lord Deal said, and wondered if his own color was rising, for absurdly, he felt as discomfitted as a schoolboy. So he gave her truth for truth. "Perhaps if you'd looked several years ago, you might have. But even then you'd have had to go to the upper regions of the house and throw open a door in order to do so, I'm afraid. I've never thought lovemaking was an art for public exhibition. I believe an audience of one is sufficient for any man," he said primly, while privately he was scarcely attending to his own words, as he was rapidly realizing this was becoming the most unorthodox conversation he'd ever had with any female, lady or not.

It was decidedly titillating, while it was not intended to be, since knowing he couldn't touch her he didn't speak with the purpose of arousing her, although it was definitely having the opposite effect upon himself. He was, he discovered, enjoying the experience enormously. It was novel and liberating, as well as exciting to speak with a woman as though she were a man and yet all the while remain acutely and delightfully aware that it was a warm and beautiful female he addressed and not a male friend.

But then she brought him down to earth.

"It certainly isn't for public display," she agreed vehemently, remembering the scene and pleased to see that a man agreed with her, most especially this man whom she wished very much to explain herself to. She went on rapidly, forgetting all her humor in her anxiety to make it clear, "It's frightening to see such violence of emotions, such lack of control in ordinarily proper people, such wild abandon. And that's only what there is to see," she laughed nervously. "The noises, the racket they make, they could wake the dead. Such ugly noises, and the protests, the promises, the florid, half-finished threats, I find that perhaps as terrible as . . ." Her voice trailed off as she heard what she'd been saying, and saw, even in the dim light, that he was no longer smiling. He sat before her, very still, his clear, knowing eyes suddenly studying her keenly. Yet when he spoke he seemed as troubled as he'd been when he'd first tended to her.

"Faith," he said softly, looking at her so steadily she could not drop her own gaze through the force of his, "Mother Carey's is always crowded. Mother Carey's is so noisy, there's such a constant party in progress, that I doubt you heard very much from the unlovely couple, even if they were coupling in such an abandoned fashion— which I very much doubt, since you said you only saw them for a moment before you turned away. Faith," he said seriously, "will you tell me about it? If it was not seen on the mythical tour we jested at, it was something similar, and very real to you. Don't retreat from me. It's late and dark and there's only the two of us here. What does it matter, after all? Just speak it as you recall it. What was it you were telling me about just now?''

It was indeed late, and dark, and she'd had a great many things happen to her in a very short space of time. And something this night had disturbed something in her memory. Something had been rudely jogged loose and would not fit back into place again, and that was an excellent excuse to deafen herself to all the warning voices and at last this late night let the dark thing out into its own element for him, as he'd asked.

''Well,'' she said in an attempt to be flippant, but very quickly so that she'd have the thing out and said before there was any help for it, ''I was young, you see, and visiting with my mama at my father's home in Virginia. They'd gotten together for my birthday. I was ten, and that was the last time they tried a reconciliation at his house, so I remember it well. There was a thunderstorm that woke me in the night, and I went wandering the halls, because I never sleep well in strange surroundings, and the slave that was supposed to watch over me was dead asleep, poor girl.

''I found them in the salon,'' she said on a brittle, artificial laugh, ''though they never saw me, of course. And then I ran back to bed, that was all there was to it, it was never so much actually, but still you see, I suppose that's why it's true I've always disliked the thought of that sort of behavior. It's an unlovely thing to witness. At Mother Carey's, or anywhere else.''

She lowered her head and gave her empty glass sudden acute scrutiny, unable to speak another word lest her heart leap from her mouth, as she was amazed to discover it beating so rapidly she thought it must burst its bounds.

All the while, he attempted to think very fast. He'd asked for the moon and gotten it, and now wondered at whether he could bear up under its weight. For if he knew anything, it was that whatever he said next would be of prime importance to them both.

''Not quite like Mother Carey's,'' he commented with forced casualness. ''It's not as though you went looking for the experience.''

''I heard voices,'' she said at once, in a little voice, with such a palpable plea for absolution in it that he knew that somehow he had stumbled across the right path to take to lead her to reassurance, at least, "and noises, dreadful noises, too. At first, I thought he was beating her. She looked in pain. I didn't see his face, but he seemed insensible, unreasonable. Luckily, even though I was only a child, something in the drama of it, something in the steady pace of it, alerted me, so that I knew it was none of it for me, and ran."

"You weren't snooping, love," he assured her gently then. "Unfortunately you were only looking for comfort at the same moment they were."

Heedless of her gasp, he went on lightly, never giving a hint as to how he groped for wisdom, knowing only as he heard each word he said that he was saying the right thing because it sounded very right to him. He could do no more for himself, and no less for her, than to trust his own innate good judgment now.

"It's odd actually," he said thoughtfully, "because when we imagine our ancestors' lovemaking, it's the epic stuff of high romance. When we consider it between our grandparents, it's quaint, but when we think of in between our parents, it's obscene. It's not, of course, it's only shocking. And in your case, unfortunate. Still, it's strange, even for you bold Americans, to find a couple, bare as Adam in the garden, disporting in the salon at midnight."

"Of course they weren't bare," she snapped at once, surprised to find herself defensive. "They were completely clothed, or as much as they could be under the circumstances, I think. Well, I'm not an expert in the matter, and it was night, and there wasn't much light, only now and again lightning flashes, but there wasn't much question what was happening. Or," she admitted more quietly, seeing at last just why she'd finally told the thing she'd never let herself so much as reflect upon before, "well, when I saw that couple tonight, I finally knew exactly what it was I'd seen then, only I suppose at that time I'd guessed and heard more than I'd actually seen."

"I'd suppose," he said carefully, "that you guessed a great deal more."

He wished he had the age or sagacity or expertise to explain the matter to her and himself, because he so badly didn't want to fail her. And then, because it meant so much to her and to him, he told her precisely that, and added, "I'm at a disadvantage, because it's scarcely the sort of thing gentlemen and gently bred women are supposed to talk about together, although I imagine they should. But Faith, I don't think it really mattered what you saw that night, not at all. It's what you thought you saw that matters. And I believe that would depend on what you saw afterward. If, in the morning you'd seen your parents smiling and behaving lovingly or even pleasantly to each other, you'd have put the thing away and counted it a dream. But if you saw them battling still, your father swaggering and triumphant, and your mother bitter and resentful, for example, why then . . ." He let his voice trail off.

"I'm no all-seeing eye," he admitted as she stared at him astounded. "Will told me how it was with them. But good heavens, girl, if their entire life together is an angry contest, what would you expect their lovemaking to be like? It isn't how it should be, or could be, or is, for everyone. Faith, no more than every marriage is the same. Or every act of love. But you never saw an act of love, my girl. Methley took you to see what money can buy. Those years ago you chanced upon an ugly glimpse of sudden lust. Neither night had anything to do with the way it could be for you."

And me, he thought, but there his courage failed him.

"Faith," he said seriously, "we humans don't learn everything by direct observation of our parents. It may well be why we make so many of the same mistakes, but," he grinned unexpectedly, "it may also be why we make so many wonderful new discoveries for ourselves as well. I should be very surprised if you looked forward to wedlock after witnessing the battle your parents were locked in for years. But," he added, determined to be absolutely frank with her, "I'd also be more astonished if you threw over the whole idea of it because of them.

"And," he said with conviction, "if you've used what you saw one stormy night as a reason to shun all of us fellows all of your life, why, Faith, I tell you, you disappoint me. Because it was never those few moments you spied by chance that was half so obscene as what went forth between that man and that woman for all those days and nights, through all those years of your life. And that, my dear, is what you oughtn't to have seen.''

Then he rose to his feet before her and spoke like a pretentious orator because he was weary with solemnity. "And as a male," he intoned in aggrieved accents, "I speak for all of us when I say that it's hardly fair to us. We're an excellent group, as a class, and just because some of our efforts in certain physical matters aren't always considered to be particularly picturesque, we oughtn't to be dismissed as totally unseemly. Besides, most of us are wonderful creatures. There may, of course, be a few whose behavior doesn't speak well for the rest of us. But I resent your being so prejudiced against us because of the actions of one, or perhaps two . . . or maybe three, no more, surely than four . . . or possibly five or six of our number."

She didn't know how she could laugh so heartily now. She'd supposed he'd guessed it might have been her own attitude that had prompted the earl's actions. She'd as much as confessed her aversion to intimacy to Barnabas, and he hadn't turned a hair. Then she'd told him the most dreadful thing, and immediately experienced deserved shame and embarrassment, along with feeling terribly traitorous and foul-minded. But then he'd taken the incident as commonplace and when it was discussed as a commonplace, for the first time, it seemed to become one. Then he made her laugh at the absurdity of it, and himself, and herself, and the whole foolish world she'd taken too seriously, it seemed, for far too long.

"Now," he said, nodding in approval at her merriment, and then listening to his mantel clock strike two long, lonely notes and looking down at his bare feet, "time to prevent your peeking further at my lovely ankles, wicked thing. I'm going to get dressed and roust Will up and tell him about this night. Not all about it, of course, there's things in it that only concern we two," he said at once, before she could ask him to keep her confidence, "and I want you to sit back and be comfortable, and do not stir, and certainly do not leave this room under my threat of several instant and extremely creative forms of death.

"And oh," he added, as he began to exit, making a show of wrapping his robe around himself with such exaggerated prissiness that she had to hold her hand to her mouth to smother her mirth, "if any young women happen by on the way back from an abduction, with a pressing problem or two to thrash out, please give them each a number and a chair, and tell them to wait for me. I shan't be long."

He'd reached the door when he heard her say in a small voice, "Barnabas?"

"Yes?" he answered, instantly serious, instantly concerned.

"In the morning, in the daytime, shall you be shocked at me?"

"No, Faith," he said, the warmth in his voice as evident as his relaxation, "no. The time of day makes no difference in my attitude. I'm tediously constant, unvarying as the evening star, which shines in the day just as it does in the night, whether you can see it or not. I'm not shocked at you now, nor will I be tomorrow."

I only shock myself, he thought as he took the stairs two at a time, and congratulate myself, too. For in all this time, from the moment you sat in my chair, I never once touched you, as I longed to do.

At three hours into a new day, Lord Deal and Mr. Will Rossiter escorted Miss Faith Hamilton to the Duke and Duchess of Marchbanks' London home. It was a quiet, if a spectacular reunion. There seemed to be a great deal more left unsaid than ever was spoken by any of the persons in the ornate and echoing entry hall.

Lord Deal explained simply and smoothly the great good fortune of their happening to meet up with Miss Hamilton shortly after she'd gotten separated and lost from her companions in the crush at the Vauxhall Gardens. As he went on to explain, it seemed quite natural then that the three of them should have decided to order dinner and wait for the duchess, Lady Mary, and the earl to return. After the concert and the dancing, they'd waited until almost every last soul had strolled out of the gardens and the management had almost begun to fold up the tables, stars, and grass about them before they'd decided they'd not likely find her companions at Vauxhall again this night. Then they set out to return to the noble Bolton townhouse.

And then, of course, only foul luck, in the form of a shoe cast by the leader of the team that graced Lord Deal's carriage, prevented them from carrying out their plans immediately. After the horse had been tended to, after it had been replaced, of course, they'd come directly to their destination. But how time flew!

A red-faced, confused duke accepted the tale, the trio seemed sincere, Lord Deal was a nobleman, and there was no evidence of anything else besides. It was irregular, but it would do. But all during the narrative the duke continued to dart suspicious glances to the others who'd been standing watch with him for Miss Hamilton's return.

The duchess then explained again, with a self-correction as frequent as a stammer to impede her speech at every other word, that as Miss Hamilton had gotten herself lost, she and her daughter had gone on to their appointment at the Swansons' in the hopes that the earl, who'd stayed behind to find their guest, would soon deliver her to them there. The earl, strangely subdued, only said that it was incredible he'd not come across the trio, since he'd thought he'd covered every inch of the place twice over in his night-long search for the young woman.

And Lady Mary said nothing, not even to Will when he looked at her with all his heart plain in his eyes, but only stood whitefaced and hangdog until Miss Hamilton bade everyone good night and begged and got leave to go to her bed.

"Faith?" Lady Mary said in a choked voice as she touched the other girl's sleeve tentatively when they'd reached the top of the stair. Her guest wheeled about so sharply that the fair-haired girl almost toppled over and tumbled down the stair, and wished she had done when she saw the look blazing in her American guest's eyes.

"Not a word," Faith managed to threaten through her tightly clenched teeth. "Tonight, please not one word from or for you, my lady. I dare not begin. I am, after all, a guest in this, your house. But tomorrow, perhaps. Now good night, my lady, and," she spat with enough force to make her listener wince before she spun around and marched to her room, "sleep well!"

The duchess said nothing further to her husband on the matter, but left him to a lonely glass of port, protesting a headache so profound that he might have been forgiven if he'd called a surgeon to see to her on the instant. Instead, he made no reply, but sat glowering and thinking deeply for another long hour of the night.

Will Rossiter went alone and silent as well, but only to a seat in the carriage outside the Boltons' door. For his host had stayed a moment to speak with the other departing gentleman, The Earl of Methley.

"We need to meet, I think," Lord Deal said coldly as he faced the other gentleman on the pavement.

"Is it to be pistols or sabers? At dawn tomorrow, or the next day?" the earl asked humorlessly.

"I have no wish to be exiled at the moment," Lord Deal replied in a tone of voice that was in itself an insult, "so it is to be now, and for the time being at least, only to exchange words. And a very few of them at that. You don't require me to tell you how ugly a trick it was. But perhaps you do need me to tell you that I will finish you if you ever attempt such a thing again—if you ever come near her again."

The earl was paler than was even his natural wont, and his long frame stiffened as he gave in reply, just as tersely, as deep an apology as he was capable of ever giving this gentleman, even though it was delivered in as harsh a manner as a snub might have been.

"It was never intended to be more than a lesson, and it was, I can see now, a miscalculated and miscarried one. I shall apologize to her for that. Indeed, I think I have never been so sorry for any mischance I've caused. But I did not touch her. And I will see her again, I don't think you have the right to prevent me. Only she does, and if she does, I'll not trouble her again. But if she does not, I can only assure you that I intend to go on as I should in the matter, as a gentleman."

"And as a suitor?" Lord Deal asked icily, his last word as sharp as a slap.

"And as a suitor," the earl replied coldly, and then he smiled bitterly as he added in farewell before he turned and ended the interview, "I may be only a mundane earl, and not a dashing farmer, but stranger things have happened, Deal, odder pairs have formed beneath your, and my, very noble noses, as you and I may do well to remember.''

''Methley,'' Lord Deal murmured unheard after a pause, to that gentleman's retreating back, ''she is long dead. Bury her, as I have done, perhaps only just tonight.''

Then he joined the sorrowing Will in the carriage and they rode home in silence. For Will was busily making up excuses for his lady so that he would not grieve for her lapse. And Lord Deal was preoccupied with his lady, who was never a lady, but rather something, he thought, a great deal better.

It had been a extraordinary night for discoveries, for himself as well as for his wild Indian maiden. Because, as he'd always lamented the fact that he was not susceptible to such a tender passion as love, he supposed it was only fair that he now found himself to be suffering from the malady. It was also ironic, after all his smug complaints about his imperviousness to the disorder, that he should find the particular strain afflicting him to be a virulent one that was not only incurable, but doubtless fated to presage a long and painful lingering ailment. For it appeared that even if she could ever learn to reciprocate his feelings, his poor love could not bring herself to physical love with any man.

And for all his supposed wit, he had no more idea of how to help her from that state than he had of how to cure himself of the condition he could have sworn he was immune to, but which would now doubtless bring him low.

FOURTEEN

On a sultry August morning in London, a young American girl known to very few members of the *ton* established a record in society that was never to be broken, although it was also never to be known. For on a humid summer's day, Miss Faith Hamilton, otherwise known as "the Wild Indian," received three splendid, bonified offers of marriage within as many hours, and although one of them might have only been from another American, he was a nabob, and the other two were from accredited members of the *ton*, and both noblemen, no less.

This successfully bested an achievement of a previous generation, in which a certain Miss Camille Plunket, opera dancer, received four offers from four wealthy, titled gentlemen all in the same day, since two of them were being blackmailed, and the other two had wagered a monkey on which of them could win her, and a case of champagne on which of them had fathered the babe she claimed to carry. But that was in a gaudier generation, and all those offers came during the course of an entire day. And that statistic was also never to be verified by all the gentlemen involved. As was the case two years previous to Miss Hamilton's triumph, when a Miss Jessica Eastwood also received three worthy offers all in a day, but they too were issued in a time period lasting from morning until dusk and so also would have failed to qualify, even if they had been made known by the lady, who generously kept the tally to herself even after she'd wed the gentleman of her choice. Thus, even Lady Elizabeth Porter's famous claim of having received four offers in a row at a riotous ball, all refused, still stands as the goal to which young women should aspire, although, as it was a very long evening and a very inebriated company, clearly it does not merit such attention.

But Faith had no idea of how she would be so singularly honored when she opened her eyes too soon to a dank and sullen summer's morning. Had it been a cooler day perhaps she would have slept longer and so missed her chance at making history, but the clammy touch of the bedclothes and the thick warm air roused her as thoroughly as a bracingly chill wind might have done. It was no pleasure to lie abed on such moist sheets no matter how late she'd laid herself to sleep on them. So she woke and washed herself thoroughly in cool water, despite her country-bred maid's repeated muttered misgivings about the unhealthiness of such frequent immersions, hot or cold, as the American girl favored. Then she dressed in her lightest, lowest-cut cotton gauze gown, sat at a little table by an open window, and frowned down at her toast as though it had somehow offended her.

She'd had too much new information received, and too little time in which to assimilate it all. It would have been to her advantage, if not to history's, to sleep this day away. For dreams, and the sleep which brings them, help the mind to digest an overload of information. But she'd woken prematurely and found the same problems on her plate, perhaps only a little smaller than when seen through night's magnifying eyes, but no less real and no more appealing.

She'd been betrayed by her hostess and her daughter, been made a figure of fun for society to scoff at, and then been compromised by a gentleman who sought her hand and her purse. Though she'd been saved by her own wit and solaced by another gentleman who meant, she discovered, a very great deal to her, she'd confessed the unthinkable to him and no matter how he dressed it up, there could be little question she'd taken herself down in his estimation by it. Add to that the fact that she'd been made to observe unseemly things that had recalled to mind a similar sight which had also changed her life after she'd seen it. And then, multiply her woes by the fact that somehow now in retrospect, quite incredibly, her remembrance at least of the sight of the previous night's ardent strangers seemed more titillating than terrifying, and the sum of it was one confused and very angry young woman.

But clearly nothing mattered anymore. Not if half the

world giggled at the thought of her as a naked wild Indian, and the other half soon would when they heard of her latest exploit. She wasn't willing, not now, to delve too deeply into the matter of Lord Deal's charity to her, except for the fact that she knew that she'd keep the memory of their shared secret hours of the past night close to her always, whatever, she thought ruefully, became of her misled, mismanaged, and miserable life in the future.

Thus it was that her first visitor on that historic day quailed at the first sight of her fierce expression. Lady Mary had hoped that the passage of the night had muted her visitor's rage, but one look at the cold, immobile features and the glittering eye her guest turned coolly upon her when she entered the room caused her words to catch in her throat. She only managed a "good morning," and then had to sit in shame-faced silence until the maid, all curiosity, as all good maids were, finally found no further excuse to linger and left them alone together.

"I came," Lady Mary said with supreme bravery, "to apologize." After a silence greeted this, and since she discovered she still lived, she gathered up a bit more courage and said, "I was against the idea, truly I was, Faith. But Mama said it was all for the best. And since I agreed that the earl is all anyone might wish for in a husband, I went along with Mama. But still I felt dreadful when she hurried me away last night, I actually felt ill when we ran off from you, like thieves in the night. I didn't want to go, but what could I do? Oh Faith, please don't be cross with me. I meant it all for the best. And there was nothing I could do, even if I did not."

"Nothing you could do?" asked Faith, her voice the only clear and cold thing in the overheated room, since her anger caused her temperature to rise to match the atmosphere. "Nothing you could do?" she repeated caustically, adding the glow of her fiercely burning bridges to the heat of the day. "Nothing you could do only if you were indeed the child they treat you as. But you're not. Mary, that was a low and dirty trick you played on me, and if that's how you folks go on in high society, well then, I'm glad I'm halfway on my way home now. Because my mind is made up even if my luggage isn't."

Faith fixed her visitor with a direct stare, and shook her

head until her silken hair began to slide from its neat knot. "I'll be honest with you then, Mary, because I reason that I've one foot aboard ship right now, and it's easier to be candid when you know you'll soon be gone. You're a pretty enough girl, and friendly too, but all surface, like all the rest of this society you've been so pleased to try to get me caught up in. When I'm safe and home again I'll feel sorry for you, Mary, yes I shall. Because whatever else befalls me in the future, at least I'll always know that it's myself I can blame, or myself I can praise for it.

"But you," Faith said, more in sorrowful appraisal than anger now, looking her white-faced visitor up and down, "why, Mary, you live a life you don't even own. It's all on borrow from your mama, and then, no doubt, it will be your husband that orders it. I expect you'll be exactly like your mama too some day, because I really think the only chance that you'll ever get to live a life will be when you live your daughters'.

"Well," Faith said philosophically, standing up and going to the door to let her guest out before she let all the rest of her anger and contempt out into the open as well, "I hope for your sake that you have daughters, then. Or, that is, that your husband lets you have them. But I hope for your children's sake you have only sons. Because," she said, as Lady Mary saw her eagerness to be rid of her and obediently rose and moved dazedly toward the door, "it seems to me that the only folks you let choose their own destiny around here are the men. I don't know if Will knows he'll be getting a little girl if you take him, and I don't know if he'll mind being a papa to his wife, along with his children. But it seems a rotten trick to play on him too, because like me, I expect he thinks a grown-up person is a grown-up person, no matter if she's a female or not.

"And," Faith said, just before she closed the door on her erstwhile friend, "I don't want the earl for a husband, and I think you knew that right enough all the while. So I think if you thought he was such a worthy fellow, you should have had a care for him as well, and not tried to foist an unwilling wife on him. But Mary, I expect you can't be a good friend to anybody until you're a good friend to yourself. And that, you're surely not, because if you were, why then, I think you'd let yourself grow up, and get on with your own life.''

Then, closing the door, having unburdened herself of this excellent advice, Faith quite naturally felt even worse than she had before. Although she was sorely tempted to call her visitor back and take everything she'd said for kindness's sake, she knew you could never take back truth, since it had a way of sounding so exactly right that any attempt to rescind it always failed, just as attempting to improve on any perfection did.

She decided to pen a quick note summoning Will, for she was sick of this house and more than eager to put her plans into motion at once. There was no place to go but home. But even as she wrote the words she began to realize that having at last achieved the goal she'd set when she'd arrived here, it had become no victory but only an ignominious retreat. And as she wrote the word "home" on the paper, she discovered that it seemed more distant than ever now in both memory and desire, and further from what she really wanted than she would ever have believed possible.

So it was that her second guest of the day saw only deep and abiding sorrow in her large gray eyes, and none of the rage and contempt that it had been Lady Mary's lot to observe.

But then the Earl of Methley was more subdued than she'd ever seen him to be himself, and after he bowed over her hand and she seated herself in the salon and waited for him to speak, his voice was so serious she scarcely recognized its deep and somber tones. His long white face was grave, and there was no scintillation in his eyes, they were, this morning, unusually for him, as innocent and gray as the first moment of dawn.

"My behavior last night," he said straightaway, "was despicable. I know it. Perhaps I even knew it then. But I'd convinced myself it was all for your own good, knowing all the while it was all for my good as well. I wanted very much for you to accept my suit, Faith, and was anxious enough for our union to try anything that might facilitate it. Whatever," he said dismissively, as though the subject bored him, though from how painfully he spoke it was apparent that was the only thing it did not do, "it was a cur's trick, and I more than apologize. Whatever satisfaction you wish from me, you may have. Although the only thing I have to offer you is myself, and that is precisely what I was attempting to give to you with all my mechanations. I still want very much to marry you, Faith,'' he said solemnly.

She remained very still, but when it became plain that he would say no more until he knew her mind, she spoke at last. Her voice was low and thoughtful; all anger having been burned out earlier, she now was capable only of sad reflection.

"No," she said thoughtfully, looking up at him where he stood awaiting her judgment, "you were not looking 'to give me yourself,' my lord. You were wishful of receiving me. It appears to me," she went on reflectively, "that the duchess and Lady Mary had me all wrapped up like a gift, and you were all ready to unwrap me. But," she grinned unexpectedly, looking up at him with a cynical expression very much like ironic amusement sitting oddly on her gentle, lovely face, "I do think you wouldn't have been at all pleased with your present, my lord. Oh no. For I'm not at all what your sort of gentleman expects. Oh, I would have come with all the trimmings, I'm dowered just as lavishly as you'd think. And really, I can't blame you for being interested in that part of the bargain—I'm aiming to be a merchant, remember. But the rest of me would be no bargain for you.

"I'm not at all the soft and agreeable sort of female you've been brought up to look for in a wife, like Lady Mary. Why, I think you'd have to beat me every morning to get me to agree with you every night, and likely you'd have to hang me by my thumbs or starve me out regularly to get me to sit in the shadows and obey your every command, as you'd expect of a good wife.

"And it's not just that I seem to have been fearful of lovemaking," she said with a small smile, pausing for a moment, diverted by the discovery that once an unspeakable thing has been said, it becomes increasingly speakable, and that repetition seemed to kill shame as surely as it slew wit, before she went on to muse aloud, "it's that I guess I can't seem to understand how all of you gentlemen think of young women as commodities. You mock me for wanting to be a merchant, my lord, but you and the duchess, who both made it clear you wouldn't stain your hands with trade, why you trade off daughters and wives like we deal in cotton and tobacco at home, seeing the whole matter as one of profit and loss. And I guess,'' she said, her accent becoming more pronounced with each revolutionary thought she voiced, ''I just don't think of myself and my future as being part of a business deal. If I ever wed, it will be for the pure joy of it, my lord, and dollars and cents just wouldn't figure in. It doesn't,'' she said at last, summoning up a real smile for him, ''add up that way for me.''

The earl looked at her, she thought, as though he were seeing her for the first time, and something in that thought and in his gaze disturbed her, so she rose to her feet and put out her hand. ''I wish you luck, my lord. And as for your apology, no need. I think you did me a favor, after all. Because I'll be going home now, where I belong.''

''The Viking,'' said the earl suddenly, as Faith jumped at the name, though she told herself it was only in surprise, ''cultivated you at first because you were suspected of being a spy and he was set to find out if you were. My besetting sin is gossip, but sin can give birth to worthier things, you know. At least,'' he shrugged, ''that's how I discovered it. But did you know that?''

''Yes,'' she said, though she hadn't, though it made perfect sense.

''He has no interest in marrying,'' he went on. ''We are old rivals. That may explain his interest now, it may not. I only attempt to make you see that mine is a present, real, and valid offer, and I cannot say that he would ever offer.''

''I know all that,'' she said dully, for that too made sense—she'd expected little else.

''Is there no way I can prevail upon you to stay, and perhaps get to know me on your terms?'' he asked seriously, taking her hand into his large one and not releasing it at once.

''No,'' she said. ''No way,'' she agreed quietly, withdrawing her hand.

Thus, when Miss Hamilton's third visitor was announced, he came out to the small economical garden in the back of the house where she sat in the shade of a single plane tree, and he discovered her fanning herself in desultory fashion, looking sad, lost, and languishing, and as regretful as if she were the one that had caused this warm and airless day.

He was all done up in autumn hues, from his brown jacket to his dark brown inexpressionables to his red and brown checked waistcoat, and when she saw him Faith sighed.

"Good heavens, Will," she said weakly, "you make me warm just looking at you."

"I can't let you go home alone," he said at once, tightly, as though the heat gave him difficulty in speaking.

"Of course, you can," she sighed, "but if you can't, it doesn't matter, because if you know me, Will Rossiter, and it would be passing strange if you didn't, you'd know I'm going anyway."

He seated himself next to her on the wicker settle and took her hand in his. She stopped fanning herself and looked at him in some alarm. He looked older and infinitely weary. There were deep shadows beneath his troubled brown eyes and there was a grim cast to his usually laughing mouth.

"When I discovered what happened last night, Faith, I was beside myself," he said. "I would've called Methley out because of it, but Barnabas kept me up for the rest of the night convincing me he had the matter in hand. It *is* his country and in the end, toward dawn, I had to agree he'd know best what to do about it. But do you want me to stand for you in this matter, Faith?"

"Indeed, I do not," she cried in alarm.

"Then marry me, Faith," he said with great sincerity, nodding as though she'd confirmed something to him, "and we'll return together."

"Don't be a nodcock," she said angrily, shaking off his hand and glowering at him.

"I understand," he persisted, "that you were shocked at what you must have seen last night, and that, of course, you're probably even more reluctant to wed because of it, but Faith, listen, I of all people wouldn't expect more from you than friendship in marriage, and we'd make your grandfather very happy, and who knows what time and maturity will bring to us?''

"Only gray hairs and the grave, Will," she snapped. "For heaven's sake, stop being such a gapeseed. Methley took me to see the goings-on in a bawdy house, he didn't employ me there. Oh now just look at you, Will, you're redder than a beet, you're a symphony in overheated colors, my boy. You ought to go douse your head in cold water and then change to something nice and cool before you visit Mary. I think she can use some cheering up far better than I can use a human sacrifice today, thank you. I . . .'' she went on in less confident tones, "was rather cruel to her this morning.''

Upon hearing this, the look upon her companion's face was so far removed from that which one would expect of a gentleman who had just offered her his life and fortune that despite herself, Faith began laughing. Then, at his aggrieved expression, she giggled, "But Will, you oughtn't to look like you were going to murder the lady you'd just asked to marry you. It doesn't speak well for your good intentions. And at that,'' she said, sobering, "maybe I did you a good turn. Because I gave her a great deal to think about and if she's got any kind of head on her pretty white shoulders, she should be thinking about thinking for herself right now.

"Yes," she said suddenly, eagerly, "if you can get an audience with her alone, and maybe you can," she said excitedly, "because I believe the duchess has taken herself off on her rounds all day today, she's that anxious to avoid me. And you know I won't interrupt you. So go. This would be the perfect time to confront her with the truth of your intentions at last, Will, along with a nicely worded sincere offer.''

And in a very short order, she related the whole of her morning's conversation with Lady Mary to him, especially the part where nothing was said, but where she'd read volumes into the expression on the other girl's face as she'd finally crept from the room.

The butler at the Duke of Marchbanks' townhouse was sorely grieved. It was not for a servant to know better than his betters, but this day no titled one in the establishment seemed to remember what was the thing to do. The American guest, of course, could be expected to know nothing. But no one else appeared to be doing much better. A stream of gentlemen seemed dead set on having audiences with various females in the house, and the duchess wasn't there to forbid it, the duke had been gone since morning, and even Lady Mary had gently but firmly overruled any hints on propriety given by himself, the housekeeper, or her abigail.

The only good thing about it, the butler sighed as he went to usher yet another gentleman into precincts where a gentleman ought not to be alone with a young lady, was that it was summer, and in the summer in London there were few around to carry gossip through the heat, and so one could do a great many things that might never be heard of again. Or at least, so one could only hope.

The warmth had grown with the day, and so this time Miss Hamilton was to be found sitting alone on a spindly chair in a corner of the anteroom. The room was hers by default. The garden had grown too sultry, she knew that Lady Mary was holding an audience in the salon, and she didn't dare be so bold as to requisition the library or the drawing room or the grand salon for her personal use. The choice of the anteroom had been a happy accident, since she soon discovered that the high ceilings and tiled floor made it one of the few areas in the house that had any claim to coolness.

The gentleman, however, had no place to sit, and the butler, after having shown him to Miss Hamilton, retreated speedily so that he would not be called upon to provide any seating either. The servitor vowed to tell the footmen not to hurry if they were summoned to do the job. It was enough that he must cater to ill-bred whims, he thought righteously as he beat a rapid withdrawal to servants precincts, it would be more than too much if he were asked to pander to them.

But no one sat, or thought to sit, after the gentleman had entered the room. Miss Hamilton rose, and stood and gazed upon her visitor, and the gentleman simply took her hand and appeared to be content to stand, holding it, and looking down at her. She had been neither angry nor sad nor regretful when he'd appeared, as she'd been in turn for each of her other guests this day. She'd thought herself drained of emotion, and had only been surprised to hear his name spoken, and then briefly, delighted to see his face, and now was dismayed at the sudden, unexpected force of her reaction to his touch.

She'd thought herself enormously sophisticated today. She'd handled each of her visitors with wisdom and aplomb. But one look at his tanned face and the warmth in his knowing eyes and she'd found herself tongue-tied and shy. She was so glad to see him, and so overwhelmed with pleasure at the glad welcome evident in his face and in his eager step as he'd come into the room, that she grew angry with herself for being so overjoyed and vulnerable to him. So she blurted, when she could, "I'm going home, my lord. As soon as possible."

"What a lovely greeting," he said enthusiastically, holding on to her hand as though he were restraining her from boarding the clipper ship that was about to bear her off, rather than standing with her in a deserted anteroom in a townhouse in London. "You do know how to put a gentleman at his ease. It's a lucky thing that I'm a monster of conceit or I'd take that remark personally. Or," he asked, not laughing now but looking at her keenly, "ought I to after all?"

"Oh no," she gasped, "it's never you. It's Mary and the duchess, and the mess I've made of things."

"And what Methley did?" he asked seriously, his eyes searching her face.

"Oh no," she said, in her anxiety to convince him of her earnestness forgetting to defend herself, and staring directly back into his eyes. "I'm glad he did that, though I realize," she began to smile, "that makes me sound like a monster of lechery, doesn't it? But it made me understand a great many things—no, our talk last night did that," she admitted, averting her eyes again, and so not seeing his relieved smile. "But he offered for me this morning, you see, and I refused him, of course, just as I will everyone the duchess tosses me to. Why," she said nervously, "I don't think I'll draw an easy breath here again for fear she'll find a way to strand me with another of her favorites if I don't keep a sharp watch. No, I'm going home."

But she didn't try to retrieve her hand, and only noted with a sort of distant pleasure that it was a strong and warm clasp and that it was comfortable to stand thus with him.

"Well," he said emphatically, and she grinned at him so impulsively that he had to curb an impulse to take her up in his arms, "it would save us both, Methley and I, a great deal of money, but even so, I don't think it's a good idea. No, I disapprove of the notion in the strongest terms. No, I cannot like the idea at all," he said, shaking his shaggy head sadly in the negative.

"I recognize," he went on, as he rubbed his thumb slowly across the back of her hand, "that your leaving would mean that I could stop buying up all the caricatures I've found in shop windows in Picadilly recently, but it also might mean ruin for several starving artists. You wouldn't want to account for all those fellows dwindling to nothing, would you?" he inquired sweetly.

"For I've come to realize," he explained, looking down at her confusion with an ironic smile, "that between Methley and myself, and perhaps the duke as well, we've given rise to an entirely new industry: the manufacture of Miss Hamilton cartoons and broadsheets. It strikes me that as we're creating the same market we're supporting, if we cease buying them up, they'll cease to exist. Because, not to wound you, Faith, but I don't believe anyone else in Town has the slightest interest in them. It's a question of supply and demand. As a woman with business interests, you probably see this clearly. But as a charitable human being you must also see that if you leave, they'll starve, or at the least, languish, and you may well have Mr. Rowlandson's and Mr. Cruikshank's untimely deaths on your conscience."

She laughed at that until he added, quite soberly, "And mine as well."

His handsome face was very serious, and as she could not bring herself to look directly at him just then, she found herself studying his high white neckcloth and wondering how he could look so cool and bear the refreshing scent of pungent herbs on such a sweltering day. Then she discovered herself wondering how it would be if he removed that constricting cravat for comfort's sake, and then of course, she dropped her gaze to his blue and green waistcoat so that she would not refine upon the thought of whether that long, strong torso would be tanned equally golden as the bit of throat which showed above the neckcloth.

"Faith," he said urgently, and she looked up at that and so was trapped like a fly she'd once seen cased in a bit of amber, in his clear light gaze, "I don't want you to go. Not ever. Not from me. I know you must feel something of what I do, but I also know that there are some things that cannot be grown out of season. In time, Faith, in time, I believe we might have a future together. But not if you run home. And not if you remain here, I grant you that. Faith," he began, and then looked about them.

"Not even a chair," he sighed, "and I doubt you'd permit me to share that one with you, and I refuse to get on one knee to make a declaration."

"Methley once said the same," she said, unthinking.

"Oh did he?" Lord Deal said with great interest. "What an interesting proposal this will be then. Be sure to let me know if I become derivative, I should hate to bore you. Well then," he said abruptly, "if it's variety you're after . . ." and before her horrified eyes, he dropped to one knee in front of her.

"Miss Hamilton," he said on a weary sigh as she stared down at the top of his streaked and tawny mass of hair, "will you do me the honor—"

"Oh do get up, do get up," she chanted in panic, looking about the room, dreading anyone's interrupting them. "Oh please don't remain so," she cried, trying to tug him up by the arm, and when he simply stared at her, enjoying himself immensely, she grew frantic enough to actually venture to tug at that thick crop of hair. "Oh don't get on your knees to me, I do not deserve it, oh I cannot bear it," she almost sobbed in vexation.

Then he rose, even as she realized with astonishment how very loathe she was to loose her grip on the silky, clean feel of his hair beneath her fingers. And as he rose he caught her up with him until he held her close, and then he said, all seriousness, all laughter, "Faith, marry me. At once. Then we'll have all the time in the world to work the rest of it out. I'd never force you, or hurry you or coerce you or compromise you, believe that. Mind, I don't cede the point, don't think I intend to give up that future physical delight, I only swear that I'm content to wait on it. I believe that in your time, in good time, you'll come to me, on your own, without fear. I must believe that, and so should you. For we're friends, Faith, and that's good and rare enough in this cold world, for now. I'll wait on the rest, it will come. And who knows what other joys time will bring to us?''

"But that's what Will said," she thought aloud, so that she would not have to think of an answer for him, she was so dazzled and flustered by his proximity, his voice, his words, his scent, and his arms about her.

"Oh Faith," he chuckled, looking down into her perplexed eyes, "we shall have to see to finding you some other sort of hobby. There's no way I can make a decent proposal when you've half the kingdom's offers to compare with mine. Have you done nothing today but be wooed? You can only have one of us, no matter how many gentlemen you've conquered. Don't you know we British frown on multiple marriages?" he asked, trying valiantly to keep the subject light, to keep his thoughts and his gaze from her soft, parted lips. Yet by looking into her eyes he could see that she was staring in fascination at his own mouth as he spoke.

He groaned, she may have too. It seemed they drew together. It might have been that their lips touched. It might have only been that they came so close that it was possible. But it was he who drew away instantly, ruefully, abashed.

"A fine way," he murmured, stepping back from her, "to assure you of my fine resolve. I *am* resolved though, Faith. I have faith in myself . . . good lord, there's that name again, see the trap you set for me?" He laughed briefly but then said very seriously, "I believe in myself, and value you. Nothing will change that, certainly not marriage, and not intimacy. It might only make me love you the more, in a different fashion, to add to what I already feel. Didn't you know that?" he asked tenderly, watching every nuance that showed in her face. "I came to know you because I was asked to determine if you were a spy. That's my hobby," he explained on a gentle smile. "Ah, that doesn't surprise you. Then it's as well that it's clear you couldn't carry a dire plot across a playground. Lovely security Britain enjoys. But the point is, once I ascertained that, I had no reason to continue haunting Marchbanks, except that I *had* gotten to know you.

"I generally avoid proper, unwed young women. I lost a fiancée, as you know, and for all my chatter, I've never looked to replace her. I still don't. I want only you, and you're certainly one of a kind. I find I'm even selfishly glad you've avoided men until now, though I know it can't have been pleasant for you, but it kept you safely single for me. Perhaps I needed a wife who wanted no husband. I've always been the contrary sort," he mused.

"Now," he said, continuing to choose his words with care from all the ones he'd thought up through a sleepless dawn, and then tested to himself all the morning so that when he at last spoke with her, he'd make no blunder, "be assured, if you want to involve yourself with trade after we've wed, I'll not stop you. In fact, I'll encourage it. I'm fond of funds, and not ashamed of how I've grown mine. I've American interests too, aside from you, of course. If you want to visit your homeland, I'll be happy to accompany you as well, it's a place to be proud of being from and a pleasure to go to. But I think you already know most of this.

"The important thing is that it needs that you believe in me, and trust me when I say that as you're not your mama, so you must understand I won't be the sort of husband she had either. I refuse to count either fear or bad experience as my rival. And neither will harm us. If, that is, you care for me."

Then he said no further word, nor did he touch her, but only waited patiently for her answer, observing her closely.

Now there was no escaping him. Or herself. She looked at him and understood what she'd feared all along, that to leave him would be to leave her only chance at happiness. Then she allowed herself to realize that dread and doubt and trepidation notwithstanding, where he stood, there stood her home. Then she steadied herself and fought against herself and because of her great need, wrenched, at last, free of herself.

"I care," was all she managed to breath at last. But from the look upon his face, and above the dizzying relief she felt, she knew they both knew she'd said a great deal more.

* * *

Lord Deal came into his own entry hall with as sprightly a step as though it were a brisk autumn day, although his butler, like everyone else he'd passed as he'd gone jauntily through the simmering streets, too preoccupied to notice the weather, was clearly wilting as he approached his master.

"I took leave to allow the gentleman to wait in the drawing room, as he said he sought either you, my lord, or your guest, Mr. Rossiter, who has not returned as yet," the butler intoned, and as his master frowned down at the limp card he'd picked up from the salver, he added quickly, "and offered him refreshment, it being quite warm today."

"What? Oh yes, quite right," Barnabas said distractedly. The name ought to have been familiar, but he couldn't quite place it, although the address caught and held his eye. "Mr. Franklin Godfrey, 2 Pearl Street, New York City, N.Y.," it read.

As he entered his drawing room the gentleman who'd been sitting in a chair by the window tapping his foot as he'd gazed out at the street, sprang at once to his feet. He was well, almost nattily, dressed, although clearly more a man of action than a dandy, no matter how well tied his neckcloth. He stood at average height, and his tightly fitting jacket showed an admirably lean and muscular form.

His appearance personified the American contradiction of class, for while close fitting pantaloons displayed a working man's sturdy, heavily muscled legs, his highly polished boots were a gentleman's dream of excellence. His age too was indefinable, for though his dark hair was merely brushed with gray along the temples, his decisive, chiseled features bore the mark of far more years of exposure to the sun than just the tan acquired on a recent sea voyage.

"Lord Deal?" he asked at once, putting out a strong and shapely hand that had known hard use. "I'd know you anywhere. I just arrived in town this morning, and see London's enjoying a New York summer. I looked to find Will here, but I'm delighted to meet you. As the cliché has it, 'I've heard so much about you.' "

Lord Deal took the fellow's hand and had a moment to be amused at his unknown guest's barely contained energy. It seemed that he was not the only one unaffected by the unusual heat of the day. Then, as they grasped hands, he chanced to look into the gentleman's bright gray eyes, and then he saw a vague reflection of something else in the smiling mouth, something that he knew very well from his frequent thoughts and very recent experience.

"Good heavens," he said then, as the puzzle fitted together and awareness dawned upon him, and he exclaimed, before he flung back his head in unrestrained, boisterous laughter, "it's Grandfather!"

FIFTEEN

THE SETTING SUN, like a giant yolk newly pricked, smeared a disorderly, vivid stain across the sky and it dripped gold all over the gray rooftops of London, but neither of the two gentlemen seated by the open window did more than give it cursory notice. They had been far too busily engaged in taking the measure of each other. And now that they'd ordered dinner, had it served to them, exchanged common pleasantries and queries about the one's recent ocean voyage and the other's recent activities, they sat back in their chairs and grinned. For each counted himself well satisfied with what he saw in the other.

"It's as well things worked out this way," Franklin Godfrey said, without preamble, for they'd just been speaking about the price of French brandy. "Faith has no idea I'm here, and neither does Will. Not that I wish to spy on them—I don't. But I think, my lord, that you can give me a fairer, or at least a more impartial, view of what's going on. Their letters tell me nothing and everything. I feel there's much more that never gets to paper."

"Fair perhaps," Barnabas Stratton said thoughtfully, "but impartial, sir? I'm afraid not, no, in Faith's case, not at all."

"Ah!" the older gentleman said cheerfully. "Ah well, then, there's a bit that lurked between the lines that I did read right. That pleases me, my lord, not that I make snap judgments. But I do." He laughed. "I flatter myself that it's my strength. And that bit of news pleases me right down to the ground upon which I stand."

"Ah, but there's nothing settled," his companion said with the faintest frown, "though I'm pleased to have the opportunity to go about things the proper way and announce my intentions to you. That's all I've been able to do with Faith, as well. It's early days yet for us, though I would wish it were later, or would go more quickly. But I hesitate to hurry with a girl like Faith. I reason the wait will be worth it, so I wait, but impatiently, sir.''

"Then," said the elder man, "I reckon you've figured out what ails Faith. I hear it in what you haven't said. Aye, that daughter of mine and that coxcomb she calls husband had no right having children, but I'm glad they did. At least I got Faith from them. If they contributed nothing else to the family, or the world, that would be enough. I think you're man enough, and have heart and brain enough to convince Faith marriage is not the misery they showed her it was. That's all she needs, all she ever needed. But for all we're close, I've been too busy building empires to do more than tell her the way of it. I never had time to show her. She never knew her grandmother.''

The American gentleman frowned then, and pursed his lips and shifted in his seat, and drew his dark brows together in a frown, before he sighed and breathed, on a loud exhalation, "Aye, that's why I'm here, you might say. That's why I've come.''

Then he straightened and looking Lord Deal levelly in the eye, he said more forcefully, opening his hands wide as though he were literally laying everything out on the table before him, "I've a problem, my lord, and that's why I've come.''

"I thought you might." Barnabas sighed, and when the older man gave him a curious look, he explained gently, "Things were going far too well lately, sir, you see. Why, things were going very smoothly for at least three hours.''

The two gentlemen continued their discussion as they walked the city streets from Lord Deal's club back to his townhouse, as it appeared the American gentleman was the sort of vigorous fellow who must move as he sought to express his thoughts. And in all, Lord Deal mused privately, it was better that his lively visitor had an entire city to vent his energies upon than if he were forced to merely pace the patterns out of his library's carpeting.

"I wed her grandmother early," Franklin Godfrey said, as though he were continuing a statement he'd just made, when in fact he'd kept silent for several moments, marshaling his thoughts. When he finally spoke, the words burst from him like staccato puffs of steam escaping from a boiling pot. "I was only a lad, eighteen, imagine. It was folly, of course. Mine considered itself a good family though poor, and hers, why, she was a miller's daughter. I had to wed her, and so I had to leave with her as well, to make my way in the world. But I'm not sorry a bit for it, not for her, she was the best thing that ever happened to me, not for coming to New York, for it suited me. I made my fortune there. But I lost her, you see, not six months later, to a fever while she was still in childbed.

"I didn't re-wed. I hadn't the time, nor the inclination. Not that I avoided women," he said, glancing at his companion sideways, "but not that sort of women, if you take my meaning. I was prudent, of course. I had a young daughter to raise. But she was raised motherless, and damned if our sins don't come back to haunt us—she raised her own daughter motherless as well. After a while I stepped in to make sure Faith was raised fatherless as well. A paltry fellow my daughter met through my business, damn his eyes," he said, and shook his head as if he would waste not so much as one more word on his son-in-law.

"Well," Mr. Godfrey sighed, so wrapped in his tale he never noticed his companion's fleeting smile at his interjection, "the fact is that Faith was born when her mother was eighteen; history repeats. I took charge of her and raised her as though she was my daughter. Maybe I felt guilty for the way I'd mismanaged her mother, maybe I was older and wiser. Reckon too, I had more time, as well as more money for the job then.

"Blast," he said in exasperation, shaking his head, "it's a good thing I met up with you, my lord. I find you a comfortable, quick-witted fellow, and still I can't spit it out. Imagine if I tried to explain it all to Faith, raw! I need your help, Lord Deal," he said, coming to a halt in the middle of the street.

"You have it," the tall gentleman said simply and calmly. That seemed to satisfy the older gentleman, because he nodded and walked forward again.

"Well then," Franklin Godfrey said decisively, "understand that I've six and fifty years strung together for myself now. When Faith left, I was lonely, but I was determined she have her chance. The fellows at home hadn't made much of an impression on her. But maybe that was because she was too comfortable with me. I could see her getting ready to settle down to be my partner and companion. That would've been dead wrong for her. I shipped her off for her own good, but I was left at sixes and sevens, I'll tell you.

"If she chose Will, and I admit I threw them together in such hopes, it would have suited me fine, but I'll admit, she's done far better. Not that Will's not a capital fellow—he is, he is. But you'll fit her like a glove. Ah, there's no way of gentling the thing into conversation. Lord Deal," the older man confessed, looking both shame-faced and proud at the same time as he swung his head around to stare at the younger man, "the long and short of it is that I'm getting married. And that I'm running true to form, because I have to, and I want to, as well."

He glowered at his companion fiercely, as though daring him to reply. Lord Deal stopped still in his tracks. And then, after a pause, his smile showed white in the dimming light as he put out his hand and said, merrily, "Why, sir, all my felicitations. I'm happy for you, of course, but as we've barely met, you'll understand that it's good news to me in other ways as well."

"I hadn't thought of it that way," Franklin Godfrey said, shaking hands bemusedly, "but there's something in that, all right. Maybe," he added doubtfully, "because Faith's not predictable, you know. And my bride used to be her companion, Molly Cabal. Well, I was alone," he said defensively, "and lonely and wandering about the house in search of a friendly face. And there was dear Molly, a tenant in my own house for seven years," he said wonderingly, "and I'd never passed more than the time of day with her before. But she'd a broken leg, my poor lass, and was a ready audience. And well," he said on a slight abashed smile, "you can see, she became far more. She's been a widow (blessedly, from what I've heard of the chap) for ten years, but still she's only five and thirty. I told her and I told her she was too young for me, but she denied it, denies it still," he said proudly.

"The thing of it is, and I'm still amazed at it myself,"

he said, "that I'm to be a father again, and I tell you, my lord," he said in a burst of loquaciousness, "I couldn't be more excited, I couldn't be more thrilled, no, though I can hardly believe it half the time. All I thought I had ahead of me was old age, and at the best, a chance to become a great-grandfather before I died. And now I've that, and a wife, and a whole new family coming, as well. I did a poor job with my daughter, and a better one with Faith. So I have the highest hopes for the new babe, be it boy or girl. But there's still Faith, you see.

"She's bound to feel betrayed. She's sure to feel left out. I know she'll feel displaced. I still love her, of course, and always shall. But no question, it will be different. And bless Molly, but she's no fortune-hunting schemer. She's refused to wed until Faith gives her permission, her loving permission. So I've shipped out hastily, and I'll do my best to sail back on the first fair tide. But what's to do with Faith, my lord?"

"I would hope," Barnabas said thoughtfully as they finally approached his front door, "that she'd find me consolation enough."

"But there's a difference lad—ah, my lord," the other gentleman said quickly, "and take my word for it, though you're a canny fellow, I've lived some decades more than you, there's a world of difference between taking something because you want it, and accepting it feeling you have no other choice left open to you. I may have made it that much harder for you, and I'm sorry for it, but she's a proud lass."

"Precisely her charm," Barnabas agreed on a grin. "So, as you'll be my guest tonight, of course, sir, we'll have the night to thrash it out between us. For I'll help you, Mr. Godfrey, if you'll help me."

"Done!" said the older gentleman at once, offering his hand on the bargain. "And here's to a profitable partnership, my lad . . . my lord."

"Barnaby," the tawny-haired gentleman corrected him softly as they shook hands.

The gentleman was dressed exquisitely. There was no other way to describe him. His valet was radiant as a bride, and took the congratulations of the entire staff with a becoming attempt at modesty, but then the creator of a masterpiece can well afford to put on a humble face, knowing that in no way will it humble him. Then too, whatever his artistry, even he had to admit the sum total of his efforts would have been less than perfection if the subject were less comely himself. "After all," as he so tastefully put it that night when toasted at the servants' table, "one can dress a toad to a nicety, and still not have a prince to show for it."

And there was little doubt that Florizel himself might have given a crown to have looked remotely the way Lord Deal did that memorable morning. His appearance was a tribute to the collaboration of valet and master. For though his valet may have labored over the laundering of the pantaloons so that their oyster-white purity was unblemished by so much as a flyspeck, only the gentleman himself could be accountable for the strong shapely legs, trim hips, and flat abdomen they displayed. The blue frockcoat was fitted just as precisely and tightly as the nether garment, but there again, it was the wide shoulders that showed the excellence of the tailoring. And whatever the accuracy of the scissors which had snipped away the excess from that tumbled crop of hair, it was the gentleman that had grown it, and sunned it from taffy to its present streaked and shining glory.

The valet, of course, must be credited for the glossy shine upon the high brown hessians, the intricate folds of the snowy neckcloth. The choice of a subtle glowing yellow and peach striped waistcoat was his, as was the brilliant idea of handing his distracted master a walking stick just as he was about to set foot out of the house at noon. That way, he did not refuse that final touch the way he ordinarily shunned such affectation, and with the top hat in his other hand, he set all that saw him, not only his enchanted valet, to sighs of content and admiration. If there were sighs of longing as well, they would have been balm and best payment to his man's ears, though they were wasted on their recipient.

There was only one person whose reaction mattered to Lord Deal today, and it wasn't her response to his attire which concerned him at all. It was true he'd consciously attempted to present his best face this afternoon, although he knew it was all for form's sake. For it was also an ironic fact that he'd never have been so apprehensive regarding the lady's reaction to him if for one moment he'd believed she would have altered it in any fashion because of how he was dressed.

But the sight of him did make her catch her breath and turn her head aside in that first instant so that she could control her emotions. Because it seemed to her most unfair that he should appear to be so spectacular this particular day, just as she was preparing to give him up forever.

He didn't note her moment of weakened resolve; he'd been too occupied, from the moment he'd been shown into the little salon, with controlling his own reaction to the sight of her. For she'd dressed with especial care as well. When her grandfather had done visiting with her this morning, he'd gone to confer with his partner, Will, and his sometime partner, the Duke of Marchbanks. But he'd told her that his host, Lord Deal, was planning to come to pay a call as well. And she'd gone to her room and dressed with the exaggerated care that anyone might take for a farewell performance. She might be saying good-bye, and she might be resolved that it was for the best, but she was only human, and she wished to be remembered with longing and with fully as much regret as she herself felt at the leave-taking.

She wore an apricot gown that could have been expressly designed for her purposes, since it was created to insinuate certain promises that might never be fulfilled. It was low at the breasts, to both hint at their creamy texture and boast of their buoyancy, and then it fell to drape softly about her torso to show her grace of movement. A single, simple, burnt-umber ribband caught her hair back from her pale and great-eyed face, and then let it free to fall to her shoulders in one long streaming slide like poured-out honey. It was never the fashion, and perhaps had not been since the Medicis had reigned, but then, she wished to show him that she was unique, true to herself to the last as she had been from the first.

They both had spent a great deal of time and effort for this meeting, and so had dressed with as much thought for an afternoon visit as others might have taken for a ball. Their efforts had not gone in vain, for though both were too distracted to realize it, there were several long seconds of absolute silence between them before Lord Deal, who, after all, was a very facile gentleman, took her hand, bowed over it, and said, "I realize my appearance must be an anticlimax after your surprise of this morning. I was tempted to come along with Franklin, your grandfather that is, but I wanted nothing to take the shine out of his visit, and knew you two would want to be alone. He's quite a fellow, Faith, you do well to be proud of him. But what a turn I got! 'Grandfather,' you said, and 'Grandfather,' you quoted, and all that sagacity and wisdom coupled with the name made me expect some doddering old gentleman, and never that lively fellow."

"Oh," Faith said very coolly, "yes, lively indeed. Won't you sit down, my lord?"

He took a chair opposite her and, though his expression didn't change, if she'd dared to look into his eyes she would have seen grave doubt there, though his voice was smooth enough as he said pleasantly, "He's agreed to stay with me, you know, until his business is done with here. With both him and Will in residence, it's a good job for me that the recent unpleasantness between our nations is over. I've friends, you see, in the foreign office, and I'd hate to think that whenever I paid a call on them in future they'd feel compelled to keep a sharp eye on me, or casually cast a blotter over what they'd just been writing when I walked in. I agree," he went on casually, crossing his long legs and brushing away an invisible thread on his boottop, "that it's not the stuff of immortal humor, but you might try a little smile for courtesy's sake, my dear. Nothing so elevated as a grin, mind, but a little smile wouldn't go amiss."

"I don't feel very humorous today," she said softly, and then she raised her head so that he could see her eyes so suspiciously sparkling that he frowned in concern as she said, "Barnabas, everything has changed. I can't jest, nor can I pretend it hasn't. I was so thrilled to see him, I was so glad, that I think I spent an hour just hugging him and weeping for the sheer joy of finding him here. He was so far away, that in a way it seemed like he had ceased to really exist, and then I was told I had a visitor, and came downstairs all unaware, like a child to a surprise party.

When I saw him, I couldn't believe it, though I couldn't have been happier, there was so much I had to tell him.

"But he had a great deal to tell me too," she said sadly, "as you must know."

"And it displeased you?" her visitor asked in admirably even accents.

"No, no, he deserves such happiness and certainly Molly does too. I should've thought of pairing them, my two favorite people, long ago. But," she hesitated, and then blurted, "yes, of course, it displeases me too. I never knew I could hold two such opposite emotions at one and the same time, Barnabas," she said, her eyes wide and wondering. "I think I'll burst from the strain of it, because for all I'm glad for them, I feel just awful too."

And then the proper afternoon call became a great deal less so, since the young lady found herself in the gentleman's arms, protesting, as she attempted to wipe away her tears, that she was ruining his lovely jacket, while he protested that he'd had it made just for that purpose.

When she drew away, she stood and folded her hands quietly about the handkerchief he'd given her, and she lowered her eyes and her voice as she said what she felt she must.

"Oh Barnabas, you're so easy for me to talk with. And because of that, I think you know more terrible things about me than anyone should. What a mean-spirited little cat you must think I am. You're well rid of me." But then she found she could say little more, and only dabbed at her eyes and bit at her lip, and hoped she'd soon have enough countenance back to say more.

"I don't think you're any more or less than human, thank heavens, since I don't aspire to an immortal wife," he said lightly, determined to ignore at least a part of her speech. "You're more honest than most, I'll agree, but that's all to the good for me. I'd not like to think of your deceiving me, and honesty for honesty, after my disagreeable experience with a lady's duplicity, it may be that I care so very much for you in part because I know that you could not, and would not be so treacherous.

"It's as well then that you can't dissemble very well, for I certainly wouldn't believe any normal, sane young woman who told me she was tickled that her adored grandfather was marrying her best friend and having a baby that would supplant her in their affections. But the thing of it is, my dear, you're going to have to force yourself out of that dependent role, and expect and ask for a different sort of love from them from now on.''

"Oh yes," she agreed at once, "I know that. And I'd never be the babe's rival, I've promised myself I'll be his best friend in the world, and devote myself to taking care of him. They'll find me a great help and comfort, I assure you.''

"Indeed," Lord Deal said with great interest. "And what will I find you?''

When she did not answer at once, he asked, coolly, as an answer for himself, "Gone?''

"My lord," she said very clearly then, great distress banishing easy tears, "I'm leaving. Going home, yes. Because nothing is the same now. It's not only that he's going to marry her," she said solemnly, and as her listener hung on every word, he couldn't help but note, with sorrow, that she hadn't called the gentleman Grandfather since she'd gotten his news. "It's also that I've thought ahead, and it's plain my condition's changed with this change in life. It's a lucky thing," she said on a dreadful little grimace, "that I didn't take Methley up on his offer. Because you see, I'm not an heiress anymore. I'm just an American girl with too little breeding and too many caricatures to her credit.

"Well, you see, my own father is not very wealthy," she explained, "and what he has he'll doubtless drink away before he leaves this earth. And Mama spends every penny she gets on her own clothes and entertainment. And think, now that he has a new family beginning, there'll be little left to give me, won't there? I doubt I'll even be as welcome in the business now that he may anticipate sons to pass the whole lot down to. Though I won't be penniless, I'll certainly be no prize package any longer. I've been devalued, I suppose." She grinned, humorlessly. But looking up, she was startled to see no answering smile, nor even that softened expression he so often wore when he saw her grin. Instead, the gentleman was clearly enraged.

"Money?" he demanded, so loudly that she stepped

back in surprise. "You think I care about whether or not you can bring me money?"

His tanned face was even darker with anger, his eyes flashed. He was a large gentleman in a towering rage, and a formidable sight. He looked down his long nose at her, and said, with no trace of humor or affection to temper his icy fury, "Beyond admitting my penchant for investments, I have never mentioned money to you, my dear, neither mine nor yours. But comfort yourself that I have enough for two. And had I been interested in earning more in the marriage bed, I would've done so long before now, since a gentleman's stamina there, I've heard, is far superior in his extreme youth, and I've never been a fellow to give short worth for good money."

He noted her wince, and it seemed to calm him, for he eyed her as she stood quite still and watched him fearfully, and then he said, more thoughtfully, "But do you know, Faith? I don't believe a word of it. No. On reflection, I find I don't believe you at all, and that's singular, because you're such a bad liar, and for a moment there, I did. It's now clear to see how you fooled me," he said coldly, "because it's equally clear that you lied to yourself. Think on, Faith. Would I care about your fortune?"

"Perhaps not," she said bravely, "but I do."

"Oh, there's truth," he said, "but it's also likely very true that beyond the disappointment—and there's no doubt a lady with no conceit might like to feel she's brought more than herself to a marriage—there's a lack of trust in me as well as in yourself. You think that if you haven't a fortune to wave over my head, I'll abuse you, underrate you, devalue you? Perhaps, but I think rather it's that you want to avoid the whole truth—which is that you haven't enough trust in me to marry me. And that you fear you'll never conquer your fear of me, or men, or marriage, and fear to even try.

"Poor Faith," he said, and smiled sadly at her as he took up one of her hands, "with so much fear, and so much mistrust, there's no room for love at all. Whatever reasons you fling up against the match I'll put down, but there's a limit to my patience, and none, I fear, to your invention. So, much as I love you, I cannot pass the rest of my life arguing my cause. If you were willing to let yourself love me, I wouldn't have to.

"My dear," he said with great sorrow, "I wish you well, I wish you everything you might wish, but I must let you go."

He placed cool lips briefly upon her hand, and bowed. Then he looked deeply into her confused eyes, and smiled sweetly and turned toward the door. But he'd gone hardly a pace when he heard her voice, as angry as his had been moments before.

"You can't go," she cried. "No, you cannot. For it's none of it true. Or maybe it was," she said, pausing to think as he bit back a smile and turned around to face her again. "But it don't signify," she argued, staring at him, clearly outraged. "You can't explain all this to me, and make me see that I was scared for a minute and just trying to cheat myself again—just because Grandfather's let me down doesn't mean you would as well. I wasn't thinking clearly because I've had so many things happening all together, and you can't run away from me now when I most need you, I love you most of all, and—Barnabas, you're laughing at me!"

"At us, love," he corrected her as he caught her up in his arms, "because I don't know what I would have done if you'd let me go. It would've looked wonderful if after all that drama, I'd turned around when I reached the door and said, 'Oh, but on second thought . . . ,' wouldn't it have? Yet that's precisely what I should have to have done. Did you seriously think I'd let you run off to America now to find some other fellow to wed, after I'd invested all that time getting you to be comfortable about the idea of marriage? After I'd done all that work? I may not talk about money overmuch," he whispered into her ear, "but understand, though I'm no Yankee trader, I expect value for my investments."

"Well then," she said in a small voice, daring to raise her hand to touch that tempting, shining hair her cheek rested against, "remember I'm still an American, an alien."

"So was my mother," he said happily, running his lips lightly along her cheek. "She was Scots, and the word she called my father, lovingly, but nonetheless, frequently, was 'outlander.' The most important difference between us is the most obvious and interesting one, Faith, and it isn't our nationalities. And it is, to the eternal benefit of our race, found in every marriage. And you have five freckles this side, but they're fading, poor things. I think I'll burn all your sun bonnets on our honeymoon, I'm that greedy for more of them.''

"There's all those caricatures of me,'' she said more weakly.

"I do hope there's enough to paper all the privies at Stonecrop Hall, don't you?'' he breathed, momentarily closing one of her bright eyes with a soft kiss before he smiled down into it again and balanced her by promptly attending to the other one.

But for all that he held her, and for all that he gave her so many tender salutes, he never presumed to draw her into deeper embrace, and he avoided her mouth entirely, just as his hands stayed carefully and conventionally upon the neutral surface of her back. This was so difficult for him, he discovered he had to keep his hands still and flat upon her back to ensure that they neither strayed nor trembled with the effort of not straying. Thus, he felt her take in a deep breath, and braced himself for yet another one of her protests, because for all he'd declared he'd grown impatient with them, he knew that as he'd raised them all in her mind, he'd have to answer to each of them. Still, he was totally unprepared for the one she offered next.

"Barnabas,'' she asked in a tiny voice, "don't you Englishmen kiss a girl's lips at all?''

"My dear,'' he said very seriously, "I don't dare presume. It may be too soon. I don't want to frighten you. I gave my word on that, you know.''

"But . . .'' she began, and then she closed her eyes without his kissing them shut, because since the thoughts she wanted to express had come to her in the darkest night, she had to approximate the conditions of their birth to remember them precisely. She, too, didn't want to waste all the time she'd recently invested, especially since it had been time she'd have preferred to have passed sleeping, as all the rest of the world had been doing all through the past nights.

"I've thought about that, too,'' she said, "and it occurs

to me that I wasn't the only child to have seen what I saw. Well, no one had separate rooms in olden days, and there were families with dozens of children and still there are lots of us around today, aren't there? Because, you were right, not everyone who sees what they oughtn't curls up in a corner and withers away. And I don't want to either, not anymore. And do you know, too, that once we'd talked about it together, it seemed to become less important.

"But the truly important thing, Barnabas," she said, taking such a great deal of time with the three syllables of his name that she opened her eyes at last to his complete and fascinated attention, "is that, how shall I know what to be frightened of, if you don't show me? We could wait forever, and how should I know? Be sure I'll tell you," she breathed as his smiling lips at last approached hers, "if I take alarm."

But she told him nothing in words for several moments, although by then he knew very well that whatever else he was doing to her, it was never terrorizing her.

When she spoke again, as he closed his own eyes in profound gratitude and relief as he rested his cheek against her warm hair, she said in a wondering voice, "Just think! I didn't want you to stop, Barnabas, though I was frightened, a little, I think. But not of you, oh never of you. Only because I'd never felt such things before. It's quite wonderful, but I didn't fail you, did I?" she asked anxiously.

"You could never fail me in that," he murmured, "for my lovemaking will never test you."

"But Barnabas," she persisted, "I mean, is it only me, or is it supposed to be just a little frightening for everybody, the way that one loses oneself so completely?"

"Yes," he said thankfully, "just a little, at first, for everybody. But love, that's half the fun of it. You'll see. Because you'll never guess what you will find if you do succeed in losing yourself. Oh, there's so much I long to show you, Faith, and so much I think you'll teach me, whether you believe that or not," he said on a shaky laugh. "But not, I think, in the duchess's small salon. Nor until we're safely wed. And never until you're ready. Now then," he said, sighing, but nonetheless putting her an arm's length away, "why is it that your hosts left you alone with me for so long? I can't approve such ramshackle chaperonage.''

"Oh," she said, drifting back close to him, "Grandfather's with the duke, and the duchess was brangling all night with Mary, and I haven't seen either of them all day, so I think they've got more important fish to fry. I seem to have inspired Mary to rebellion, and I'm glad of it. I only hope it benefits Will in the long run, though now I'm not too sure I did him a service, though I know I helped her.

"But you know, Barnabas," she went on, hiding her eyes beneath downcast lashes, with something in the way she drawled his name as she traced one finger slowly along his sleeve causing his eyebrows to lift, "since I have so very much to learn, I really wonder if this match is fair to you, who after all, have probably had most to do with more learned ladies in the past. After all, I shall need a very great deal of instruction and gentle handling, and careful, patient teaching . . ." But at that she couldn't bear his expression a moment longer, and began giggling even as he took her back into his arms.

"The careful handling part sounds lovely," he said, holding her securely, "but I think I've created a monster. It's very fortunate that I adore monsters," he explained happily as he proceeded with the first of his courses of instruction that she'd so clearly indicated she desired.

She was such a rapid study, he later admitted, that it was just as well that the door to the salon was soon thrown wide and the Duchess of Marchbanks tottered in, gasping in distress. She was so disordered that she didn't seem to note the sort of communications she'd interrupted, but after Lord Deal regained enough presence of mind to assist her to a chair and ring for the butler to procure her salts, sal volatile, and water, she managed to cry out plaintively, "Gone! Gone, she's gone. Do you know where she is, girl?''

"Who?" Faith asked, and received a glowing smile for her idiocy from her gentleman, who seemed to take it as proof of his proficiency and applause for his abilities.

"Mary, my Mary has gone!" the duchess wailed, almost pitiable in her bereavement, until she sat up a bit straighter and growled at Faith, "Eloped! She's run off with him. And it's all your fault."

"I hardly think so," Lord Deal said smoothly before Faith, who'd been surreptitiously attempting to straighten her gown and her hair as well as her wits, could answer, "since Faith hasn't spoken with Lady Mary all day."

"But she spoke with her before," the duchess howled, "and she filled her head with seditious things, treasonous things, disobedient, outrageous and unacceptable, rebellious thoughts."

"Oh, well of course she did," Lord Deal said with a great show of boredom, as he left the duchess and came to stand by Faith's side and put his arm around her. "She's an American."

SIXTEEN

THE NIGHT WAS cool and still, but neither Lord nor Lady Deal was sleeping. The lady lay propped against her pillows, and her husband propped one hand beneath his shaggy head as he leaned on his elbow and looked down at her.

". . . And another reason," he continued to say, as he toyed with a strand of her hair, "is that as an American you're delighted to share this chamber with me, which pleases me no end, where an English lady might think it declassé, and I do get so lonely in the midst of the night, not to mention how hideously cold my feet can become during our wretched English winters, that's no small factor contributing to marital happiness, and another reason is—"

"Barnabas," she giggled, "that's twenty-seven reasons you've given me thus far tonight."

"Of course," he said sadly, "but if you persist in saying silly things about how you worry about what people will think of our wedding, you'll never get to sleep tonight, for all the wrong reasons," he added even more sadly, "for as it happens, I'm not in the least tired, and should very much like to be, if you take my ulterior meaning."

"I do, Barnabas," she said at once, and he nodded and said, "Just so, and there's number twenty-eight, for you always do, and that's even more delightful. And what generally follows is number twenty-nine through fifty, it's that marvelous."

"Only fifty?" she said with mock despair before she held him off and said, "But truly, Barnabas, I sometimes wonder. I've no claim to title, and that's so important here."

"Where?" he asked, looking around their bedchamber

suspiciously as she laughed, for he always made her laugh, even here, in their bed, when he wasn't making her sigh with happiness. The wonderment was that once he'd freed her from the ice which had held her fast, she was discovering to their mutual delight that it had only been a surface covering and it seemed she had a molten core. But they'd been married for a week, and now she was at last beginning to wonder about how life would be when the novelty of marriage had worn off.

"See here," he said sternly, as though he'd heard her thoughts, "once and for all, if I'd wanted a title, I would have lent some money to Prinny and picked out a few more for myself. I didn't have to marry one. I married the only female I wanted, and would have done even if you'd come from another planet, not to mention another country. All right?"

"All right." She smiled as she began to believe that it might be that the novelty of this union would never wear off.

"Barnabas?" she said in a moment, causing him to lift his head instantly, for he still was always alert to her every change of mood, "just think, Grandfather is almost home by now."

He repressed a sigh and drew back from her and lay back on the pillow beside her, too wise to press his suit when she clearly was distracted by something else, too experienced to take it personally, and far too respectful of her intelligence to think it was of no moment.

"Do you miss him, Faith?" he asked softly, watching her profile in the light of the single candle they'd left to light them to pleasure. "I can't help that, I can only try to make this so much your home that you long for no other except for sentiment's sake."

"It's not that," she said at once, turning her head to look at him, "it's only that I thought of Will, and Lady Mary, and Methley, and of how my coming to England changed so many lives. And I wondered if I did the right thing for Mary, though I don't know how I could have done anything else. I told her what I believed in, not to convert her but to let her know why I was disappointed in her. And look what I caused."

"You caused her to be happy, or at least to choose her

own path, and to take charge of her own future. That's no small achievement," he said, "no matter what the duchess thinks. And be sure, by the time Mary comes back into society, the duchess will be pleased to show everyone how thrilled she is at her new son-in-law, and no one will ever guess how hard a pill he was for her to swallow. She lives on gossip and knows how to turn it to her own uses. At that, I think they'll be very good for each other; he'll keep her anger from her daughter, for she'll never blame Mary so much as she does him, and she'll, no doubt, amuse him."

"Poor Will," Faith sighed.

"Isn't there a bird in your country that says that?" he asked curiously, as she smiled, "but there's nothing poor about him, my love. His was the very best fate of all, and doubtless he'll tell you so often enough when he thanks you over and over again in all the years to come."

"Oh Barnabas," she sighed, for he'd said everything she'd wished him to, and better yet, had made it all sound as though he meant every word of it. "Oh Barnabas—do you know," she said with a sudden frown, "I don't care for that name in the least. No, Barnaby is even worse," she forestalled him by saying.

"Oh, but you've called me by some other names recently, far better names." He laughed, and bent low to whisper them to her, and was pleased to see her faint blush clear and remarkably extensive even in the scant light of the flickering candle.

"I'll grant you're not likely to use them in company, although I promise you," he said wickedly, "nothing would please me more. But if I have to put up with Faith, you'll just have to learn to abide Barnabas. Viking, you'll allow, is too cumbersome."

But hearing that old name with all its painful implications caused her to instantly reach out to him, and their spoken conversation ceased. The candle guttered out and the room was lit by the glow of a late summer's moon, when Lady Deal murmured breathlessly, with a certain amount of suppressed laughter, "Barnabas, the children."

"Really, my love," he complained, "I'm doing the best I can. We've only been married a week, though. I don't know what else you expect of me."

"Oh no," she said on a wide grin, which caused a delay before she could speak again. "But really—" she tweaked at a lock of his hair to make him pay attention—"I had the most dreadful thought. A Viking and a Wild Indian. Oh Barnabas, whatever shall our children be?"

He thought a moment. Then, just when he decided yes, that was precisely where he wished to kiss her next, he whispered before he did so, "Why, formidable, my darling, absolutely formidable."

And although he'd said it just to make her laugh, in light of present circumstances, he was just as pleased, no, even more pleased, when her only answer was to catch up her breath, and then to let it out slowly in a long, shivering, very contented sigh.

The moon shone down on the sleeping town of Edinburgh as well. And the Lady Mary lay back in her bed as well. But her husband stood at the window in his dressing gown and looked down at the old, dreaming city.

"I think," the Lady Mary said decisively, "that we can return to town any time now. I doubt," she said smugly, "that Mama will seek annulment now. A week, after all, is time enough to have started anything."

Her husband turned his attention from the window, and when she saw him gazing at her, she said, "Oh no, I have no evidence. But I have hopes, don't you?"

"Of course, my dear," he said.

"It will be odd," Lady Mary said pensively, "to meet up with Faith and Lord Deal again, but I think they intend to spend most of their time at Stonecrop Hall and travel in entirely different circles, and we, of course, will stay in Town, won't we? I don't see that as a problem. I know you've been friends, but Faith and I had harsh words before I left. Though I thank her and shall always, for giving me the courage to break from Mama, I cannot think she loves me well."

The gentleman stirred, and an unreadable expression crossed his face as briefly as a cloud shadowing over the face of the moon. He turned to gaze out the window again, though there was something faintly like regret in his voice as he said, "And her love, does that matter so much then?"

"No, of course not," she said. "Not now that I have you. But it's curious, her words made such a difference in my life. I wanted you. I had from the beginning, but I would have bent to Mama and gone elsewhere if it hadn't been for Faith. She gave me the courage to send for you, and to leave with you. Were you shocked at my proposal?" She laughed. "But really, her words went to my head. I dared. Since that day, I've been a different person. Although you," she said passionately, "are the only one accountable for making that person feel like a woman, you know."

The invitation in her words, the command implicit in her outstretched hand, were impossible to ignore. Her husband went to her. And as the Earl of Methley slipped off his dressing gown and came to his countess as he'd been bade, he said, with more of his old irony than passion in his voice, "If Faith freed you, my dear, and I made you a woman, why is it that you remind me so of your dear mama so often lately?"

"I've grown up," she said, and smiled at him as he came close, for she took it as a compliment. And the Earl of Methley, who had gotten everything he'd once thought he wanted, looked into his future and sighed when he admitted to himself, before he submitted to his wife's desire, that doubtless he'd gotten everything he deserved as well.

There was only one more day of sailing, and then the ship would dock safely in New York. Will Rossiter explained this patiently to the two young women who stood at the rail looking out at the sea that as yet had no horizon. The moon might be rising high in the land they'd lately left, but here the afternoon sun blazed a path to the New World he was telling his rapt audience about.

Franklin Godfrey had stayed in the cabin to get some paperwork done, but Will had been restless, and so had come out to the deck to pace and think about all that he had lost, and gained, and given up and left behind him.

He hadn't known the fair-haired lady he'd left at the Duke and Duchess of Marchbanks' townhouse. For surely, the Lady Mary he'd offered his heart and his name to would never have let him speak his entire heart and mind, sitting like a stone until he was done and then she never would have said, "Oh no, Mr. Rossiter. It's out of the question. You have funds, but so do I. My husband must be able to offer me something I do not have."

"Like love?" he'd asked, confused.

"Oh no," she'd smiled, looking ethereal even as she'd said it, "like a higher title, silly."

He'd been badly wounded, of course, perhaps he'd even bled a bit internally when he'd heard she'd run off with Methley. But what had Barnabas said at his wedding the day before he'd left? It had definitely staunched the flow.

The bridegroom had poured him some champagne, and then commented, in the half-serious way he said the most important things, "Will, she never was your sweet fair London lady, the one who bandaged your hands and won your heart. And it wasn't fair to expect it of her. But if you'd like, you can always search for that particular lady before you leave. I'd expect, though I don't claim to be a wizard with figures, that the female of your dreams would be about a generation older by now. And if she is, there's a chance she might be a widow, and if you don't mind wedding a grandparent (there's a great deal of that sort of thing going 'round, you know), why I'm sure you'd have a blissful union."

Will smiled at the thought now, and was pleased to discover it became easier to do so with each league the ship leaped forward. The two young women looked at him curiously, to discover his jest. One was an English lady, this one all correct, a vision in dark tresses and pink cheeks, and the other, her maid, a creature of russet curls and the whitest, most contagious smile he'd ever seen. Oh yes, Will thought, this one would do very nicely in the New World. Her mistress would be shocked, and the little maid, delighted, but they'd soon find title meant nothing in the land they approached, unless it was on a deed to property.

He felt enormously cheered at the thought, especially since he stood before them right now because he'd decided in his disappointment and chagrin to give up his dream of living in England again, and was returning to his life and home in New York.

"But ooo, sir, how can you be sure that there are no Indians to torment us?" the maid with russet curls simpered, flirting outrageously while her mistress tightened her lips in disapproval at her servant's audacity. Oh yes, Will thought merrily, some surprises in store here, before he said carelessly, "Why, because I just left the last one in England."

The girl tittered and then said, "Oh fie, sir. You're only having fun with us. For how should you know? You're as British as I am, and that's as much as old John Bull, it is."

"But there's where you're out," Will said seriously, and then he paused, because the more he thought about it, the more he knew it to be true.

"I'm an American," he finally said.

And as he heard the words, he knew he spoke the truth.

Then he grinned widely as he felt a great swell of relief, and a great weight lifted from his heart as he added, "And I'm going home now. Yes, I'm on my way home at last."

About the Author

Edith Layton has been writing since she was ten years old. She has worked as a freelance writer for newspapers and magazines, but has always been fascinated by English history, most particularly by the Regency period. She lives on Long Island with her physician husband and those of her three children who are not involved with intimidating institutions of higher learning. She collects antiques and large dogs.

The sensuous adventure that began with

SKYE O'MALLEY

continues in . . .

He is Skye O'Malley's younger brother, the handsomest
rogue in Queen Elizabeth's court . . . She is a beautiful stranger . . . When Conn O'Malley's roving eye
beholds Aidan St. Michael, they plunge into an erotic
adventure of unquenchable desire and exquisite passion that binds them body and soul in a true union of
the heart. But when a cruel betrayal makes Conn a
prisoner in the Tower, and his cherished Aidan a harem
slave to a rapacious sultan, Aidan must use all her skill
in ecstasy's dark arts to free herself—and to be reunited
forever with the only man she can ever love. . . .

**A breathtaking, hot-blooded saga
of tantalizing passion and ravishing desire**

Coming in July from Signet!